Also by Paul Dowswell

*Ausländer*

The Adventures of Sam Witchall in reading order:

*Powder Monkey*
*Prison Ship*
*Battle Fleet*

# THE CABINET OF CURIOSITIES

# PAUL DOWSWELL

**BLOOMSBURY**

LONDON BERLIN NEW YORK SYDNEY

Bloomsbury Publishing, London, Berlin and New York
First published in Great Britain in July 2010 by Bloomsbury Publishing Plc
36 Soho Square, London, W1D 3QY

A CIP catalogue record of this book is available from the British Library

ISBN 978 1 4088 0046 1

FSC
Mixed Sources
Product group from well-managed
forests and other controlled sources
Cert no. SGS-COC-2061
www.fsc.org
© 1996 Forest Stewardship Council

Typeset by Dorchester Typesetting
Printed in Great Britain by Clays Ltd, St Ives plc, Bungay, Suffolk

3 5 7 9 10 8 6 4 2

www.bloomsbury.com

*To J & J*
*and*
*D & B*

# CHAPTER ONE

*January 1598*

Lukas Declercq struggled to wake from a deep sleep. There was a heavy weight on his chest and shoulders and a pain at his throat.

At first he thought he was sickening with Grippe or Lung Fever. Then a grating voice hissed in his ear, 'That's right, my fine fellow, open those eyes.'

Lukas could smell putrid breath – an unholy mixture of rotting teeth, garlic and alcohol. He tensed, waiting for the sharp jab of a dagger in his neck.

The man spoke again. 'Give me your money belt, and your clothes, and your sword, and I might spare your life. Any funny business and I'll slit your throat.'

Lukas, wide awake now, could see the grotesque warty face of his tormentor. The man straddled him, a knee on each shoulder. One hand held a knife to his throat, in the other was a lantern. The index finger of both hands had been cut off to ugly stumps – a common punishment for poaching.

He had a weasely face and a sickly pallor. For an instant Lukas wondered whether to try to shove him off. He was quite tall for his age and his voice had started to deepen. He might be able to beat a man like that in a fight. But then, he was still as thin as a rake. Besides, he could hear other hostile voices. Intuition told him to do as he was told.

'Quick, before I lose my temper,' hissed the man.

It was so cold in the stable Lukas could see his breath in the dim lantern light.

'Move off me then,' he said – and was instantly afraid he had spoken too sharply.

But the man could see the logic in that and sprang up suddenly, quick as a hare. 'Clothes – all of them,' he growled.

'But it's freezing,' pleaded Lukas.

The man jabbed him in the arm with his knife – leaving a shallow cut no longer than a thumbnail. 'Clothes,' he repeated.

Lukas stripped, noticing the blood from his arm was splattering the white tunic he was struggling to remove.

'Breeches,' said the man. 'Stockings.'

Lukas was now stark naked and for a moment he wondered if this man and his accomplices meant to do worse to him than kill him. But the man grabbed his clothes, blanket, money bag and sword and disappeared into the night.

Lukas felt the blood hot against his cold skin. His body was covered in goose pimples and he began to shiver. With the robbers gone, he felt sick with fear and swallowed hard to keep down that evening's stew and dumplings.

The chiming of the monastery clock broke the silence to summon the monks to prayer. Lukas glanced at the night sky. It was still dark outside, with only a glimmer of light on the eastern horizon. He guessed that dawn was still an hour away.

Another voice spoke. 'If we don't find some clothes in the next few minutes, we'll freeze to death.' It was the dark-haired French boy who was a little older than him

– one of the passengers in the wagon who had joined them the day before. He too had been robbed of everything he owned.

They had not spoken much. The boy's name was Etienne Lambert. Lukas knew that much. He had keen eyes and a sharp face. But unlike the other travellers, who would while away the journey in conversation, he said very little, though he listened intently to everyone else. Lukas didn't like him.

'What about the others?' said Lukas. A German man and his wife had also been sleeping in the stable at the monastery, as the wagon had more passengers than the local inn, in the village of Momalle, could hold.

Etienne called their names softly. 'Herr Koberger! Frau Koberger!' but there was no reply. They had chosen a separate stall and, although Lukas and Etienne peered through the gloom, the moonless night made it too dark to do anything other than blunder around. Lukas tripped over a coil of rope and fell, landing heavily on his face. He cursed and said, 'Maybe they've gone for help, or maybe the thieves took them hostage.'

By now both of them were shivering uncontrollably. They glanced fearfully out of the stable door, listening hard. Once satisfied their assailants had left, they ran towards the cloisters, hoping to catch one of the monks on his way to prayer. But the eerie sound of plainsong already filled the night air. Cold as the boys were, neither of them felt they could interrupt the monastery's sacred service by wandering naked into the nave.

'There's a storeroom next to the buttery,' said Etienne. 'I saw one of the monks take a habit from there when we arrived.'

They tried the small wooden door. It creaked open and even in the dimmest light Lukas could see how ramshackle it was, rotten and almost falling off its hinges.

There were no windows to the room and inside was pitch black, so they felt with their hands. 'I think I've got one,' said Etienne. Lukas heard muffled noises as he tried it on. 'Too small,' he heard, and then felt it hit him as the French boy tossed it over. 'Try that.'

Lukas pulled the scratchy woollen garment over his head. 'We'll need two of these each, at least,' he said. 'Otherwise we'll freeze our stones off.' He could feel the chilly air gusting around his legs.

'Never mind that,' said Etienne brusquely. 'Look for some footwear.'

Lukas felt on the floor with his hands and then banged his forehead on the sharp corner of a wooden cabinet. Blood trickled down the side of his face. Biting his lip to stop himself crying out, he lifted the lid and felt inside. His hand brushed against the rough leather of some sandals and he scrabbled through them, trying to find a pair that fitted.

Clad in two habits, Lukas warmed up enough to stop shaking. 'We must find one of the monks, tell them what's happened,' he said.

Etienne shook his head. 'No. The service will go on for at least an hour. Let's get back to the stable and wait there until daybreak. Then we'll tell them.'

As they neared the entrance they heard low, angry voices. 'They're not here. You should have slit their throats. If they recognise us, we'll all be for the wheel.'

Lukas and Etienne froze in their tracks and crept

4

silently back to the cloisters. They saw four dark shadows emerge from the stable, each clutching a knife. The figures began to walk warily in their direction.

Halfway across the courtyard one of them whispered, 'We can't go searching a whole monastery.' Then he turned and punched the man next to him so hard in the chest he fell to the ground. 'Next time, do a proper job,' he snarled. Another dark shape hauled the whimpering man to his feet and they hurried away.

'I'm not going in there now,' said Lukas.

Etienne nodded. 'They might carry on arguing and come back.'

'I wonder what happened to the German couple,' said Lukas quietly. He had travelled several days with them and had grown to like them. Koberger's cabinet-making business had been thriving, and now he and his wife were taking time off to visit their family back home. She had teased Lukas about his looks, telling him he was a beautiful boy – 'like an angel' – who deserved to be painted by one of the Italian masters.

Etienne shrugged. 'Let's hope they heard them coming and escaped.'

The sound of singing and chanting continued. The two boys found a spot away from the wind and waited out the long hour until dawn, but it was impossible to sleep on the stone floor of the cloisters. When the sky lightened they decided it was safe to return to the stables. Stumbling into the hay, they fell at once into an exhausted sleep.

Lukas woke to the sound of shouting. Someone grabbed hold of him and lifted him to his feet. For a second he thought the robbers had returned, but he realised that the man yelling in his face was a monk. 'Look!' he said. 'He's got blood on him. And bruises. Look at his face.'

Etienne ran at the monk, knocking him to the ground. Then he grabbed hold of Lukas's sleeve and shouted, 'Run for your life.'

Lukas had no time to think. His instinct told him to run, and they tore past the monastery's outbuildings and winter fields, through the outskirts of the town, and deep into the woods, the early-morning frost crackling beneath their feet and the shouts of their pursuers in their ears.

Etienne gasped, 'If we can find a nook somewhere . . .'

He was breathing so hard he could barely get his words out.

Lukas's lungs were close to bursting. He didn't try to speak. They found a hollow close to a large oak and hurriedly gathered the leaves that had drifted beneath. A fallen branch from a recent storm lay close by and Lukas dragged it over.

'No!' said Etienne, and cursed him. 'They'll follow the marks in the frost.' Lukas should have picked up the branch rather than dragging it.

They hared off again. Their pursuers had gained valuable seconds.

'Quick, over here,' said Etienne, and they jumped down a small slope to another oak. There they lay down in the freezing earth beneath the tree, pulling the cowls of their garments up over their heads and hiding themselves as best they could under a thick covering of leaves. At least their brown monks' habits would blend in with the detritus of the forest floor.

Lukas was sure their winded gasps would betray them. But their pursuers took a while to reach them and by the time they passed both boys were breathing evenly.

'What was . . . ?' he began to say.

Etienne hushed him abruptly, whispering, 'Keep quiet. If you get us caught, I'll kill you.'

They waited in an oppressive silence. Melting frost began to penetrate Lukas's woollen clothing. The cold seeped into his bones and eventually he began to shiver. Braving Etienne's anger again he said, 'I'm freezing to death here.'

But Etienne was calm and reasonable. 'They've gone past us,' he said in a low whisper, 'but they'll be coming back.'

Other voices silenced them at once. Etienne was right. Lukas buried his head in the ground and tried to keep as still as possible. He could guess what the men were doing from the swishing noises that reached them – combing the ground, digging at the bushes and piles of leaves with sticks or branches.

'The spawn of Satan!' they heard one man say. 'They've vanished.' Another voice said, 'It is a punishment from God, visiting these villains upon us.'

The men sounded exhausted and dispirited. Their search was half-hearted. Their voices faded as bright winter sunshine pierced the forest, causing steam to rise from the melting frost.

The boys waited a few more minutes and then cautiously pushed the leaves away. Now Lukas could ask his burning question. 'Why did we have to run?'

'The monks think we killed that German couple,' said Etienne. 'They woke me up, screaming in my face, and dragged me over to the stall at the end of the stables. They're both there, dead as mutton. Then they wanted to know what I was doing wearing a monk's habit. One of them said it was plain we were going to escape in disguise.'

Lukas could not believe what he was hearing. Questions swam around his head. 'Why couldn't we explain to them what happened?' he said.

Etienne looked exasperated. 'Didn't you see how angry they were?'

Lukas could see there was a logic to it. Everyone in this part of the Low Countries seemed hostile to strangers. Over the past few days, they had been taunted at the roadside by local people thinking them labourers looking for work. Some had even thrown stones or clods of earth at them. Lukas had been frightened, although some of the other travellers in their party had been affronted. They were well-dressed merchants and craftsmen. Not vagrants.

What could they do now? There was certainly no going back to the monastery. Their sole possessions in the world were the stolen clothes they stood up in. They didn't have a penny to their names, and they were both cold and hungry.

Lukas tried to hold in the sob that was rising in his throat. Etienne, on the other hand, looked quite at peace with the world. Dusting off the last of the forest debris he said, 'Well, I'm going that way,' and set off towards the east at a determined pace.

Lukas hurried behind him. 'Wait for me,' he said.

'Why?' said Etienne, but in a way that made Lukas think he was just playing with him.

'Why not?' said Lukas, realising he sounded desperate.

'Because we're fugitives now, and you nearly got us caught,' said Etienne.

Lukas felt even more agitated. 'If we'd stayed and explained to the monks that we had been robbed of all our clothes instead of running away like guilty thieves and murderers, maybe they would have looked after us. If I go back there now, after running away, they'll think I'm giving myself up and it'll be me that's broken on the wheel.'

Etienne winced. 'All right.' He nodded. 'You can come with me to the next town. But you'll have to keep up . . . and after that you're on your own.'

# CHAPTER TWO

Lukas traipsed behind Etienne in gloomy silence as steady drizzle turned to rain. All his papers – his passport, his permission to travel and his letter of introduction from Uncle Anselmus at his destination, Prague – had gone with the robbers, along with his money. But, he told himself, at least he was still alive, unlike poor Herr and Frau Koberger.

'Do you think the robbers were from round here?' said Lukas, just to make conversation.

'No,' said Etienne. 'Those accents were from all over – Flemish, south German – I'd guess they were soldiers. Deserters probably. They seemed too rough and ready with their blades to be run-of-the-mill vagrants. Soldiers get a taste for living off civilians . . . I think we can say for certain they weren't pilgrims.'

Lukas was surprised to find himself smiling.

'My mother told me to sew coins into the lining of my coat,' he said, 'so I'd be all right if brigands turned out my pockets. I don't suppose it occurred to her that they'd steal the coat as well. And my bag. She made this horrible ointment from garlic, hollowleek and butter and ladled it into a little box. It's supposed to cure blisters and chilblains and it stinks like a dead dog. She hid some money in that. She thought if a robber opened the box they'd be so disgusted by the smell they'd drop it at once.'

As they walked down the muddy road the wind carried a great solid stench their way. Two or three furlongs ahead was a sprawling encampment. Choking smoke drifted from spluttering wet wood fires, and the inhabitants sheltered in makeshift tents of tattered canvas and branches. 'Put your cowl up, quickly!' said Etienne, and they both raised the thick woollen hoods of their habits over their heads. 'Don't look at them.'

It was a wise precaution. Lukas knew from his travels that most of them would be farm labourers desperate for work and food. They could guide an ox and plough the earth, but that was little use in a foundry or builders' yard.

A small group of men was loitering by the roadside, sitting on a fallen tree. Lukas noticed with horror that one of them was wearing his tunic. Closer to, he could even see the blood on it. 'Is that them?' he whispered to Etienne.

'Keep going. Don't stop for anything,' said Etienne.

Two of the men began to walk towards them. Lukas could just see them on the edge of his vision and fought the urge to remove his cowl so he could get a better look. His legs felt stiff with fear as he willed himself to keep moving. What could he do? He had no weapon. Even if he managed to outrun these men, he would be scurrying straight back to the monks who were also pursuing them.

Children's voices rang in his ears. A handful of ragged urchins rushed towards them, hands cupped in the universal gesture of the starving beggar.

'I am sorry, my children,' said Etienne. He was trying to sound grown-up and benevolent, but Lukas could hear the fear in his voice. 'We are as poor as church mice.'

The men clearly thought them not worth the trouble and walked sullenly back to the edge of the road, watching them pass with dull, resentful eyes.

The boys listened for any sound that would indicate the men had recognised them. Lukas could sense their eyes boring into his back. But there were no cries or footfalls. The urge to turn around and look was so powerful he had to pinch his hand hard to distract himself from doing so.

The road took a turn, and when he felt they were safely out of sight Etienne said, 'The man in your tunic – he was the hog's turd who robbed me.' He looked white with fear. 'He's obviously bullied it off the one who stole it from you.'

Lukas nodded, too frozen with fear to answer.

Two hours later they arrived in Rocourt. Within minutes they were sitting in a tavern by a roaring fire, tucking into a hot stew. Lukas marvelled at Etienne's knack of getting people to give him things.

He had explained to the innkeeper that they were penniless disciples of God, going north to a monastery in Aachen. When the man had asked them why they had not shaved their heads in the customary monk's tonsure, Etienne said that, as he could see by their youth, they were novices and would do so only when they were fully admitted to the order.

The keeper told them it would be an honour to provide them with board and lodgings and would they please say prayers for the good of his soul. Lukas thought this was a fine place to stay but Etienne, anxious to get away from Momalle, said they had to move on.

'So where are we going to sleep tonight?' Lukas

muttered. He could see them shivering in a barn some-where, or even a ditch, when they could have been curled up in front of a roaring log fire.

'We?' scoffed Etienne. That was enough to remind Lukas that he had promised to travel with him only as far as the next town. But then he winked and placed his hands together in prayer. 'The Lord will provide,' he said.

As they scraped their bowls clean, Etienne asked where Lukas was going. It was the first time he had shown any curiosity about him.

'Prague,' said Lukas.

'Why?' asked Etienne.

'My Uncle Anselmus is taking me as his apprentice. He's a physician at the court of Emperor Rudolph.'

'The mad one?' said Etienne, his eyebrows shooting up in delight and surprise. 'I've heard the Emperor has an army of overpaid alchemists searching for the elixir of eternal youth.'

'And I've heard the Emperor is a generous master,' said Lukas, 'although he is also a man of dark humours. And where do you plan to go?'

Etienne smiled and said, 'I don't know. Where it suits me.' He turned and looked directly at Lukas. 'I might even go to Prague.'

Lukas felt uneasy. 'What would you do there?'

Etienne moved his head from side to side. 'This and that.'

They finished their meal and thanked the innkeeper. Lukas noticed how charming Etienne could be. He made a point of asking the man for directions to Aachen.

'That should send them in the wrong direction,' said

13

Etienne, 'if someone from Momalle comes here looking for us.'

They took the main road south. Etienne did not mention Lukas's tagging along.

'I once contemplated a life in medicine, but lost patience with the Latin and Greek,' he said. 'It's quite enough to speak French, German and Italian.'

'So what did you choose to do instead?' asked Lukas.

'Swindle people,' said Etienne boldly.

Lukas laughed but Etienne was looking at him without the trace of a smile.

'It's called trade – my father was a merchant – and it's all within the law. Well, most of it, anyway.'

'And what does your father do now?' Lukas asked.

'He's dead, I think. Murdered, probably. They say he crossed someone over a consignment of furs and then he went missing. Ended up in the river, most likely. The body was never found. But everyone in Amiens thought the worst.'

As they walked, Etienne became quite animated. 'It's a golden age we live in, Lukas. These days you can buy goods from around the world. In the big market towns and the cities there are merchants to sell you furs from Muscovy, glass from Venice, spices from the Levant, even potatoes from the Americas! But there's only so much you can say with your hands and a shrug.

'So that's where I come in. I can speak German and Italian, and a lot of people speak a little French – even you,' he mocked. 'I'm going where I can learn to speak another couple of tongues and I'm going to make my fortune helping one merchant speak to another. The world is my oyster. Every quayside, market square and merchants' fair will find me invaluable. And if I can do a bit of my own business on top of that, then I'll soon be rich.'

He was clearly enjoying having such an attentive audience.

'And more people have money to spend on things to make them feel important – not just their next meal and a roof over their head,' he went on. 'Pride is one of the seven deadly sins. But business would be nowhere without it! Nor greed, nor envy, nor gluttony. Wrath and sloth I can do without, and murder, although I'm willing to make an exception for some people, but I'm all in favour of the other deadly sins. You're not pious, are you, Lukas?' he said with a raised eyebrow.

'My father was burned alive by the Inquisition,' said Lukas quietly. 'I'm not pious at all.'

Etienne gave him a sympathetic smile and they walked along in companionable silence. As dusk began to fall he said, 'I shall make an arrangement with you, Lukas. We shall travel together. But you must help me. Here we are, with just the clothes we stand up in. Only human kindness stands between us and starvation. But, as you can see, I am not troubled, because the world is full of people who are kind.'

'And what will you expect me to do?' said Lukas warily.

'You're going to be a physician. So you'll speak Latin, won't you?' said Etienne. 'Well, you can start by teaching me some of that. I know it's not as common these days among the merchants, but I hear it is still a necessity in the east, where the tongues men speak are far more varied. As for any other favours, I shall tell you when the time comes.'

Lukas looked anxious. Etienne smiled. 'Nothing nasty. You are to be your uncle's apprentice. Well, first you shall be mine.'

He placed an avuncular arm around Lukas's shoulders and, as they walked down the road together, Etienne hummed a merry gavotte.

That evening they reached a small town, but only the third inn Etienne approached would offer them hospitality. And then only the stables.

The keeper showed them a space among the horses and gave them a blanket apiece. 'Now, good sirs,' he said, 'come and sit by the fire and we shall find some refreshment for you.'

'You are most generous,' said Etienne, 'but our holy orders forbid us to drink and to frequent taverns. If you could provide us with water and a plain meal here in the stable, we shall pray for you.'

Lukas was cold, and a warm fire was just what he needed. As soon as the innkeeper had gone he said, 'What did you say that for?' He could barely keep the anger from his voice.

'Listen and learn, young sir,' said Etienne. 'At Rocourt I told the innkeeper we were heading north. Many people saw us dine at the inn. Soon, maybe even now, word will arrive of two youths dressed as monks, wanted for the vile crime of murder back in Momalle. Here, if we keep to the stable, only the landlord will know we are travelling this way. Tomorrow we shall need another disguise.'

Lukas understood. He thought at once of the wheel. He had seen robbers and murderers executed in this manner – their limbs tied and tangled to the spokes of a large wagon wheel and broken with an iron bar. The wheel was hoisted into the air on an axle, like a malevolent giant hogweed, and they were left to the elements to die a slow, agonising death.

As they ate, Etienne asked Lukas if he had been happy to leave home. Lukas lied. He wasn't going to tell a virtual stranger anything that might be used against him by the Inquisition. 'I can't let an opportunity like this go,' he said cheerily. 'An apprentice to a physician – who would say no?

'So why did *you* leave home?' he asked Etienne. 'There must be work for interpreters in Amiens.'

'After my father disappeared, my mother took up with another man,' said Etienne. 'He didn't like me. We fought.' He shrugged.

It was a cold night and, despite his exhaustion from a day on the road, Lukas slept badly. Etienne snored like a boar so Lukas moved his blanket to another stall. When he woke in the morning, his companion had gone.

# CHAPTER THREE

Lukas tried not to panic. He was alone in a part of the Empire he knew nothing about and had no idea which way to go, except south. Grabbing a carrot from the pig trough to keep his hunger at bay, he started to walk quickly down the edge of the road.

It was a mild morning, with none of the rain that had soaked the ground for the previous three days. Ten minutes later he heard a low voice in the undergrowth at the side of the road. 'Lukas! Over here!'

It was Etienne. He was wearing a thick fur-lined coat, breeches and a woollen smock, all a little big on him.

He had a large bag with him. 'I've got something for you too,' he said, opening the bag to reveal a blue tunic, brown breeches and a hooded cloak.

Lukas was perplexed. 'Why did you disappear?' he said, trying not to sound petulant. 'I thought you wanted me to come with you.'

'I woke up early and thought I'd have a nose around the inn,' said Etienne. 'Found these clothes in one of the rooms. They even left an empty bag for me to carry them! Unfortunately the owner began to stir, so I thought I ought to vanish. Didn't even have time to go back to the stable and wake you up. Sorry. I thought you'd probably leave as soon as you knew I was gone. So I waited. And here we are!'

Lukas was still angry. He could have been blamed for

the theft. He wondered if that had been Etienne's plan.

As they talked, another problem occurred to Lukas. 'How are we going to get lodgings for free, if we're not monks any more?'

'This lovely coat has a lovely purse in it, with some lovely money,' said Etienne. 'We shall pay for our own board and lodging for the next few days. We'll bury our habits in the woods, and when we're far enough away from Momalle we'll take a carriage again.'

Lukas decided he would forgive Etienne. Especially when he thought about the fuss the good citizens of his hometown, Ghent, had made about him – all for a few outspoken words. He didn't like to think about what would happen if they were caught, but he had a strange confidence in Etienne. And the bolder they grew, the greater the sense of elation he felt when they managed to get away with it.

They stopped at an inn that evening and listened with interest as the landlord told them to look out for two desperate young brutes dressed as monks who had murdered seven or eight travellers.

Setting off at first light they walked half a day under a pale winter sky to the next town. Although they were able to walk along the smooth cobbles of a Roman road, the entire route was up and down a series of steep hills. 'Tomorrow,' said Etienne, 'we travel by wagon.'

They reached the town shortly before the church clock struck midday and retired to a gloomy inn where Etienne ordered two plates of stuffed eggs. When they finished eating he said, 'Watch this. And get ready for a speedy retreat!' Taking up the plates to carry them back to the kitchen, he passed a stout middle-aged man who was supping alone. Etienne slipped and his spoon fell and bounced off the man's back.

Etienne was very apologetic. Taking a rag from his pocket, he pretended to clean the man's fur-lined tunic. In truth there was no food there at all – the spoons and plates had been licked clean.

'What was that about?' said Lukas as they left.

'Keep walking, and I'll tell you when we're a good distance away.'

Out of sight of the inn Etienne said, 'He had a plump purse at his belt. I have it now.'

Seeing the worried look on Lukas's face, Etienne laughed. 'I'd be more worried if we didn't have any money.'

'But that man will go to pay for his next tankard of ale,' said Lukas, 'and he'll realise he's been robbed.'

'Maybe,' said Etienne, 'but that won't be for a while. His tankard was freshly filled, I noticed, and he might just think he's dropped his purse. I know how to pick my targets!' he added brashly.

They stopped by the road and counted their prize. Six gold florins, and plenty of silver. Enough for several nights' board and lodging, and the opportunity to travel by wagon, if they could find one that was going their way.

As they travelled on, Lukas's fascination with Etienne slowly grew. He didn't entirely trust him, and sometimes wondered why he wanted him to tag along, but as they approached another town on their route, towards the end of a warm early-spring day, Etienne said, 'It's good to have a companion. I never had a brother or sister.' The remark touched Lukas. His parents had had a child before him and one after. But both had died young and only he had lived long enough to learn how to talk.

Lukas wondered if Etienne really would come with him to Prague. They talked about it one night around the blazing log fire of a tavern.

'I like the sound of it,' explained Etienne. 'There is wealth – as you'd expect with the Emperor there. And where there is wealth there is trade. And trade brings opportunity! I'm always open to opportunity.'

True to his word, whenever their funds ran low Etienne would concoct some money-making scheme. They played the same trick whenever they were with a fresh bunch of travellers, especially if they were among people just going from one village to the next. They would always sit separately in the wagon, giving no indication that they knew each other. People talked on the journey, as they always did, and Etienne would sit there in silence, pretending to doze while listening intently to his fellow passengers. Then he would join in the conversation. A while after that he would let on that he had the gift of second sight. Lukas would immediately challenge him to tell his fortune.

Etienne would take his hands and examine his palms. 'You are an adventurous young man,' he would say, 'who has travelled far and who does not wait for life to happen to him – he goes and seeks his fate and fortune.'

Someone would always scoff, usually a young man. 'He's travelling – of course he's adventurous. And he has travelled a long way – with an accent like that I'd say he was from way to the north.'

Others would shush the scoffer. Etienne would ignore him and carry on pontificating, knowing that everyone in the wagon was listening.

'You have the hands of a healer,' he would say to Lukas. 'Your destiny is in the healing arts.'

Then Lukas would gasp and say, 'Well, that's extraordinary. For I am travelling to be apprenticed to my uncle, who is a physician.'

That would really get everyone's attention. Then Etienne would say, 'I see a beautiful woman with long dark hair and eyes like sapphires. She will bring you much happiness and many children.'

Lukas would look delighted and offer Etienne a silver crown. By then the rest of the carriage would be clamouring for this exceptional young man to tell their fortune too.

Etienne would play them like a fiddle, telling the man with a local accent, whose hands were ingrained with soil and as rough as his clothes, that he toiled in the fields but did not get the rewards in life he deserved. One day he too would become a farmer with his own land.

To the plain girl with no wedding ring, who was fast approaching middle years, he would say she had had many disappointments in her life and that someone as good and kind as her had not been properly appreciated. But he could see that her heart line pointed to a promising future, perhaps with a gentle man who was older than her.

To the elderly woman dressed in black he would ask, 'And have you had a recent loss?' If she shook her head he would say, 'I thought not,' although this rarely happened. Death was usually a safe bet with the elderly.

That was the way of the world.

Lukas would tie himself in knots trying not to laugh at these obvious guesses and note how easily Etienne gained the confidence of his victims by flattery and carefully worded questions.

And then, after each telling, they would all reach into their purses or pockets. At the end of that day's journey, all the passengers would go on their way confident that their lives were soon to change for the better. And Lukas and Etienne would have enough coins for a meal and a bed for the night.

When the River Main grew narrow and what had been a broad waterway turned to a fordable stream and then a brook, Etienne declared their journey was coming to an end. 'We follow the Main into the highlands and then pick up the River Eger into Bohemia. We're still two or three weeks off our destination, but there's not long to go now.'

They passed Leitmeritz and when the Eger flowed into the Vltava, they followed it all the way south to Prague.

# CHAPTER FOUR

It was a sharp spring morning when Lukas and Etienne first caught sight of the city. Everything on the skyline seemed sharp too. There were churches with pointy spires, towers with pointy spires and even some of the spires had smaller spires. The roofs and walls of the densely packed buildings glowed in brilliant sunshine, and smoke from a thousand chimneys rose straight into the still air.

A stout crenellated wall encircled the entire metropolis, which sat on a bend of a river spanned by a vast stone bridge with two great towers. Lukas had never seen a bridge quite so impressive.

As they grew closer the smoke and stench of the place began to catch in their throats, and the sheer volume of people coming and going through the city gates was bewildering.

Lukas had committed to memory the letter from his Uncle Anselmus, which he had carried with him when he left Ghent. He had lost it, along with everything else, when they had been robbed in Momalle.

Etienne, with his instinct for such people, had met a forger in a hostel shortly before they reached the capital, and had asked him to run up a replacement of Anselmus's letter. He also had a 'letter of introduction' made for himself, under a false name of course, purporting to be from a Prague merchant, offering him work and accommodation in his business. Both were essential to get them into the walled city.

Lukas had been told to bring his letter to the palace gate and announce himself to the guards as apprentice to Anselmus Declercq – court physician to His Imperial Majesty the Holy Roman Emperor.

He had wondered if the palace would be difficult to find, but it was obvious where he needed to go. High above the houses and churches, atop a steep hill, the Castle loomed huge over the rest of the capital.

As they approached via the North Gate Lukas bade Etienne goodbye. With both of them carrying forged documents, they had decided it would be best to enter the city separately.

'When you have found lodgings send word to me at the Castle,' Lukas said, then thanked his friend for helping him reach his destination.

Etienne gave him a warm hug and assured him they had helped each other. He promised he would contact him within the week. He wished him well in his new appointment and then strode briskly away.

Lukas wondered if he would see Etienne again. He had grown fond of him over the last few months.

Seeing that Lukas's destination was the Castle, the city guards waved him through almost immediately, and he wandered along the narrow streets staring open-mouthed at the strange buildings and people. It had been many months since he had walked the streets of a big city. The stench was suffocating. Ghent never smelled as bad as this.

As the city closed in around him he tried to remember

the direction of the Castle. Almost at once he bumped into someone, who shoved him aside so hard he fell on the cobbled ground. The man said something heatedly in a language he could not understand and hurried away. Lukas noticed his assailant had only one ear.

In the fall he dropped his bag. As he gathered his senses a young boy ran up to him and picked it up. Before Lukas realised he was stealing it rather than handing it back, he was gone, disappearing into a narrow alley.

There was little in the bag that Lukas would miss – just a change of clothes. But the suddenness of the theft shocked him. Wisely he had had the good sense to carry his money on his belt.

The North Gate took him into the heart of the Jewish Quarter. While many countries had expelled their Jews they were welcomed in Prague, and Lukas looked with interest at the curiously fashioned temples of their faith.

He reached a grand square overlooked by a vast church with magnificent soaring twin towers and was distracted by the wailing coming from two tiny baskets left by one of the church doorways. No one was paying them any attention.

Across the square, heaving with market stalls and people, there was another tower. Lukas guessed it was Prague's famous Astronomical Clock. A crowd had gathered around the side and as it chimed midday Lukas could see why. The clock itself was a bewilderingly intricate set of dials, hands and strange figures that came to life when the hour was struck. He watched with wonder, but there was something sinister about it.

The crowd's attention was suddenly caught by a

commotion on the other side of the square. Lukas stood on a pillar in front of one of the grand buildings to see over people's heads. A bear with a spiked collar around its neck was chained to a sunken pole. Lukas could hear the yapping of hunting dogs and the laughter of the onlookers.

Lukas watched for a while, unable to drag his eyes from the spectacle. As he turned away a great shriek rose from the crowd. The bear had broken free, and Lukas could see it lumbering across the square, dragging the broken pole behind it, while two men with whips and gauntlets tried to catch up.

Lukas hoped this was not an omen. He quickened his pace, sensing he would be safe only once he reached the security of the Castle. He was ashamed to feel so unnerved. Here on his own, he felt a long way from home.

It was easy to get lost in the narrow streets. When he passed for the second time a shop with a large green wooden lobster hanging over the door, he knew he needed help.

He had picked up a few words of the Bohemian tongue and approached a young beggar with a peg leg and asked, 'Kamenný most?' – the Stone Bridge. The man held out his hand and Lukas reached for the purse on his belt. It was gone. Someone must have lifted it as he watched the clock or the bear. There hadn't been much money in it, but Lukas felt stupid for having it stolen. He had thought he was sharper than that. Lukas shrugged to show he had no money and the beggar turned away.

*

Eventually he emerged from the maze of streets and one of the great bridge towers stood before him. The bridge spanned the broad river and was wide enough for two hay wagons to pass.

With dismay, Lukas spotted a tollbooth. Buttoning his coat against the bitter river breeze, he stood by the entrance for nearly an hour – begging with his hand held out – before someone gave him the pfennig he needed to cross.

Stepping on to the bridge, Lukas could see trails of golden water plants catching the sunlight. All along the waterline were sawmills, tanneries and boat-building yards.

'Out of my way,' shouted a harsh voice above the clip-clop of hoofs and the grinding of wheels on cobblestone. Lukas darted into one of the passing points on the bridge as a large wagon trundled past. 'You dolt!' shouted the red-faced man who drove the wagon, and lashed his whip down on Lukas's head. The whip caught his cheek and drew blood.

Lukas waited for a gap between wagons and ran. Catching his breath at another passing point he looked up to admire the great tower that marked the western side of the river. Something ominous caught his eye. On the upper ramparts were heads on spikes. Some were rotten green, some were skulls picked to the bone by carrion birds, others were fresh with slivers of tendon or a dribble of dried blood still dangling from the severed neck. Who were they? Criminals? Traitors? Feeling a little sick, Lukas shivered as he thought of all the things he and Etienne had done. Guiltily he glanced around, even though no one in Prague knew him.

Beyond the bridge was the great bulk of the Castle, big enough to be a prosperous-looking town in itself.

The road leading from the river was quite different to that on the other side of the bridge. It led past grand buildings with cloistered pavements and all manner of shops. There were fewer people here and they were better dressed.

Wondering where to find the entrance to the Castle, Lukas thought to try his Czech again 'Hrad?' he said to one man, who hurried past without even looking at him.

Another did stop – and pointed to a steep hill to the right of the square. Lukas climbed until the cobbled street narrowed, then stopped at a broad stone staircase. This twisted steeply to a large open square where the Castle lay before him, with a magnificent view of the city below. Lukas felt a great rush of excitement. This amazing palace was to be his home.

# CHAPTER FIVE

The Castle stood above the city's smoke and filth and stench. Like the streets and the people, the air here was cleaner.

It seemed extraordinary to Lukas that one man should have such a vast fortress to call his home. But then, he was the Holy Roman Emperor – successor to the late great Roman Empire. Rudolph was lord of half of Europe.

The closer Lukas got to the Castle the more his apprehension grew. He had never met his uncle. His father had spoken fondly of him, but said there was always something going on inside his head that the rest of his family were not privy to. He would begin a sentence and never finish it, because something more interesting had intercepted his train of thought. They had mocked him roundly for his absent-mindedness when they were children, said his father. But what now? wondered Lukas. Now Anselmus was an accomplished fellow of great standing, would he be prickly and impossible to understand? He would soon find out.

The entrance gate was modest for such a grand building – only a small carriage could pass through. Approaching it, Lukas regarded the palace guard with a flutter of trepidation. They had pikes with vicious spikes and stared directly ahead. There must still be blood on Lukas's face where the wagon driver had caught him with his whip. He wished he'd thought to wash it off.

Lukas walked up to the nearest guard and stood in front of him. The man ignored him. He coughed, looked him straight in the eye, and still the man ignored him.

'Stand away,' came a ringing command from within the gate. Lukas looked over, and there was another guard, an officer by the look of his uniform, with sword drawn.

'Hello, sir,' said Lukas. 'I am come here to meet with my uncle, the court physician.'

'Be off with you,' said the man. 'You insult the office of the Holy Roman Emperor. And if you come back on my watch I shall run you through.'

Feeling very small, Lukas gathered the courage to speak again. 'Sir, I have travelled from Ghent to meet with my uncle. His name is Anselmus Declercq, and I am his nephew, Lukas Declercq.'

'Off,' said the officer. 'Off and do not return.' He advanced with his sword pointing directly at Lukas. 'It is only the thought of your wretched blood soiling the Castle portal that stops me from killing you.'

'Please let me show you the letter from my uncle,' begged Lukas. He fumbled in his coat and produced his forgery of Anselmus's letter of introduction. At least that hadn't been stolen when he arrived in Prague. The officer was looking dangerously impatient.

Lukas opened the letter and held it out for inspection. The officer plucked it away from him with the point of his sword.

'Where is your baggage? Where are your servants? You do not even have a purse to your name.'

Lukas started to explain that he had been robbed on

his arrival in the city, but the officer was examining the letter and clearly not listening.

'Arrest this vagrant for impersonating a relative of the court.'

The forged letter might have fooled the guards at the city gate, but it was not good enough for the palace.

'Take him to Daliborka Tower.'

Surrounded by four soldiers, Lukas was dragged into the Castle. As he turned a corner into a dark alley he saw the officer rip his letter to shreds and let them scatter in the wind.

Lukas was hauled through a series of grand courtyards and portals, then past the narrow northern wall of the Castle along the yawning face of the Cathedral nave. When they reached another great courtyard he screwed up his courage and shouted, 'Uncle Anselmus, help . . .' but the 'me' was squeezed from his lips into a strangulated squawk.

'Shut up,' said the guard, holding him by the throat.

At the bottom of the hill was another guarded gate and for a few glorious moments Lukas thought they were going to throw him out the other end. But they turned sharp left and he was dragged up a steep flight of stairs and through a small maze of passageways. Below them was an ancient stone tower. Down they went and Lukas had to move his feet very quickly to stop them bashing against the stone steps.

At the entrance to the tower one of the guards banged three times on a black wooden door fortified with heavy iron struts and bolts. In the pause that followed Lukas could hear shouting, or was it screaming? His stomach turned over and he thought he would be sick.

The tower reeked of unwashed bodies and human effluent. A voice behind the door demanded to know who was there. 'Imperial guard with a prisoner,' came the reply. Bolts were drawn back. The door opened with a billowing fart of heat and stinking smoke. In front of them was a narrow staircase. Lukas heard a high, unnatural shrieking, and something in the smell coming up the stairs reminded him of burning meat.

'Down we go,' said a guard with mocking cheeriness. Lukas was shoved almost off balance and stumbled before he regained his equilibrium. What were they going to do to him?

The scene that greeted him at the bottom of the stairs was beyond his imagination. Lukas fainted.

Another scream brought him abruptly to his senses. He was soaked through. He wondered if he had wet himself in fright, but then recalled the sensation of cold water being thrown over him. He was in a small enclosure built into the side of the wall, facing a wooden door with a small iron grille. The cell had no ceiling and was like a large chimney breast with an open top about twelve feet up, through which he could see the wooden joists of the floor above.

He steeled himself to peep through the grille. He was in the Castle torture chamber. There were body cages and all manner of tongs, prodders, stocks and chains. Some half-starved wretch was tied spreadeagled to a rack and a gross, sweaty, bare-chested man with a black hood over his head was prodding him with a red-hot poker.

The scrawny prisoner did not scream again and Lukas marvelled at his courage until he realised he was unconscious or worse. Despite his own terror, Lukas wondered what the poor man had done to deserve such hellish treatment.

He heard the door at the top of the staircase burst open and a small spring of hope fluttered in his breast. Uncle Anselmus? Surely someone would have told him his nephew had arrived.

There were several sets of footsteps clattering down the stairs. Lukas craned his neck to see.

A gaunt, severe-looking man with cropped white hair swept into the room accompanied by three soldiers and a priest. 'Has the wretch confessed?' he said to the fat man.

'No, Grand Inquisitor,' he replied with a bow.

The gaunt man ordered water to be thrown over the unconscious prisoner. Lukas watched with mounting terror. Was this what they were going to do to him?

The prisoner began to groan and then came to. 'Do you admit to consorting with Satan and all his minions?' said the Inquisitor.

The man gibbered hysterically.

'See how he mocks us,' said the Inquisitor. 'See how he laughs in our face.' He turned to the hooded man again. 'Apply the iron.'

Lukas turned away and heard a ghastly scream.

When he could bear to look he saw that the prisoner had passed out again.

'He is being assisted by Satan,' said the Inquisitor. 'The dark one has lulled him into sleep. See how he has not a care in the world. Apply the iron.'

Lukas steeled himself for another scream, but none came.

'Even my poker cannot raise him from his slumber,' said the man in the hood.

'More water,' said the Inquisitor. The man was doused again.

After a pause the Inquisitor looked at the prisoner, then stepped forward and held his wrist. He placed a brass ear trumpet on the man's chest and listened.

'He's dead,' he snarled, and struck the fat man with the trumpet, denting it with the force of his blow. 'If you kill any more of the prisoners, I shall begin to suspect you are an agent of Beelzebub – sent to spare his disciples from the wrath of the Inquisition.'

'My lord,' said the man fearfully, 'I have taken every care. This one must have been weakened by his wickedness. Perhaps the succubi have been visiting him at night?'

It was strange to see the torturer so afraid. He could easily have picked up the Inquisitor and thrown his spindly body against the wall or even the bed of spikes that was propped upright close to Lukas's cell.

'And who else do we have?' said the Inquisitor.

'One from the country, accused of bewitching his neighbour's cattle,' said another, more confident voice. Lukas guessed it was one of the soldiers. 'And a vagrant. Tried to enter the Castle under false pretences.'

'Well, he's no concern of mine,' said the Inquisitor, 'and the sorcerer can wait a little longer.' He turned on his heels and left.

Lukas sat down in his cell and tried to ignore the gnawing in his guts. He felt exhausted, and the warmth from the braziers used to heat the irons was making him drowsy. Despite the terrible scenes playing in his head he fell into a fitful sleep. As he dozed he became aware that he was being sprinkled by something. At first he thought it was rain from a leaking roof, but he quickly recognised the sour smell of urine.

Lukas looked up, disbelief etched on his face. There, in the shadows above him, unnoticed before, was a cage with another prisoner in it.

'Stop it,' he shouted, his fear briefly exceeded by revulsion.

'You should have to worry about far worse things than that,' said a sheepish voice above his head. 'What else am I supposed to do? Let my bladder burst?'

'Silence,' said a guard somewhere in the dungeon.

His misery complete, Lukas fought back tears. There was another clatter of boots on stone stairs. 'Present me with the boy and hand me a leading stick,' said a stern voice.

The cell door was unbolted and Lukas was grabbed by the shoulders. He was held upright by two burly guards while another slipped something over his head. It was a heavy iron hoop on a long wooden pole. Lukas could not see what was inside the hoop but he could certainly feel it. The whole thing was lined with sharp spikes, pressing into his soft skin.

The man holding the pole gave a little tug and the spikes bit into the back of his neck. Lukas tried to be brave, but as the hoop gnawed into his neck again he gasped in pain. 'Silence,' said a man behind him. He wanted to turn and look, but moving his head even a little made the spikes bite.

'Advance,' said a guard.

Lukas yelped as he struggled upward. Aside from the spikes, the hoop was heavy around his shoulders and its rough iron rim chafed his skin.

It was getting dark now – early evening, he would guess – and lights burned from every window.

'To the palace court,' said the voice behind him. They walked up the hill towards the huge Cathedral, and as they reached the large courtyard that lay before its southern exterior Lukas was jerked into a doorway and up a sloping ramp. He felt like that bear he had seen on a chain and understood why it had been so desperate to escape. He could feel a wet trickle down his neck now, where the spikes had drawn blood. He didn't look down to see how much. It was too painful to move his head.

They entered a courtroom with an imposing wooden platform where a handful of officials were sitting solemnly under the soft glow of hundreds of candles.

An elderly bearded man in an impressive cloak sat at the centre of the platform in a great wooden chair. Lukas had seen men in similar dress at his father's trial, before he was burned at the stake.

'And what is the nature of the crime?' the elderly man enquired.

The palace gate officer stepped forward. 'Vagrancy and impersonating a relative of the court in order to gain entry to the palace.'

'And on what do you base this charge?' said the elderly man.

'Despite having the appearance of a vagrant, the youth here claims to have travelled all the way from Ghent, sire. Yet he has no baggage and no retinue. He also has no money at all. Following recent attempts on the life of His Imperial Highness, I have good reason to suspect he is an assassin, come to infiltrate the court. And the letter of introduction he produced was plainly a forgery.'

'A wise precaution,' said the old man. He turned his gaze to Lukas. 'And what do you have to say?'

Lukas could barely speak. He could not believe the grave charges levelled against him.

'I am the nephew of Anselmus Declercq, court physician,' he said.

The old man looked upon him with contempt. 'Anselmus Declercq? How do you know of a court physician with such a name? A wretch like you. You are not related to such a prominent person.'

'Please, sir,' said Lukas, 'can Anselmus be summoned so I may talk to him?'

'Such impertinence,' the officer scoffed. 'His Eminence is away from the Castle on imperial business. It is not known when he will return.'

'Your story is nothing but lies,' said the old man to Lukas. He turned to the officer. 'Take this vagabond back to the Daliborka Tower and put him to the torture. I want to know who else was conspiring with him to kill the Emperor.'

The leading stick twitched again. This time Lukas felt its spikes in his throat. 'Please,' he gasped in desperation, 'I tell the truth.'

'To the torture,' thundered the old man, and waved a hand dismissively.

Out into the evening air they went and back down the narrow road to the tower. Just as they came to the staircase that led to the northern wall, a group of people came in through the Eastern Gate. Lukas searched their faces, seeking a likeness he might recognise as family. He had never met his uncle, but he supposed he might look a bit like his father.

It was difficult to see in the evening gloom, but just at the end of the party Lukas saw a well-dressed man of middle years with a nose just like his father's. 'Uncle Anselmus,' he cried out. 'Anselmus Declercq!'

The man turned. 'Who is this brat?' he asked.

'A vagrant assassin,' said a guard.

'Please, sir,' Lukas pleaded. 'I am your brother's son.'

'I have no brother,' said the man with a shrug, and walked away.

The guards continued with their prisoner, not concerned now to keep the spikes from piercing his neck.

Daliborka Tower loomed before them, and Lukas could see the heavy wooden door that led to the dungeon below. Now he knew what was down there, he could barely keep his legs from collapsing beneath him. Only the thought of tearing his neck on the spikes of the collar kept him upright.

They shuffled down the stairs, the heat from the dungeon fires rising up in a pungent miasma. The collar was removed and the guards flung Lukas back into a cell. He sat there in his own bubble of misery, wishing he could magic himself away.

Time passed. There was a banging at the door. Footsteps approached his cell. Lukas did not peer out to see who was coming. His cell door creaked open and he cowered against the wall, his eyes tight shut in terror.

'Some supper for you,' said a kindly voice.

Lukas look up in disbelief. One of the guards had brought a pitcher of water and a wooden plate with bread, cheese and sausage.

'You can't torture a man without a proper meal inside him,' he said.

Despite his fear, Lukas wolfed down the food. He had had nothing to eat since the morning.

'When will they come to torture me?' asked Lukas.

'Later,' said the man plainly. Then he looked around to see who else was in the dungeon. 'Look, lad,' he whispered close to the grille, 'just tell them what you've been up to. Everyone talks eventually. Save yourself all that nastiness. If you tell them right away, they'll kill you quickly. Beheading . . . probably. It'll be over in no time. But if you won't tell them, then it'll just go on. Nobody likes that. Well, most of us don't.'

'But I haven't done anything,' said Lukas desperately. 'I've come to see my uncle, Anselmus Declercq.'

The man shook his head and let out a weary sigh. 'Let's be having that plate and pitcher,' he said.

'Thank you for your advice,' said Lukas, grateful that someone had spoken kindly to him. Now that he was a little stronger for eating, he dared to look again through his cell door. There were two fires in braziers and a selection of iron bars and pokers. Feeling faint, he looked elsewhere.

His eyes settled on the most terrifying piece of apparatus, which looked like a bed frame with iron chains and a pulley and rope attached to the lower end. This was a rack. His father had been tortured on a similar device. Victims were stretched by their arms and legs until the bones came out of their sockets. Lukas wondered what sort of man would make use of such a thing.

The door banged again and Lukas heard footsteps and a commotion on the stairs.

'Hey there,' cried a voice before them. 'Hey there.'

Lukas peered again through his door. A tall, spindly man of middle years was hurrying towards them. A shock of white hair sprouted over his ears, below a gleaming bald pate. A great white beard grew down to his chest.

'Is this the prisoner who asked for Anselmus Declercq?' he said to the guards. He was quite out of breath.

The guards nodded. Lukas began to speak. 'Uncle?'

'You must be Lukas,' said the strange man as he peered through the slit in the door. 'You are the image of your mother.'

# CHAPTER SIX

For one giddy moment Lukas thought his uncle might take him away then and there. But the guards were having none of it.

'Eminence,' said one, 'we cannot release this boy on your say-so. We have to consult the officer of the watch.'

There was renewed banging at the door.

The officer who had first arrested him arrived with an enormous sinister figure, wearing a hood that covered his face. Lukas guessed it must be the torturer he had seen earlier.

The big man swept off his cloak with a theatrical flourish. He was bare-chested and a broad black leather belt held up his considerable breeches. Although he was running to fat, which fell in wobbly folds around his middle, he gave an impression of possessing great strength.

'Prepare the prisoner for torture,' said the officer. The fat man picked up some bellows and began to fire up the coals in the braziers.

Anselmus spoke up. 'There has been a mistake, Freiherr Svoboda. This boy is my nephew. He has come to the Castle to serve as my apprentice.'

'Your Eminence,' said the officer arrogantly, 'how can you be sure he is not an imposter? Have you met the boy before? The only way to discover the truth is to torture him.'

'You will do no such thing,' said Anselmus. He sounded alarmed, which made Lukas even more afraid. 'Who is the officer of the watch? He must be informed at once.'

Svoboda turned to him and said curtly, 'The officer of the watch is fully informed of the situation.'

'Then I shall go to him immediately and –'

Svoboda cut him off in his tracks. 'Save yourself the trouble. You are speaking to him.' He turned to the guards. 'Bring out the prisoner.'

'You must stop at once,' said Anselmus, as Lukas was dragged from his cell.

'Your Eminence,' said Svoboda, 'I have jurisdiction in this matter. I ask you respectfully to withdraw.'

One of the guards placed a mailed hand on Anselmus's shoulder and the physician was firmly marched away, spluttering angry protestations.

Lukas watched in despair as his uncle disappeared up the winding staircase. Guards on either side hauled him up. He was so terrified his legs had collapsed beneath him.

'Chain him up,' said Svoboda.

Lukas's hands were placed roughly in manacles attached to chains that hung down from the ceiling.

'Haul,' ordered Svoboda.

Behind his back Lukas could hear a clanking noise. Then his arms were jerked tight and he was lifted off his feet. The manacles bit into his wrists and his hands fumbled for the chains above them to take his weight. At once, his shoulders began to ache.

His shirt was ripped off and he felt the heat of the braziers on his bare back. They left him there for a few minutes. Then Svoboda approached him, his brow beaded with sweat. He leaned so close Lukas could taste his stale breath.

'Who persuaded you to commit treason? Was it the Duke of Freiberg? Was it the Lutherans? Was it the Jews? The Turks?'

Although he knew it would not help him, Lukas could not bring himself to lie. 'My story is true, sir. I am come to serve as apprentice to my Uncle Anselmus.'

'Ready the iron,' said Svoboda.

Lukas felt the scorching heat of the fire iron on the small of his back as the torturer held it close, waiting for his moment. He imagined his skin was already blistering in its scarlet glow. It was like some glassy nightmare. Everything around him, his every sense, was pin sharp – the manacles cutting his wrists, the acrid smells of the dungeon, the flickering light from the braziers – as he waited for the agony to come. Was this what hell was like? He fought the urge to gabble out a confession. What could he tell them?

Another voice butted in. 'Enough, Freiherr Svoboda. Release this youth.'

It wasn't his uncle, but Lukas recognised the voice from somewhere.

'But, Your Excellency, the boy was about to confess.' Svoboda sounded almost petulant.

'I'm sure he was,' replied the newcomer. 'I'm sure he was.'

Lukas felt the chains lower. As soon as his feet touched the ground he twisted round. His uncle was with a man he recognised as the head of the court. The one who had sent him here to be tortured earlier that evening.

44

Anselmus took off his cloak and wrapped it round Lukas's shoulders. 'Come,' he said. 'It's over.'

As they walked out of the stifling heat of the dungeon, Lukas began to shiver in the cold air. He was grateful for his uncle's cloak and pulled it tight around his body. His two rescuers held on to him on either side, not speaking. Lukas sensed there was an awkward atmosphere between them.

They turned into a large doorway with guards on either side. This was where they had taken him to the court. The doorway led into an impressive passageway – large enough to accommodate a carriage and team of horses.

Anselmus and the judge parted company. 'Thank you for your intervention, my lord,' said Anselmus briskly. The judge nodded but made no reply.

Anselmus led Lukas up another winding staircase to the side of the hall, up and up, until they could go no higher. 'Here are my quarters,' he said, indicating an ornate wooden door with elaborately cast silver hinges and handle.

Behind it was a large, well-heated room. Thick blankets hung at every door, and the walls were covered in tapestries.

'Sit down by the fire,' said his uncle. 'I shall fetch you a shirt and some supper.'

As Anselmus banged pots and pans around in the kitchen and muttered to himself, Lukas stared into the fire feeling supremely glad to be alive. He was bewildered too. This was the city where he had come to be safe, yet he had faced death within hours of arriving.

His uncle returned with a damp flannel for Lukas to mop the dried blood around his neck. Then he brought a steaming goblet of mulled wine and a thick woollen shirt. Lukas expected him to look relieved, but could see he was deeply angry instead.

'You are lucky that I returned. I have been in Zidice these last few days and only arrived back this evening.'

He paused, then looked sad. 'This is an unpredictable place, Lukas,' he said. 'There are many traps for the unwary and each one of us at court must be vigilant. The palace is home to men of widely differing beliefs and opinions – all of them vying for the Emperor's attention and approval. I learned of your arrival only because my friend Ruzicka told me he had encountered a frightened youth on a leading stick who asked after me.'

'Who is the Inquisitor?' asked Lukas. 'I had heard this city was free of the Inquisition.'

Anselmus sighed. 'Monsignor Gerwald Mach. He's the Inquisition's representative here and a very bitter man!' Anselmus laughed scornfully. 'Our venerable Emperor, long may he prosper, won't let him persecute the Jews, or the Protestants, or the alchemists and astronomers, so he's just left with witchcraft.'

Lukas slept on a couch in front of the fire. He woke frequently from nightmares, and the aches and bruises from his ordeal left him restless. When dawn came he was disturbed by the clatter of pots and pans in the kitchen. He turned around and pulled his blanket over his head and drifted back to a blissful sleep, almost delirious with relief that he had been spared from torture. Later he was woken again, by someone close by, raking the ashes from the fire.

He peered over his blanket to see the slender back of a young woman on her knees at the fireplace. Her clothes were rough and he supposed she was Anselmus's maid. He coughed to draw attention to himself. She turned and shrieked.

He guessed she was in her early twenties. She was small and dark, and once she had recovered her senses she curtsied formally and said something to Lukas he did not understand. He sat up in bed and introduced himself. But she seemed desperately anxious to be away.

Undeterred, he repeated his name. 'Lukas,' he said, pointing at himself.

'Otka,' she said, and fled.

Lukas heard her agitated voice outside the room. Anselmus appeared soon afterwards. 'Met Otka, have you?' he said with a chuckle. 'I didn't get the chance to warn her I had a visitor.'

'I frightened her,' said Lukas bashfully. Actually he was quite amused by her reaction.

'She comes in every morning,' said Anselmus, 'then goes after supper. Her stepfather works in the alchemy workshops. He's not a natural philosopher,' he said loftily. 'He just tidies up, keeps the fires burning – that sort of thing. They live on Golden Lane, a bit close to Daliborka Tower for my liking.'

'And Golden Lane is part of the Castle?' said Lukas.

'Yes, yes, of course.' Anselmus sounded testy. Lukas felt confused. How was he supposed to know? Perhaps Anselmus noticed the hurt look on his face. 'I will ask Otka to show you around the Castle after you have eaten,' he said.

They had a long and pleasant breakfast, Lukas still light-headed with relief. Anselmus told him he had been expecting him since March. He was anxious for news of his sister-in-law and keen to know as much as possible about his new apprentice.

When he asked about the medicinal properties of camomile and Lukas looked blank, Anselmus snapped, 'I knew all about camomile when I was your age.' Clearly there would have to be a great deal of learning in a very short time.

Having been assured that Otka would not disturb him, Lukas took a bath in front of the fire and then dressed in some of his uncle's clothes. He was tall for his age and Anselmus was only a little taller. The clothes felt big on him, but not uncomfortably so. 'When you earn your first wage you must buy your own clothes,' said his uncle, 'but until then you can make do with mine.'

When he was ready, Anselmus called for Otka. She appeared immediately and gave them both a little bow. Lukas thought she had a nice face, although she was not what he would have thought of as pretty. Anselmus spoke to her in the Bohemian tongue. Lukas had picked up a few words on his travels, but not enough to hold a conversation or understand what was being said now.

'She speaks a little German too,' said Anselmus. 'I'm sure you will be able to manage.' Like many Netherlanders, Lukas had grown up speaking both Flemish and German.

Otka looked at him and smiled, showing her large white teeth, which seemed slightly too big for her mouth. 'Follow,' she said.

# CHAPTER SEVEN

They walked out to a bright spring morning. Only now he wasn't terrified could Lukas begin to enjoy his extraordinary surroundings. He passed through a great stone door and out into a square that most prosperous towns would be pleased to call their own.

But instead of the usual bustle of a town or city, this square was almost empty except for a small squad of soldiers and a few hurrying courtiers. Lukas felt like a trespasser.

Otka pointed at the huge Gothic structure immediately to their left. 'St Vitus,' she said.

Most big cities had a cathedral. The Castle had one to itself. The size of it filled Lukas with awe, but there was something a little sinister about the knobbly buttresses and arches that rose like a great thicket of thorns into the sky.

They walked through two vast courtyards separated by an enormous building. Otka pointed to some windows above a magnificent fountain. 'Emperor sleep here,' she said, and put her head to one side on her clasped hands.

She pointed to another building. 'Shhhh,' she said with a finger to her pursed lips. 'Treasure!'

'What sort?' said Lukas.

'All sort,' she said. 'Everything. Amaze! But shhhh-hhhh! Otherwise . . .' She mimed a knife being drawn across her throat.

Lukas was curious. He would ask his uncle about it.

Another passage led to the Western Gate of the Castle. It was here, Lukas recalled with a shudder, that he had been seized by the palace guards.

They walked up to the ramparts and stood before a bridge spanning a great empty moat. A landscaped park lay beyond, with its own stone wall.

Otka pointed to the park and began to make animal noises. 'Grrrrrr.' She grimaced and clawed the air with both hands. Lukas looked puzzled. Then she put an arm up to her nose and waved it about, making trumpeting noises. Lukas wondered if she'd gone mad.

She was enjoying seeing him look bewildered. She stooped low and swung her arms around in front of her, making grunting sounds.

Lukas knew all the great palaces of Europe had their own menagerie. At last he realised Otka was mimicking the animals in this one. He growled and clawed at the air. 'Lion?' he said. She nodded. He made a trumpeting noise. 'Elephant?' He swung his arms. 'Monkey?'

'Go back,' she said, and ushered him back inside the Castle. They approached a large round tower on the great north wall and an assortment of pungent odours, predominantly sulphur, assaulted Lukas's nostrils. He could hear strange clattering and shouting, and behind one window were intermittent flashes and sparks.

'Powder Tower,' said Otka. She mimicked the long hair and beards of the natural philosophers and pretended to pour material from one container to another. 'They take dirt,' she pretended to scoop up earth. 'Then, *PRRRRKKKHHH*, is gold!' She shook her head. 'Is nonsense.'

Lukas had heard about alchemists. Everyone with a little learning knew about them. In some parts of the continent they burned you at the stake for dabbling in alchemy, but it seemed Emperor Rudolph encouraged it.

'Can we see?' he asked Otka.

She beckoned him to go in. Her stepfather worked there, she said.

'Does your mother work in the Castle too?' asked Lukas.

Otka shook her head and pointed to the sky. 'Heaven,' she said.

They walked up a steep spiral staircase into the stifling heat of the laboratories. Lukas was immediately reminded of Daliborka Tower and wondered how anyone could bear to work in such a place. Most of the first floor was taken up by a large circular room, with one or two smaller rooms off it. There were bubbling flasks and cauldrons and bizarre many-tentacled receptacles that resembled strange glass sea creatures. The smell of burning coal, woodsmoke and chemicals was suffocating. Lukas covered his face with the sleeve of his shirt and tried not to cough. Men, most with spectacles and beards, bustled and mithered over their experiments, like mother hens with chicks. Thin slits let in a little natural light to supplement the candles and fires, but most of the walls were taken up with shelves stuffed dangerously full of glass and earthenware jars. Each one had a label on it – strange words Lukas half recognised: *Phosphor*, *Brimstone*, *Amalgama*, *Vitriol* . . .

Close to the implements were open books. Lukas peered cautiously at the nearest one. The instructions were handwritten and although they were in plain language, rather than code, they made no sense to him at all:

*The greater the quantity of the Eagle opposed to the Lion the shorter the combat; torment the Lion until he is weary and desires death . . .*

Accompanying the text were extraordinary illustrations – in beautiful greens, reds and blues. One showed the torso of a naked woman with the wings, neck and head of a swan, emerging from a cauldron of boiling red liquid.

'Father,' shouted Otka, and waved excitedly. The alchemists at work in the laboratory looked up disapprovingly. A dark-haired burly man, with several days' stubble, rushed over. He was stripped to the waist, his body covered with soot and grime. 'Otka, my love,' he said gently, 'you shouldn't shout, disturbing the gentlemen like that. A wave would do.' She looked crestfallen and he squeezed her hand to show he had forgiven her.

'Now, who's this?' he said, smiling warmly at Lukas.

'Apprentice to Doktor Declercq,' said Otka.

Lukas bowed. As he was about to speak there was a commotion across the laboratory. Two assistants were carrying the body of an elderly alchemist from one of the smaller rooms. 'Get him outside,' said one of them, 'away from these fumes.' As they passed, Lukas noticed the elderly man's face had an unusual pink flush about it.

'That's Doktor Benisek,' said Otka's stepfather. 'He asked me to fetch him some zincum a couple of hours ago and not to bother him.'

'Does this happen a lot in the Powder Tower?' asked Lukas.

Otka's stepfather shook his head. 'Once or twice every few years. Who knows what it is. I'm sure some of them summon the Evil One to help with their experiments. Maybe that's why he wanted to be left alone.'

This talk of the Devil frightened Otka, and Lukas too. She tugged at his sleeve. 'We go!'

They emerged into the cool fresh air outside the tower. Doktor Benisek's lifeless body lay on the cobbled floor, surrounded by a small group of assistants. Lukas decided not to ask his uncle if he could work with the alchemists.

Otka tugged at his sleeve. 'More,' she said. They walked past dense buildings that blocked the sun, and two more churches.

'How many churches does a palace need?' muttered Lukas. God had taken his father, for no good reason that he could see. He was sick of being told that God moved in mysterious ways. But he still feared the Devil. The flames of hell seemed more real to him than the pastel blue and pink visions of heaven he saw in church paintings.

Otka was looking at him. She could see he was lost in thought. She quite liked this funny boy from the west. She showed him the vineyards out past the East Gate, then took him past the stairway leading to the dungeon. There was something she wanted to show him. Lukas caught a whiff of Daliborka Tower and his stomach turned over. He did not need reminding there was a dark side to the fairytale world of the palace. They arrived at a long narrow street on the edge of the northern wall. Here were the tiniest houses he had ever seen.

'Golden Lane,' she said with a flourish.

The doors were so small only a child could pass

through them without stooping. Each house was slightly different from the others in its arrangement of windows and doors. 'Who lives here?' said Lukas.

'Me,' she said proudly. 'And Father, and Emperor's servants, and . . .' She made that booming explosion noise.

'Alchemists?' said Lukas, guessing she did not know the right word.

She nodded and tapped her head. She thought they were mad. They both laughed and Lukas turned his face to the warm spring sunshine.

His reverie was broken by an impatient presence, eager to pass them as they blocked the archway into the lane. A man squeezed past. He was dapper in his black velvet robe and starched white ruff, and with a smattering of grey in his neatly trimmed hair and beard.

'Doktor Krohl,' said Otka with a wave and a grin as he hared past them. He turned impatiently. 'Lukas,' she announced proudly, pointing to him. 'Doktor Declercq's apprentice!'

The man gave them a brusque nod as he placed a key in one of the tiny doors.

Otka shrugged. 'Grumpy Doktor Krohl,' she said, giggling.

On the way back there was a great commotion in the street leading up to the palace. A party of travellers had just arrived with their great wooden caskets and cases. Lukas and Otka watched from a distance. The newcomers looked austere, with dark complexions and long, solemn faces. The men sported beards of medium length at the chin but shaved on the cheeks. Even their clothes were dark. Black was obviously the fashion

54

where they came from, despite the high cost of the dye to colour the fabric. Their tunics and dresses were richly embroidered with silver thread.

Lukas felt uneasy. They looked like the Spanish officials who ruled over his country. Then a snippet of conversation, snatched by the wind, reached his ears. His gut tightened a little. He had travelled halfway across Europe to be free of such men.

# CHAPTER EIGHT

While Otka prepared his midday meal, Lukas had a look around his uncle's apartment to take his mind off the new arrivals. Anselmus's living room was full of books. Many were magnificently bound in gold-embossed red or white leather, some with delicate floral motifs painted on the spines. Books like these cost more than an ordinary man would earn in half a lifetime. Most concerned medicine, but there were travel books too, discourses on natural philosophy and works from the ancient world.

By the window was a large table, spread out with books and papers and a bulky parchment register. A bleached human skull, a selection of feather quills and an ivory inkpot lay among the clutter. Lukas took a peek at what his uncle had been writing. It was an inventory of some sort, with neat, descriptive entries under the heading 'Purchases on behalf of His Imperial Highness':

**Mining compass, wood inlaid with bone ivory . . . Acquired January 9, 1598. 100 crowns.**

**Scourged Christ standing by a column – linden wood, painted, fine detail . . . Acquired March 18, 1598. 175 crowns.**

**Armour from Japan, iron, cord, leather, black lacquer . . . April 12, 1598. 300 crowns.**

The sun came out. The room was flooded with light and Lukas noticed a small oil painting nestling among the books on the far wall. It was his father, Thomas Declercq. The artist had caught his strong features and that unbending integrity – his mother called it stubbornness – that had seen him burned at the stake, refusing to recant his heretical beliefs.

To look on his father again, a year after his death, was like seeing a ghost. Lukas fought back his tears as a distant memory of home stirred in his mind – his father sitting for the portrait painter a few years before. 'Your uncle is doing very well in Prague,' he had said to Lukas. 'Anselmus can even afford to pay for my painting!' It was rare for ordinary people like them to have their portraits painted. Thomas Declercq's printing workshop kept them fed and clothed, but there was nothing left over for luxuries of that kind.

Thomas had been burned for publishing pamphlets that dared to question whether the purchase of holy relics and prayers to the saints were good for the soul. Thomas had come to believe these well-established rituals were flawed, and that only someone's faith – what was really in their heart – would save a man or woman from perpetual hellfire.

Lukas sensed the anxiety in his mother's voice when she warned Thomas that this philosophy would be the death of him – as it had been for so many other 'heretics'. Thomas reassured her he would be careful and publish his pamphlets anonymously.

Betrayal swiftly followed. Thomas Declercq was tortured on the rack and condemned as a disciple of Satan. The Sunday following his death the Bishop of

Ghent himself had preached a stern sermon on the dangers of heresy and a warning that a single spark of hellfire caused greater suffering than a thousand years of torture. Enraged by spiteful schoolyard taunts, Lukas had declared he found it hard to believe in any God, after what the church had done to his father. From that day on, his days in Ghent were numbered.

Otka returned with a bowl of soup and some bread. She could see Lukas was upset and put a maternal arm around his shoulder. She looked over at the painting and nodded. She knew who was portrayed there.

After a pause she said, 'Eminence. He come back at night. After,' she mimed spooning up his soup, 'you read.' She gave him a book with herbs and flowers painted on the spine.

'No,' said Lukas with a laugh, 'I sleep!' He wasn't sure he wanted his uncle's chambermaid telling him what to do.

She tried to look stern. 'No, you read. Eminence very angry if no!' She shook her fist.

So when he finished his soup he picked up the book *Tacuinum Sanitatis* – The Tables of Health. The crisply printed pages had hand-coloured illustrations of medicinal plants. Lukas was fascinated by the lists of herbs and the maladies they were reputed to cure, but eventually his eyelids drooped.

There was a commotion at the door and Lukas awoke from a deep sleep. Judging by the light against the wall it was already late afternoon. Anselmus had returned.

'Lukas, dear boy,' he said, 'has Otka ensured you attended to your studies?'

'Most conscientiously,' said Lukas.

He was struck by his uncle's outfit: a blue silk robe trimmed with velvet and a magnificent fur-lined cloak. Whatever his uncle did here, he was handsomely paid for it.

Anselmus turned to Otka. 'Now, my child. Supper, if you please. We shall eat in half an hour.'

She gave a little curtsy and left.

Lukas still had the new arrivals at the Castle on his mind. He wondered if they would persecute him if they knew about his father. 'Uncle, I saw a party of Spanish gentlemen arrive at the Castle today. Do you know why they're here?' he asked.

Anselmus gave a little shrug. He didn't seem particularly interested. 'People come and go all the time,' he said, 'and from all over the Empire. They may leave tomorrow or stay a year.'

He shuffled off to the kitchen and began to bring plates and cutlery in. Lukas had expected Otka to do this.

'Lukas,' he said, 'you may open a bottle of wine.'

All three of them sat around the large oak dining table, tucking into a venison stew. Lukas was surprised when Otka joined them. Anselmus could see it in his face. 'She cooked it. Why should she not enjoy it?' he said when she went into the kitchen to fetch a bowl of vegetables.

While they ate, Anselmus talked to Lukas about one of his great theories – that precious stones and crystals could cure sickness. 'Sapphire is the most reliable cure for ague,' he said, 'and cornelian mitigates the heat of the mind.'

Lukas nodded, but behind his look of earnest interest he did not have the first idea what his uncle was talking about. Otka was lost in her own world and hummed softly between mouthfuls.

Anselmus said, 'I am due to see the Emperor tomorrow, for his weekly examination. He also has a collection of precious gems he wishes me to inspect.' He paused, then added, 'Would you like to come with me?'

Lukas nearly choked on his stew. Aside from his brush with Prague's Grand Inquisitor in Daliborka Tower, he had never been in the presence of anyone more important than a town magistrate.

'What would I have to do, Uncle?'

'Keep your mouth shut. Stay absolutely still. Do only the things I ask you to do. Can you manage that?'

Lukas gave a big grin. 'And what will I have to wear?'

'We will find a suitable robe for you. I will ask Otka to cut one of mine down to size.'

Lukas couldn't believe what was happening to him. Only yesterday he had faced torture in the Castle dungeon. Tomorrow he was going to meet the Emperor.

# Chapter Nine

Anselmus and Lukas arrived at the door to the Emperor's quarters ten minutes early. Lukas liked the feel of his new silk gown. It was much smoother than scratchy wool. And he was fascinated by the way the colour shimmered in the light. He was also very nervous. So was Anselmus. He was muttering to himself, running over what he was going to say. Lukas was under strict instructions not to talk. So he looked around the gloomy Castle portal and at the mysterious crests and coats of arms that had been painted on the walls.

The Castle clock struck eleven. Anselmus snapped out of his muttering trance. Confidently advancing towards the great iron and wooden door, he banged its ornate silver-plated knocker with great authority. The sound echoed through the stone corridors.

There was a scuffle of feet behind the door and the rattle of several locks and bolts. A tall, imposing figure ushered them into the vestibule, then a larger room beyond.

'His Majesty will summon you shortly,' said the courtier.

Lukas looked around. The Emperor's quarters were grander than Anselmus's but the clutter was much the same. Every horizontal surface was covered with piles of books or ornaments or strange objects. Despite the carpets, tapestries and fires that burned in two fireplaces, the room had a dismal chill.

There were several paintings stacked around the room and hung on the wall. Most had a disturbing eroticism about them – depictions of naked women, with flushed, lascivious faces. Rosy cheeks and rosy bottoms. One great canvas that immediately caught his eye showed the Last Judgement. On the left of the picture, scores of naked men and women rose up to the blue skies of heaven. On the right side, hordes of equally naked people were being corralled by demons with pitchforks and driven into burning pits. That wasn't all they were doing to them either. Lukas blushed. Above it all, surrounded by a halo of sunlight, a beatific Jesus gazed down with benign indifference.

Lukas noticed a small gold timepiece resting on top of a pile of open books by a large windowsill. It would be easy to slip it into his robe. The temptation was huge, but Lukas resisted. That was the sort of thing Etienne would do.

A courtier appeared, and Anselmus and Lukas were ushered into another, larger room. This one was even more chaotic. Among the books and ornaments stood an impassive figure.

'Your Excellency,' said Anselmus in German, 'may I introduce to you my apprentice, Master Lukas Declercq.'

Lukas shot to attention and, as instructed, bowed low and long. When he stood upright again, the Emperor was holding his gaze and gave a small, almost imperceptible nod of his head.

On his travels to Prague, Lukas had seen Rudolph's likeness every day on coins. Now here he was, in the same room as the most famous man in the Empire.

Lukas was mesmerised. Draped over his shoulders Rudolph had a great fur and velvet cloak. Beneath he wore a finely embroidered tunic of a rich brown hue. His breeches were fashioned from the same material. Fine white silk stockings and buckled suede shoes completed his outfit.

His beard and hair were cropped short, in the Roman style. He had a great thrusting jaw and fleshy lips, which gave him the look of an obstinate bulldog. But what struck Lukas most were his eyes. There was a great sadness there, he thought.

Lukas was taller, he noticed, but the Emperor still presented a fine figure and strode with vigour towards an elaborate cabinet with many small drawers, each intricately decorated with mother-of-pearl motifs.

'We have gemstones, just arrived from Asia Minor,' the Emperor said to Anselmus. 'Can you tell us of their worth? And we should like to know if these stones have healing properties.'

Anselmus examined the gems. 'They are of exemplary quality, Your Excellency,' he said, 'especially the lapis lazuli. You might have noticed the rare intensity of the blue, comparable with the jewellery from the Pharaoh's tomb which I acquired for the Cabinet last year. There are gold flecks in the rock, as one would expect, but no trace of calcite veins. Such material would have a marvellous restorative effect, Your Excellency. Lapis lazuli is especially renowned for its capacity to cure melancholy.'

The Emperor listened intently. 'And how should these stones be made use of?' he asked.

'I would suggest that the largest piece be polished and then fashioned into a pendant to be worn close to the heart. It is said that the life force within the stone is effective in keeping the soul free from error, fear and envy. The smaller pieces should be mixed with honey and wine and ingested.'

Rudolph gave a gentle smile. 'Then see to it, my dear Declercq. We leave it with you.'

Lukas was pleased to note that the Emperor did not have a haughtiness about him – such as he would have expected from the most powerful man in Europe. Instead he seemed to have a mighty, impenetrable detachment.

Anselmus then began to examine the Emperor, as he did on every visit. He checked his pulse, eyes, posture and skin for any signs of disorder. Then he asked for 'the samples' and Rudolph clapped his hands. Another courtier appeared with two containers. The first, a narrow-necked flask, contained a pale yellow liquid. Anselmus held it up to the light, swilled it around, then took out the cork and sniffed it. Lukas, standing next to him, caught a whiff of urine. The second container was a covered pale porcelain bowl. Anselmus held his breath, quickly lifted and replaced the lid, and pronounced the Emperor's stools to be healthy.

The routine inspection over, Anselmus assured the Emperor his body was in good health. Lukas realised with disappointment that it would soon be time to leave.

Rudolph reached for a small handbell and rang it. The courtier who had let them in appeared and within a few minutes they were back at Anselmus's apartment.

'So, Lukas, what did you make of our Emperor?' asked Anselmus, almost eagerly. Lukas wondered whether he had been glad to have someone else with him.

'It was a great honour, Uncle,' he said diplomatically,

but what he really wanted to say was that he felt perplexed. He had expected Rudolph to radiate some kind of luminous superhuman presence, but beneath his splendid clothes the Emperor seemed all too human. And after the hardship and poverty of his journey it was bizarre to be surrounded by so many things that were worth many months' food and shelter. For a moment he thought of Etienne again. He would love to be able to tell him about what he had just seen.

'Who are the "we" and "us" he talks about?' asked Lukas.

'It is a royal tradition,' said Anselmus. 'Monarchs of all descriptions refer to themselves as we and us. They mean "God and I", I suppose, or "We, the living embodiment of the realm and its people".' He laughed at the absurdity, then looked sad. 'His Highness suffers greatly from melancholy. It has grown worse in the time I have been observing him. And he is bedevilled by hypochondria.'

'Uncle,' said Lukas gingerly, 'I know what melancholy is, but not hypo . . . whatever it was.'

Anselmus's eyes widened in irritation, but he checked himself and spoke in a firm, calm voice. 'Hypochondria. It is a Greek word. It is a disease of the mind where the patient fears they are suffering from ailments that are in fact imaginary. Today was a good day. Sometimes we have rages and sometimes we have dark silences.'

# CHAPTER TEN

That afternoon Anselmus sent the largest of the lapis lazuli stones to the royal jewellers, to be polished and attached to a silver chain so it could be worn around the neck. Then he showed Lukas how to make the Emperor's new medicine. He had him grind the remaining gemstones to a powder, 'the finer the better'. Then he mixed it with wine, honey, cinnamon and olive oil. Lukas took it at once to the Emperor's quarters.

He returned to see Anselmus welcoming a visitor to his apartment. 'Lukas, my dear boy,' he beamed, 'this is my esteemed colleague and companion Doktor Albrecht Grunewald!'

Lukas bowed. Grunewald was as stout as Anselmus was lean, although he had an almost identical long white beard.

He smiled warmly at Lukas. Then a shadow crossed his face. 'I was sorry to hear of your father,' he said. 'I have some sympathy for his beliefs. You will find in Prague, with our good Emperor to rule us, that men are left to follow their own faith without fear of the Inquisition. Indeed, they are allowed to do many things in the spirit of natural enquiry that would not be permitted in most other Christian realms.'

He paused in thought then said to Anselmus, 'Which reminds me, did you notice a party of Spaniards arrive earlier this week?'

'My nephew brought this to my attention,' replied Anselmus.

'Court ambassadors by the look of them,' he said to them both. 'I wonder what they're doing here. I shall make it my business to find out.'

Then he turned back to Anselmus. 'Look at this,' he said excitedly, holding up the book he was carrying. 'It contains Guarinonius's formula for *Elixir vitae*.'

Lukas looked baffled. Grunewald turned the pages until he came to the section he wanted.

'I doubt it really is the *Elixir vitae*,' said Grunewald. 'Immortality from a medicinal concoction – that would be too much to hope for. But I hear Pope Clement VIII took it when he was very ill, and he made a full recovery.'

Anselmus's face lit up with fascination.

'I entrust it to you, the great medicine maker,' said Grunewald. 'You must restore our Emperor to good health. This would be an unhappy realm without him.'

He took his leave with a pleasant smile.

'This will be just the thing for the Emperor,' said Anselmus. 'I must wean him off the absurd treatment Doktor Krohl is subjecting him to.'

'Who's Doktor Krohl?' asked Lukas. He had forgotten he had already met him in Golden Lane.

Anselmus sighed. 'His Excellency has several physicians. Grunewald is one. He principally attends to the Emperor's children and mistresses. Krohl is another. He has a rather grand idea of his own importance . . . and he doesn't like me because I live here in the Castle –' he smirked – 'and he has a little cottage in Golden Lane.' He went on. 'His greatest flaw is his enthusiasm for magnetic remedies. I have no time for them. A lodestone may indeed point north, and attract iron particles, but I cannot see how it would draw the black vapours that cause melancholy from His Excellency's body . . .

'Anyway, look at this.' Anselmus pointed excitedly at the text. 'Guarinonius learned of the remedy in a dream. And now we have it here. Let me see what we will need.'

Anselmus paused and wiggled his finger about, pointing this way and that and talking quietly to himself. 'Zedoary, calamus, elder root we have in the garden . . . the Emperor's apothecary has nutmeg and ginger . . . cinnamon I have in my kitchen . . .'

After supper Anselmus donned his fur cloak. 'We must go to the Castle herb garden to gather our ingredients tonight,' he said to Lukas. 'As I'm sure you know, the effectiveness of medicines is very dependant on the time of day they are harvested.'

Lukas was excited. He was keen to visit the gardens that lay beyond the northern wall.

On every stage of their route through the ramparts, over the bridge and into the Royal Gardens, guards bowed and opened any barrier that lay before them. Lukas felt proud of his uncle, recognised wherever he went, having doors and gates opened on his command.

'We are in luck,' said Anselmus. 'The elder root must be plucked just before a full moon. And we are at that exact stage of the lunar cycle.'

It was a warm, bright night. The moonlit Castle looked beautiful and the Royal Gardens were bursting with extraordinary smells.

The quiet of the place, as they walked there, was unnerving. Apart from the call and response of hooting owls, all Lukas could hear were their own footsteps scrunching on the gravel path. The trees were beginning to sprout summer leaves but they still had something of their skeletal winter look in the pale light of the moon. Lukas drew in great lungfuls of night air.

Anselmus told Lukas how to recognise each herb, and what it did for a patient. 'Elder root: excellent for quinsies, sore throats and strangulations. Calamus: a sure cure for the intestinal worm.' He knew exactly where to look and they found their herbs quickly.

'Back to our warm fire,' he said. Lukas was disappointed. He was enjoying being out in the night air.

A low growling noise stopped them in their tracks. It came from somewhere close to the gate.

'What was that?' said Anselmus. His fear was infectious and Lukas was immediately afraid.

'Walk back to the gate. Don't run, but be quick,' whispered Anselmus.

'But it came from by the gate,' said Lukas.

'So it did. So it did.' Anselmus grabbed his nephew by the arm and hurried him further into the garden.

The growl came again. A guttural snarl Lukas could feel in his chest.

Anselmus now looked terrified. 'Nothing makes a noise like that . . . apart from the Emperor's lion.'

They could hear snuffling now and panting.

'A tree. We've got to climb a tree,' fretted Lukas.

The garden was full of extraordinary trees. There were several close by that looked easy enough to climb. 'Help me up,' said Anselmus, pointing to a slender trunk covered in beautiful white blossom. The panting was getting closer.

Lukas made a stirrup with his hands and Anselmus

hauled himself up into the thin branches. Then he leaned forward, offering his arm to help Lukas to pull himself up. But as he took Lukas's weight, the branch began to creak and Anselmus instinctively released his grip.

Lukas heard a great roar right next to him. He looked over to see a young lion, somewhere between a cub and an adult. In a second the creature was upon him. But rather than maul him, it rubbed its mane against his legs. Instinctively Lukas began to stroke its fur. The lion gave a contented yawn, his sharp teeth glistening in the moonlight. An awful catty stench filled the air, worse than any animal Lukas had ever smelled before.

'He wants you to give him something to eat,' whispered Anselmus.

'What do you suggest?' said Lukas desperately.

The lion was growling now, and snuffling around Lukas's crotch. He was getting restless. 'Uncle, pull me up, before he takes a bite out of me.'

Anselmus relented. He reached down an arm and pulled with all his might. Lukas scrambled up, distracting the lion with a snowstorm of white blossom dislodged from the tree.

They both clung to the trunk, resting their feet on the sturdiest branches, so close they were almost nose to nose. The lion sat below.

Lukas shifted his weight and the branch beneath his feet cracked and broke right off, leaving him dangling by his hands. The lion was on his feet in an instant. Lukas could feel the wind from its wafting claws on his swinging foot.

Anselmus pulled Lukas back as yet another branch gave an ominous crack.

'This tree isn't going to last much longer with the two of us up it,' said Anselmus. 'We need to distract this creature while you run to another tree. There's one close by.' He looked guilty. 'I would go myself, but I am not so agile.'

Lukas took off one of his boots. He called down to the lion and swung the boot by its laces. The creature stretched out its body and began to paw at it.

Then Lukas threw the shoe as far as he could and the lion galloped after it into the darkness. Taking his life into his hands he leaped down and sprinted to the next tree. By the time he scrambled up it, the beast's claws were reaching for his feet.

As he reached the safety of the lower branches, a startled bird fluttered up in panic. Lukas almost lost his grip. As he clung on tight he saw the bird was tied to the tree by a tiny golden chain. When the chain pulled tight, the bird gave a shriek of alarm and fluttered down to the top branches.

'What's that?' he hissed.

'One of the Emperor's parrots,' said his uncle.

Their voices carried easily in the still night air.

'What do we do now?' said Lukas when he had caught his breath.

'We wait, nephew,' said Anselmus.

'But it's cold,' said Lukas. It was too. April nights were cold enough to produce a frost in the morning. 'Can't we call for help?'

'No,' said Anselmus. 'The Emperor might be sleeping in the Summer Palace. You can see it there, at the far end of the garden. If we wake him, he will be very angry with us. Being eaten by a lion is probably preferable.'

# CHAPTER ELEVEN

Dawn came with a light frost. Anselmus and Lukas worried that they would fall from their perches like frozen sparrows. But soon after first light, the lion keeper entered the garden with a piece of meat. 'Taman,' he called. The creature lolloped over to him and even let him fuss with its mane as it began to eat.

While the lion was distracted the keeper placed a heavy iron chain around its collar. Then the two of them trotted back towards the lion cage in the Emperor's menagerie.

Anselmus called, 'Ahoy! Are there any more lions loose in this garden?'

The keeper came over and stared up, bemused. 'Your Eminence . . .'

'We came here last night to pick medicinal herbs. Then we were set upon by a lion,' said Anselmus, in a tone that suggested this sort of thing happened to him all the time.

'Taman does break out of his cage some evenings,' said the keeper. 'He hasn't eaten anybody yet. I keep telling the Custodian of the Royal Gardens we need to strengthen that door . . .'

They found Lukas's boot close to the gate. It had been chewed to pieces – a fate they both felt they had narrowly avoided.

That afternoon Lukas spent a tedious hour grinding

roots and herbs with a pestle and mortar, and carefully separating each one into a small bone-china dish. The herbs were boiled and the oils siphoned off, then mixed with lemon juice and spirit of wine.

'The medicine must be drunk before meals, and only when the moon is in Cancer, Leo or Virgo,' said Anselmus.

Lukas was not really paying attention. He was tired and in a foul mood. Anselmus had offered to lend him money to buy some more boots. Lukas thought it wasn't his fault he'd had to throw his boot away. His uncle had brought him to the garden. Surely he should buy him another pair. Lukas didn't feel brave enough to mention it, but he did think ill of Anselmus for not offering.

At supper that evening Anselmus was in high spirits. He ignored his nephew's surly mood. 'When we have done the preparation, I will present this new medicine to the Emperor and tell him of its effectiveness. If the Pope himself recommends it, I am sure that Rudolph will be prepared to take it. Besides, he must surely be growing tired of Doktor Krohl's magnetic remedies.'

Lukas could not be angry with his uncle for long, so he smiled and told him how much he was enjoying his studies. He knew he was living in a privileged world. Anselmus had even cleared some space in one of the smaller rooms for him. It was barely big enough for a rickety bed and table, but Lukas thought it was marvellous to have a room of his own. He felt that all he lacked was someone his own age to talk to.

He liked being his uncle's protégé and he didn't even mind Anselmus's determination to teach him good manners. 'You must have picked up some bad habits on your travels. If you live and work at court, you cannot behave as you would in a low tavern full of villains and women of light behaviour.'

Every mealtime he provided a running commentary on Lukas's more regrettable behaviour. 'Do not fall on your food as though you were a hungry dog . . . Do not fart and belch as if you were performing to an audience . . . Do not sneeze in people's faces . . . and when you blow your nose, do not look into your handkerchief, as if you were expecting to find diamonds or emeralds.' Lukas paid close attention. He was clever enough to realise this was the way to advancement in the world.

The medicine was prepared and ready for the Emperor's next weekly examination. As they walked to the imperial chambers clutching several bottles they passed two Spanish courtiers, who watched them with clear curiosity.

'They're still here,' said Anselmus, when they were out of earshot. 'No doubt wanting an audience with the Emperor. They'll have to be patient.'

As they waited for their summons Lukas had never seen his uncle in such a state of excitement. 'I am convinced this is the remedy for His Highness's melancholy,' Anselmus said.

They were ushered into the royal presence and waited for Rudolph to turn away from the window and acknowledge them.

'We hear you have met our friend Taman,' said the Emperor. When they looked puzzled he chuckled. 'Our lion,' he explained. He obviously found the episode amusing.

'It was a most . . . remarkable . . . evening,' said Anselmus. He was doing his best to hide his exasperation, but the Emperor noticed and his mood changed in an instant. It was like a chilly draught stealing across the room.

Anselmus braced himself. He was determined to mention his new remedy. 'Your Excellency,' he said, 'might I recommend a cure for your condition which I have just discovered.'

Lukas tried to hide a smirk. Clearly Grunewald was not going to get the credit for this.

'It comes from the Pope's physician. His Holiness greatly benefited from it.'

But Rudolph was no longer in a receptive frame of mind. He turned his back on them again.

They waited in awkward silence. The sun came out, then went in. A horse and cart scuttered across the cobbled courtyard below. The fire crackled in its grate.

Eventually the Emperor turned to face them.

'Cure? We are weary of your cures, Anselmus Declercq,' he said, his voice a low, threatening hiss. 'We followed your advice on the lapis lazuli stones we received. We wore this confounded necklace –' he wrenched it from his neck and threw it at the window, which cracked but did not break – 'and it has made not the slightest difference.

'Then we took the ground-stones potion – as you suggested. If you think two days of chronic dyspepsia and a day of burning flux a fine cure for melancholy, then we have to disagree with you.'

Lukas looked at Anselmus from the corner of his eye, trying to gauge his reaction. His uncle was standing there, head cocked to one side, wearing his usual 'listening' expression.

When he was sure the Emperor had finished speaking he said, 'I am sorry Your Excellency has experienced an unfortunate reaction to my cure. I can assure Your Highness that the remedy has benefited many of my previous patients.'

'You have many patients who have the wealth and opportunity to ingest lapis lazuli?' said Rudolph incredulously. 'Then you hardly have need of our patronage.'

He stood glowering. The sun had come out again and was shining directly through the window, leaving him in silhouette so that Anselmus and Lukas could not see the expression on his face.

After a further silence Anselmus perkily suggested the Emperor might still like to try this new concoction. 'There are no ground stones – only herbs picked at the most advantageous moment of the lunar cycle.'

'This medicine does not interest us,' said Rudolph wearily, his rage spent. 'Doktor Krohl's cures may be equally ineffective, but at least they do not cause such unpleasantness . . . And if we ever experience a similar disorder of the innards again, from anything you may prescribe, we shall suspect that our most favoured court physician is trying to poison us and have him sent to Daliborka Tower.'

He turned his back, picked up his little handbell and rang it. The examination had been forgotten and the audience was over.

As they walked back to his apartment, Lukas noticed how Anselmus had gone a chalky colour.

'The symptoms His Excellency describes are not

unusual in any course of medicine. He must know that . . .' he said. Then he lowered his voice, as if imparting a great confidence. 'That was him on a bad day, but I've seen worse – babbling, tears, tearing hair. He'll probably be pleasant the next time we see him.'

# CHAPTER TWELVE

Rudolph was cold with them when they came again, but on their following visit he was anxious to show Anselmus his latest acquisition: a polished brass armillary sphere for studying the heavens. They fell into conversation about the difficulties of stellar observation and the strain staring at tiny dots of light placed on the eyes. Anselmus had been forgiven. As they walked back to their chambers, Lukas noticed his uncle seemed almost giddy with relief. Otka was waiting for them, and her face lit up when she saw Anselmus looking happy. Lukas sensed a strong bond between them.

Lukas increasingly missed having friends his own age to talk to. The Spanish party was still at the Castle and one of them in particular had caught his attention. She was around his age and had jet-black hair, but unlike most of her compatriots who were olive-skinned, hers was milky-white. Whenever he saw her, he could not take his eyes off her. She even began to visit him in his dreams – little interludes that he would remember in fragments throughout the day. He longed to be able to talk to her – to show off about the extraordinary things he was seeing and doing.

Aside from Anselmus and Otka, the only other person he saw regularly was Anselmus's older sister – his Aunt Elfriede. Once or twice a week he was sent to her house with bread and meat. She lived close to the river in Mala

Strana, twenty minutes' walk from the Castle. Her home was as cramped as the tiny houses on Golden Lane. The only good thing was you could heat it with a small kitchen stove.

Elfriede made her dislike obvious, greeting Lukas sourly and never asking him in. He didn't mind. She was old and frail. Every day he visited her with provisions was another day when she wasn't living with him and his uncle. Anselmus was devoted to her though. She had taught him his craft. Even now, at her age, people would come to see her when they fell sick. She cost a lot less than a real doctor, and her cures were just as effective.

This was a mixed blessing for Elfriede. She made enough money to keep her independence, but she also courted trouble. A few months before Lukas had arrived, a boy had fallen ill with a fever. The parents were too poor for a doctor. Their prayers and offerings to St Nicholas, the patron saint of children, had come to nothing. So they went to Elfriede, who gave a potion to the child, but he died soon after. Wild with grief, the parents whipped their effigy of St Nicholas and threw it in the Vltava. Then they turned on Elfriede, accusing her of wishing their son dead.

No one took them seriously enough to bring her to trial, but her customers were not so plentiful and the taint of witchcraft hung in the air. She even had a black cat – Marushka. It was the only living thing she seemed to have any affection for.

Lukas was shrewd enough not to complain about her. Anselmus seemed increasingly pleased with him and he wanted to keep things that way. 'You are an inquisitive young man,' his uncle had told him. 'That is important in a boy. Intelligence and quick-wittedness are all very well, but God has also given us brains to think and to question!'

If Lukas continued making progress, Anselmus had said, he could soon take his first-stage apothecary's examinations.

A month after he arrived in Prague, Lukas came home to see Otka curled up on his uncle's lap, her head resting in the crook of his neck. They were sitting by the fire and were both fast asleep.

As Lukas came into the room Anselmus woke with a start. He seemed flustered and embarrassed to be caught this way, but he put his index finger to his mouth to tell Lukas to keep quiet. Lukas crept to his room, feeling confused. Otka was young enough to be his uncle's daughter. Lukas thought of the paintings he'd seen showing a lecherous old man embracing a scheming young woman – it was a popular subject.

That evening conversation did not flow. Anselmus was more formal than usual and Lukas went to bed feeling lonely. It was time he started to make some friends around the Castle. He had barely thought of Etienne over the last month and felt a twinge of guilt. But then, Etienne had not sent word to him at the Castle either.

But that was probably a good thing. Lukas had done nothing he felt ashamed of since coming to the Castle – but he had done something bad almost every day when he had been travelling with Etienne.

Late the next afternoon, Anselmus sent Lukas to Aunt Elfriede's with provisions and then into Prague to replenish his medical supplies. He was to go to an apothecary's shop close to the Old Town Square.

His uncle was lacking opium, hemlock, gall from a castrated boar and treacle. 'You must take a note with you, from me, or they will not give you these things.'

Lukas walked into the centre of Prague and found the apothecary easily enough. He felt wary of the inhabitants of the city and very conscious of the two gold crowns he carried in his purse. He could feel them chink with each step and felt sure that every ne'er-do-well within fifty paces would hear them too.

And ne'er-do-wells aplenty roamed the streets of Prague. The late-afternoon gloom seemed to bring them out. There were beggars and prostitutes on every street, but Lukas wasn't afraid of them. It was the villains he had to watch out for.

They said that the creatures of the field grew skittish at dusk, for that was when the hawk was most likely to strike. As he turned back to the Castle, clutching his bags of medicine, he didn't know which was worse – carrying money or carrying hemlock and opium. He knew these substances had illicit uses.

The Stone Bridge was a lot quieter in the evening, so he began to cross without fear of being killed by a horse and wagon.

Lukas tripped on the uneven cobblestones as light rain drifted down from the dark sky. It was warm for late April. Overhead a flock of birds wheeled by, the underside of their wings catching in the flare of the torches atop the mighty tower on the north side of the bridge. Their plaintive cawing reminded him of the seabirds in Ghent and evening walks on the beach near Vlisseghem with his mother and father when he was younger. He glanced briefly at the rotting heads on the tower parapet and wondered if the robbers at Momalle had had their heads stuck on poles yet.

'Hey, Lukas,' came a shout from further up the bridge. As the voice called again he recognised it as Etienne's. They strode briskly towards each other and hugged. 'You can buy us a pitcher of beer,' said Etienne, 'and I know just the place where we can drink it.'

Lukas did not have any money of his own, just what Anselmus had given him for the medicine. There was enough left for ale, but he felt uneasy about spending it.

The tavern was in Mala Strana, downriver from the bridge, in a side alley and staircase close to the sawmills and tanneries. It was reached by a door that gave little indication of what lay behind. But the Three Violins did not need to advertise for custom. Inside, the low ceiling ensured there would be a comfortable fug, and the log fire in the grate gave off enough heat to thaw the most frozen nightwatchman. Candles on every table and a torch or two on the walls threw out a dim but comforting glow.

Although the place was cosy, the customers were anything but. Lukas immediately felt ill at ease. These were people his instincts told him to avoid. When he ordered a pitcher of beer even the serving girl was awkward – huffy and not eager to please, although she was very pretty.

'That's Jenka,' said Etienne with a wink. 'Come and join my friends.' Lukas felt his stomach tighten. He didn't want to meet any of the people who drank here. Etienne paused and said, 'Don't tell them what you do at the Castle. It's best they don't know. Say you're a lowly servant. Errands, sweeping up the horse droppings, that sort of thing.'

He led Lukas to a table close to the fire and introduced him one by one to the five most frightening-looking men in the inn – Radek, Dusan, Oldrich, Strom and Karel. They were all a little older than Etienne and as he ran through their names each one ignored Lukas or gave a curt nod. Lukas could never remember names but they looked like men who would not easily forgive someone who forgot them.

Etienne beckoned Lukas to sit down opposite him at the end of table. As he sat he was startled to hear a low growl. There was an enormous brown dog lying at their feet. Lukas's toes were nestling under its haunches. He felt glad they weren't anywhere near its slobbery jaws. 'That's Belphegor,' said Etienne. 'Belongs to Strom. He's a lurcher. He'll love you if you buy him a plate of milzwurst.'

Lukas didn't want anything that size dribbling over him.

The men fell into conversation, showing no interest in Lukas. His attention was drawn back to Jenka, who seemed almost heroically stroppy. A customer on the next table pointed to the chalked menu on the wall and asked, 'Is the herring hot or cold?'

'How quickly are you going to eat it?' she said without a smile.

After a while he realised he was starting to relax. It was good to be away from the palace and back in the company of Etienne and other young men. He always felt he needed to impress his uncle with his intelligence. Here it was quite the opposite. Etienne's friends' conversation was punctuated by the sorts of oaths that Lukas's father had assured him would guarantee a place in hell.

Radek and Dusan were built like berserker warriors – with fierce, angry faces and biceps the size of Lukas's head. Five or six hundred years ago, it was said, the Vikings had travelled down the waterways of Europe to Bohemia. Maybe these men were their descendants. He could imagine them both leaping from a longboat, swinging great double-headed axes.

Then there was Strom. He had strange tattoos either side of his face – slender geometric patterns, like those found in a book about page motifs that Lukas's father had kept in his study. Strom said little, which made Lukas uneasy. He watched and waited, occasionally leaping into the conversation to reprimand one of them when he thought they were being foolish. Lukas guessed he was their leader, especially as several of them made a point of ordering milzwurst sausages for Belphegor. It seemed to be their way of paying homage.

Oldrich had long black hair that fell down his back. But when he took off his hat he was bald almost down to his ears and the top of his head was as white as a boiled egg. He sat there looking inscrutable – or maybe there was nothing going on in his head at all.

Finally there was Karel – a wiry man with gaunt cheeks. He was the butt of the others' jokes, not least because of his name – one given to both girls and boys in Bohemia. Karel began to seethe at their mockery and eventually took out a long curved knife, the sort market traders used to gut fish, and began to clean the dirt from his fingernails.

They turned their attention to Lukas, and he tried not to shrink in his seat.

'So, what's a twerp like you doing with a fellow like Etienne?' said Strom.

Lukas froze, not knowing how to reply.

Etienne answered for him.

'Lukas is all right,' he said with a grin. 'We met on the way to Prague. Ask him nicely and he'll buy you all a beer.'

Lukas kicked Etienne under the table. He had calculated that Anselmus would not miss the minor outlay of a pitcher of ale, but drinks all round would be far more difficult to explain.

'Tell him you gave the change to a beggar,' said Etienne, reading his mind.

'You'd be telling the truth,' said Strom, who had instantly understood what their conversation was about. 'Especially with Karel.'

They all laughed until Karel brought out his knife again and carried on cleaning his nails. Lukas wondered if he was going to draw blood from one of his tormentors, then realised they were looking at him with impatient expectation. He decided it would be safer to buy the drinks and worry about the money later. He would have to earn it back somehow, or tell a lie about losing it.

He left the tavern late in the evening. They had been friendlier to him after he had bought them a drink – even asking him what he did. Remembering Etienne's advice, Lukas was deliberately vague. 'I sweep the courtyards, feed the horses,' he shrugged. 'Nothing fancy.'

He swaggered alone along the dark streets close to the Castle, no longer feeling the unease that had haunted him earlier in the evening. He had been mixing with villains! Now *he* was someone to be frightened of!

Yes, they had mostly ignored him, but they had been happy to let him sit with them. And it had been good to see Etienne. As he left, his friend had said, 'You can find us in here most days. We'll see you again?'

Then Dusan had come out with his bags full of medicines. 'Hey, you dolt! You forgot these!' he had said, and slapped him cheerfully on the back.

Lukas's footsteps echoed around the empty courtyards of the Castle. As he entered the deserted Cathedral square he let out a belch thunderous enough to startle the starlings from their perches. This amused him so much he did not begin to fret about what his uncle was going to say until he approached the door to their quarters.

What would he tell him about his missing change? How angry would he be about his late homecoming? Fortunately Anselmus had retired for the night.

Lukas slumped into bed and was asleep in seconds. The next morning Anselmus casually asked him where he had been and seemed unconcerned when Lukas said he had met an old friend and they had gone for a drink. He thought it best to say nothing about the money he had failed to return and, sure enough, as the day wore on, it seemed that Anselmus had forgotten about it.

# CHAPTER THIRTEEN

Lukas decided he should not go back to the Three Violins. But as the week wore on he thought how much he'd enjoyed meeting his old friend. It was a shame the tavern was the best place to see him.

He was beginning to find his evenings with Anselmus something of a chore. His uncle always wanted to talk about serious things, and by nine o'clock Lukas was keen to escape to his room. But Anselmus would often ask him to stay up a while longer to keep him company. He especially enjoyed a game of chess. Lukas did not have the patience to play well, and his impulsive manoeuvres would make his uncle tut with scorn. Then Anselmus would sit there stroking his beard and spending an age deciding on his next move, as the clock ticked away the evening and Lukas's eyelids began to droop.

A fortnight after he had been to the Three Violins he saw Dusan and Radek – the Vikings – in the Old Town Square. They slapped him on the back and greeted him like a friend.

After that, whenever he had a bit of money to spare, Lukas would venture into the Three Violins. He would peer cautiously around the inn to see who was there. If Etienne was with Strom and his gang, and he usually was, he would join them. If he wasn't, he would slink out again, hoping the others hadn't seen him.

He didn't go very often. Much of his meagre apprentice wages had gone on buying a new pair of boots, and he had to ask Anselmus for money for the most basic essentials. '*The man who's careful when he borrows has few cares and fewer sorrows,*' recited Anselmus. 'You must learn to live within your means.'

He pointed out that Lukas had a place to live and food on his plate, so what else did he need to spend money on? Lukas wanted to say, 'My friend,' but sensed this would lead to awkward questions.

Etienne was always good company but the rest of the gang still made him feel uneasy. Now they knew he worked in the Castle, they wasted no time asking about the 'Treasure' reported to be kept there. Lukas wondered if this was what Otka had told him about. He played it down, saying, 'Aren't all castles full of treasures?'

Strom leaned forward to speak in a low voice. 'This one has a series of chambers they call the Cabinet of Curiosities. It's got everything you could ever imagine. Pearls from the Orient, gold from New Spain, jewels from the four corners of the Earth . . . And then there's the really special stuff. Nails from the cross . . .' Here he crossed himself, which surprised Lukas as Strom was one of the most ungodly people he had ever met. '. . . all three of them. The eye of the Cyclops, the Golden Fleece, the robe Judas was wearing when he betrayed Jesus in the Garden of Gethsemane . . . it's all priceless. They say there are thousands of treasures up there, and any one of them could keep a man fed for the rest of his life.'

Oldrich elbowed Lukas in the ribs and gave a dim chuckle. 'You keep your eyes peeled, our friend Lukas.' He paused to belch noisily. Lukas was surprised to hear himself called a friend. It was the first time Oldrich had spoken to him. 'Anything you see there that's lying around, you bring it to us. We'll get you a good price for it.'

Lukas couldn't imagine Oldrich getting a good price for anything. He was relieved when an altercation at the next table distracted them. A Flemish couple were talking loudly in their own language, assuming no one else around them would understand. The woman was drunkenly berating the man for his wandering eye. 'She wouldn't be interested in a flabby old goat like you,' she said, her head cocked towards Jenka. She thumped him hard in the gut. The man doubled up, spilling his beer, and let out a string of curses.

Lukas translated the tale into German to his new friends and felt pleased with himself when they roared with laughter. Unfortunately the man spoke German too and stood up angrily, challenging Lukas to come outside and fight him in the street.

Strom looked him over and told him he'd have to fight all of them. The man started swearing in Flemish, half to himself, half at them, and his wife grabbed him by the arm and pulled him towards the door. Passing Radek, she spat at him, but he just looked at her as if to say, 'Is that the best you can do?'

As Lukas was leaving, Etienne sidled up to him. 'If they knew you were apprentice to the Emperor's physician, you'd never hear the last of it. And don't think you'll get a fair price for anything you bring to them. If you want to make some money, let's go fortune-telling again.'

Lukas walked home feeling uneasy. In his heart he

knew he was keeping dangerous company. But he was lonely at the Castle, and these men were the nearest thing he had to friends. And he felt bad about the incident with the Flemish couple. The man had been humiliated for a cheap laugh. He also worried about the gang finding out what he really did. He hoped Etienne would never tell them.

'Uncle,' said Lukas the next afternoon, when Anselmus had been particularly pleased with an elixir he had prepared, 'is it true that there is a room in the Castle full of extraordinary things?'

Anselmus was evasive. 'Hmmmm? Most of the Castle is full of extraordinary things. What made you ask such a question?'

'I just remembered Otka telling me, when she showed me round, that there was a room full of treasure. I've been curious about it, that's all.'

'Never could keep a secret, that girl,' said Anselmus indulgently.

'Have you seen the treasure, Uncle?'

'Seen it?' Anselmus was affronted. 'Of course I've seen it. I'm curator of the collection!'

Lukas was astonished. 'So you go out and collect things for this treasure?' he said. 'What a fantastic job! Can I come with you when you do it again?'

'It is not a treasure, it is a Cabinet of Curiosities,' Anselmus said rather sniffily. 'I serve the Emperor in many ways,' he continued. 'Attending to the Cabinet is one of them. Collectors and charlatans are always coming to the castle with items for the Emperor. It is my job to decide whether or not to purchase. My friend

Doktor Grunewald sometimes assists me. He has a special interest in the manuscripts and printed books of the collection.'

'I should very much like to see the Cabinet,' said Lukas.

'It is open only to imperial scholars and artists. It is not a fairground attraction,' said Anselmus.

Lukas was due to take his first Pharmacy exam in a week's time. 'Uncle,' he said tentatively, 'if I succeed in my examination, will you show me the Cabinet?'

Anselmus said he would consider it.

The week after Lukas's glowing report from the Board of Apothecaries, Anselmus casually mentioned over breakfast that His Imperial Highness the Emperor was on one of his rare trips away from the Castle, and that this afternoon they might, just might, pay a visit to the Cabinet. After all, he said airily, 'I have duties to attend to therein.'

For the rest of the morning Lukas could not sit or stand still. His friends from the tavern had talked about it again with wide-eyed wonder – how it was the most extraordinary collection of treasures on Earth. It was said that some who gazed upon it were so overcome by its magnificence and strangeness they went mad. Now he, the disgraced printer's son from Ghent, was going to see this wonder of the world too.

Lukas was still unsure where the Cabinet was – or even what it was. It couldn't possibly be just a cabinet. The collection was too large.

That afternoon they headed off on their usual route towards the imperial chambers. But instead of taking the stairs to the second floor, where the Emperor's quarters were, they stopped at a large door on the first floor.

Anselmus produced a bunch of keys from his cloak and unlocked the door. It opened with an unearthly groan and they entered a modest anteroom, with a high vaulted ceiling. The walls were painted with brilliant and beautiful images of earth, fire, air and water. The twelve astrological signs of the Zodiac also decorated the room, each one magnificently depicted in bold colours. Overlooking it all was a vast painting of Jupiter. 'His Highness feels a close affinity with the King of the Gods,' said Anselmus, as Lukas gawped in astonishment.

In front of them was a huge double door. Anselmus reached again for his keys and unlocked it. He leaned on the handle on the right and pushed with all his might against the great weight of the door.

As it swung open Lukas could see a space the size of a ballroom, flooded with light from great south-facing windows and crammed from floor to ceiling with everything he could ever have imagined and many more things besides.

The room was like a vast repository of missing treasure troves. It was impossible to take in what he was seeing. Every one of the thousands of things that assaulted his senses would have made a fabulous ornament and endless talking point for anyone who possessed it.

On the floor, where space allowed, there were statues from Ancient Greece and Rome, and a great marble sculpture of a lion mauling a horse, its eyes wide and nostrils flared. It was so real Lukas could almost hear the poor creature neighing in terror. Then there were strange stuffed animals of dragon-like appearance, and massive antlered beasts that Lukas had never seen before. They stared at him with sightless eyes. Propped up, or hanging from the walls, were huge lurid paintings of naked women.

Great solid wooden tables ran down the centre of the room, covered in astronomical instruments. 'Look through here,' said Anselmus, indicating a strange arrangement of lenses, one larger than the other, held in place along a brass rod, and Lukas peered through the smaller lens.

In the swimming, distorted image he could see a detail in a painting at the far end of the room, almost as if he was standing right next to it. The experience startled him. 'It is as if the eye has been transported thirty paces ahead!' explained Anselmus.

'What a strange phenomenon,' said Lukas. 'Perhaps it could be used to examine the heavens.' He was remembering the conversation about the difficulties of stargazing that his uncle had had with the Emperor. But Anselmus had wandered off and Lukas thought no more about it.

Most arresting of all were the great cases. There were at least twenty in this room alone. Some were shelved with glass doors, so the objects within could be seen. Others were like an apothecary's storage cabinet, with scores of little drawers, each with a tiny parchment label slotted into a minute iron frame. All of them were beautifully decorated with inlaid mother-of-pearl or different types of wood.

'I could spend years in here and still not see everything,' Lukas said. Anselmus beamed indulgently. His nephew was a bright young lad, he thought. It was only right to expose him to these wonders while his mind was fresh and ready to absorb it all.

They walked along, each step revealing further treasures. There was a violin made of glass, and a bizarre timepiece which drew their attention as it rattled and whirred as they passed.

'Look, here is the very dagger used to kill Julius Caesar. This has long been one of the Emperor's favourite artefacts.' Lukas was disappointed to see there was no blood on it, although it still looked sharp enough to cut your meat at table.

His eyes alighted on a sinister-looking monkey, dressed as a court musician and clutching a life-size violin. All at once it gave a strange creaking noise and turned its head towards him. He nearly jumped out of his skin.

'What the devil is that?' he said to his uncle, trying hard to quell his fear.

'Ah, the Emperor is a great admirer of automata,' said Anselmus. 'His collection of mechanical creatures is the greatest in Europe. This one was built in Prague. I met its maker once – a strange man. There was something missing about him; I can't remember what.'

'But that *thing* turned to look at me,' said Lukas, who wasn't really listening. He pointed to the monkey with a trembling hand.

'A last contraction of the mechanism. Like the final spasm of a dying man. It must have been operated recently,' said Anselmus. 'The spring must have had a certain amount of life force left in it.'

'You mean it's alive?' said Lukas. He was feeling a little revolted.

'All cogs and flywheels and chains and levers, my boy,' said Anselmus. 'If you wind the spring inside, it gives artificial life to the mechanism. It is most ingenious.'

Lukas looked at the monkey again. It was so lifelike he supposed it had been made from the stuffed body of a real monkey. What a strange fate that would be. To be killed and then have your body reanimated by a mechanical contraption. To have your limbs and mouth and eyes move again in a way they had never been able to while you were a living, breathing creature.

Lukas didn't like the monkey at all. He much preferred the peacock standing on the floor close by. It was an iron creature, mechanical in every way, save for its tail, which was fashioned from real peacock feathers.

'That one is my favourite,' said Anselmus as they passed it. 'It struts around and makes its mating call, then fans out its feathers.'

'Can we see?' said Lukas.

'Perhaps I will show you one day,' Anselmus replied.

The monkey had unnerved Lukas. 'Uncle,' he said, 'maybe we should go. I feel privileged, but perhaps for now I have seen enough.'

Anselmus nodded. He too was feeling uneasy, with no real business to be there.

# CHAPTER FOURTEEN

Over supper Anselmus announced that he had been invited to dine with his friend Doktor Grunewald and some of the Spaniards. 'Perhaps Grunewald has asked them to discover why they are here at the Castle.'

Lukas listened with great interest. Whenever he saw one of the Spanish party around the palace he felt a shiver of unease. Apart from that beautiful girl, of course.

Anselmus continued: 'There is one, a Señor Don Jenaro Dorantes, who particularly interests me. He has lately returned from the New World and I would like to discover as much as I can about this fascinating realm. They say the Spanish conquered an entire country with less than two hundred men, two score horses and a single cannon. How extraordinary!'

The day came, and Lukas was surprised and uneasy to discover he was expected to attend too. 'It will be good for your education,' said his uncle. 'You will find it fascinating, I am sure. Do you know much of Spain and its people?'

'I know about the Spanish Inquisition,' he said warily.

Anselmus tutted. 'We cannot assume that all Spanish gentlemen agree with its methods and purpose. I shall make it my mission, where discourse allows, to suggest to our visitors that the Inquisition is too blunt a tool for its purpose. If you wish to win men's minds, you must persuade them by reason and example.'

'You know what happened to my father, don't you?' said Lukas.

'Your mother wrote and told me the worst,' said Anselmus. 'See how the Devil takes on many forms – even claiming to do God's work. But what I really want to know about concerns the New World, so I shall not let intercourse with our Spanish guests degenerate into sullen reproaches.'

That afternoon they bathed, then dressed in their finest apparel. Lukas felt very grown-up, accompanying his uncle to a meeting of such august men. He was a little intimidated too, until he reminded himself that he met with the Holy Roman Emperor each week.

Grunewald's chambers were close to the West Gate and a five-minute stroll through the hot late afternoon.

When they arrived everyone was ready for the feast, which was announced in grand style when Grunewald waddled into the room with a beautiful gilded copper model of an ocean-going galleon. From the bottom of its flat hull to the top of its highest mast measured three-quarters of a man's arm span. Grunewald placed the model on the long dining table and released a little switch. The machine immediately trundled along the table, tipping up and down in its voyage, as if swayed by the motion of the waves. Music filled the room as tiny drums and a pipe organ inside the galleon played a sea shanty. Little figures atop the masts started to strike the crow's nests, and the air rang with the sound of chiming bells.

Grunewald ran to the end of the table and turned his

extraordinary contraption around before it plunged off. 'Not quite the edge of the world,' said Anselmus, thinking himself very witty.

The galleon carried on until it reached the middle of the table. Then it stopped and, as the music reached a climax, miniature cannons on both its starboard and larboard sides produced loud explosions and smoke.

The guests were entranced and clapped and cheered. Grunewald had got his party off to a fine start.

A place of honour had been kept for Anselmus, at the centre of the table opposite Don Jenaro Dorantes. Grunewald introduced his friend to the Spanish guests as 'His Imperial Majesty's most esteemed physician'. Lukas was ushered to a place at the end, facing an empty chair.

Next to him was Doktor Krohl. When Lukas sat down, Krohl gave him the merest glance before turning his back to him. Cursing his luck, Lukas resolved to just enjoy the food and try to learn as much as possible from the conversation of the others.

From the start it was apparent that Jenaro Dorantes was the most interesting of the Spanish guests. The other two made little attempt to do other than listen to their countryman.

The meal started on an awkward note. Speaking in fluent Latin, Dorantes said he was surprised that there were so many Jews in Prague. His own country, he remarked, had expelled their Jews a century before.

Anselmus and Grunewald both gently suggested that the Jews of Prague had contributed much to the wealth of the city. As Christian teaching held that it was wrong to make money from money, it was Jews who lent money to merchants and enabled them to prosper. Of course they were paid interest, but why should they not be rewarded for their risk?

Grunewald said, 'People resent the Jews for lending money. It is unjust. It's like hating a doctor because you need to pay him money to cure you.'

Dorantes nodded and agreed that his host presented a persuasive argument. An awkward silence fell over the room until Anselmus invited Dorantes to tell his fellow diners about the Incas of Peru. He smiled indulgently.

'They had no writing, but instead recorded their daily business by a system of knots in slender ropes. The wheel also was unknown to them. Yet they cannot be dismissed as savages, for their buildings are constructed with extraordinary precision. And they farm their land, which is mostly steep hills, so the arable fields are layered in terraces, with ingenious systems of irrigation.'

Anselmus asked Dorantes if he knew of the Fountain of Youth – whose waters made the old young again. It had been discovered in one of the new lands, he had heard. Was it the one the Spanish call Florida?

Dorantes shook his head. He had heard of such a marvel but did not know where it was.

Lukas was so fascinated he did not notice someone had sat down in the empty chair opposite him. Only when she tapped him lightly on the arm and said, 'Would you please pass me the water pitcher?' did he actually look across the table.

It was her. The girl he had seen around the Castle. Up close he could see that she had deep brown eyes. She was wearing a black velvet gown with silver and gold embroidery and pearls sewn around the neckline, which was cut in such a fashion as to reveal the soft skin of her neck and the swell of her breast.

Recovering his senses, Lukas bowed his head low. She gave him a little smile and offered him a hand, which had a faint scent of flowers, to kiss.

'It is an honour to meet you,' said Lukas, dimly remembering what he was supposed to say on such occasions to a girl he had never spoken to before.

'My name is Celestina Dorantes,' she said. 'I am the daughter of Don Jenaro Dorantes, ambassador to the court of Philip II. That's my father in the middle of the table, doing most of the talking.'

She was speaking in Flemish rather than Latin, much to Lukas's relief. He knew Latin well enough to listen, but he was not fluent enough for rapid conversation.

'And I'm –' began Lukas.

'You're Lukas Declercq. I know!' she said with a giggle. 'You're the nephew of Anselmus Declercq, the greatest physician in the Castle, or so I've been told.'

Lukas flushed with pleasure, knowing that she had gone to the trouble of finding out who he was.

'And do you like Prague?' he asked her.

'This whole country is not to my liking,' she said quietly, looking around to make sure no one was listening.

'Don't worry,' said Lukas with a smile. 'I don't think anyone else here speaks Flemish, apart from my uncle, and he's paying far too much attention to your father to be eavesdropping on us! So why is it that you speak Flemish?'

'I was born in the Low Countries. We moved back to Madrid when my father was posted to the province of Peru.'

'Did you and your mother not think to go with him?' said Lukas, uncertain whether he was prying or just making conversation.

'Oh no,' she said. 'My mother refused to go. I can still remember them arguing about it. She said it was suicide. The crossing is terribly dangerous – pirates, storms, scurvy, shipwrecks – well, you can imagine. She said if he wanted to risk his life then that was his business, but she wasn't risking mine or my two brothers'. And even when you got there, heaven knows what might happen. You could die of some strange sickness. Or get yourself murdered by savages.

'The sad thing is, my brothers died anyway. We went back to Madrid and we hadn't been there three weeks when they caught the smallpox.'

She looked distant and a little sad. 'So, anyway, there's just me left now.' Lukas felt for her.

'I had a younger sister,' he said. 'I'd feed her bread and milk in front of the fire. I don't know why she died – I was still very young – but I remember the funeral on a freezing winter's day, and the tiny coffin, and feeling it was wrong to place her in the cold earth when what she loved most was to play close to the hearth.'

It was a painful memory. For the rest of his childhood Lukas had felt an emptiness, especially when he lay awake at night in his room, listening to the children in the house next door running around in their excitement and roaring with laughter.

She reached over and squeezed his arm. Then she gave him a cheery smile. 'It's so nice to be speaking Flemish again,' she said. 'When we left the Low Countries I thought I might forget it. But we had a neighbour in

Madrid who had a Flemish wife, and she and I would talk together when she was homesick. So I haven't forgotten.'

'So you don't like it here?' said Lukas. He was surprised by how easy it was to talk to her.

'Don't like the food, don't like the people, don't like the weather, don't like the clothes, don't like our rooms. Can't understand a word of their wretched language. Even when I say "yes" or "no" in Bohemian they look at me blankly – I might as well be snorting like a pig or braying like a donkey . . .'

'I can teach you a bit of Bohemian,' said Lukas, rather too eagerly. She ignored his suggestion and carried on talking.

'. . . and I get so lonely here now my mother has departed this life. All I have is my little dog, Chico. He keeps me company. What about you? How did you get here? Do you like it?'

Lukas wanted to tell her how his father had been killed by the Inquisition, but he remembered Anselmus's warning and bit his tongue. 'My uncle offered to take me on as his apprentice. How could I refuse?' He whispered, 'He's a bit serious, but he's been very kind to me.' Then he worried that Krohl would overhear him and changed the subject. 'I've grown to like it here. I'm sure you will, when you get used to it.'

Further up the table he heard someone say, 'And do they practise human sacrifices?' That was something most people seemed to have heard about the native inhabitants of New Spain. For a moment they both stopped to listen to Dorantes.

'There is some evidence that the natives of Peru occasionally sacrifice children,' he said, to gasps of horror, 'but they do not practise this abomination on anything like the scale of the Aztecs, to the north. But since you have enquired about the custom, will you permit me to show you something given to me by the Viceroy of New Spain?'

Dorantes placed his hand in his tunic and produced a slim item wrapped in a velvet cloth. As everyone sat in fascinated silence he unwrapped it to produce the most malevolent-looking knife Lukas had ever seen. It had a blade of roughly hewn white stone, which appeared both sharp and brittle, and an elaborately decorated handle, fashioned in the shape of a kneeling man.

Celestina pulled a long face. 'Not that again,' she whispered to Lukas. They both giggled, but he was still fascinated.

The blade was a material called chalcedony, explained Dorantes. The handle was mahogany, or some other such dark wood, inlaid with colourful stones and shells.

'Do the savages not know of metals?' said Anselmus.

'They have bountiful supplies of silver and gold,' said Dorantes, 'with which they fashion exquisite ornaments. And they are known to make edge weapons of bronze. Of the other metals they have no knowledge.'

Celestina began to talk to Lukas in a low whisper so as not to draw the disapproval of her father.

Lukas tried to listen to both conversations at once.

'They hold the victim down at the apex of a vast pyramid . . .'

'The journey here from Madrid was most wearying . . .'

'. . . and the heart is cut out of the chest . . .'

'. . . a whole month of dried peas and salted meat on the ship . . .'

'. . . and held up while it is still beating, to the morning sun . . .'

'. . . but the sunsets were very pretty . . .'

'. . . Then the body is cast down the stone steps . . .'

'. . . and my little Chico took to life at sea like a dogfish . . .'

'. . . and another is brought forth . . .'

'. . . like a dogfish . . .' she repeated, giggling. Then she kicked him under the table, annoyed at his refusal to laugh at her joke.

'And did they sacrifice him too?' said Lukas, whose interest in Celestina's dog had been completely eclipsed by his fascination in her father's account of human sacrifices.

She kicked him again, hard. 'You ought to be paying attention to *me*,' she said archly, 'not some boring old story about natives.'

'Were you disappointed that your mother was so determined not to go to Peru?' said Lukas, suddenly frustrated to be drawn away from the main conversation.

'Oh no,' said Celestina. 'My father was to be away for seven years. He only came back three months ago. I barely recognised him, and he certainly did not know me. But then I was only seven when he left.'

Lukas was getting distracted again. Dorantes was telling them how the Inca beast of burden – a long-necked donkey-like creature called a llama – could often be seen wearing gold hoops in its pierced ears.

Those brown eyes were looking straight at him and he grasped for a conversational straw. 'I'm sure your mother was pleased to have your father back,' he said.

'She died the year before he returned,' said Celestina

reproachfully. 'I told you of it – don't you remember?'

Lukas blushed bright red. 'I am so sorry,' he said.

'You're hopeless,' she chided, 'but you'll have to do. Besides, I want you to show me around the Castle. You've been here a while now, and I'm sure you know all the nooks and crannies.'

Lukas was astonished. A high-born girl would never ask to go out alone with a boy of her own age. It was unheard of. She must have noticed the look on his face. His eyebrows had almost flown off the top of his forehead. 'I'm sorry,' she said. 'I'm being too forward.' She leaned towards him and whispered, 'My father is always chastising me for it. I meant, would you be so kind as to show Perpetua, she's my maid, and me around the Castle?'

She was looking right at him, in a way that most adults would consider too bold. Something about her excited Lukas in a way he did not really understand.

As the night drew on, the guests drifted away in dribs and drabs. Celestina gave him that look again when Lukas said goodbye. He talked excitedly with Anselmus all the way back to their rooms. His uncle smiled indulgently. 'It is good for you to meet others of your own age within the Castle, Lukas. I sometimes wonder if you can be happy here in a world full of old men like me!'

Lukas assured him he was thrilled to be there, learning such a fascinating profession. He took to his bed and fell asleep thinking of Celestina's brown eyes and the soft scent of her skin.

Krohl stayed late at the gathering to finish his wine. He

did not want to return to his dreary little house on Golden Lane, among all the crackpot alchemists and servants. Dorantes came over and filled up his glass.

'I hear His Excellency is attended by the finest physicians in the Empire,' he said.

'His Majesty is attended by noble men,' murmured Krohl. 'They are good Christian souls. Indeed I know them all –' his voice dropped to a whisper – 'although it should be said that some are more tolerant of heresy than others. And they especially seem to be rewarded with His Majesty's highest affection and the most prestigious dwellings in the heart of the Castle.'

'Tolerance of heresy?' said Dorantes softly, playing the sympathetic listener with accomplished ease. '*Beware of false prophets, which come to you in sheep's clothing, but inwardly they are ravening wolves.* Surely the Emperor would not accept such men in his midst?'

Krohl sensed he had gone too far. 'It would be dishonourable to say more,' he mumbled. 'I must be away.'

'They are all good, learned men,' he added hastily, as he stumbled out of the room.

# Chapter Fifteen

The next time Lukas saw Celestina she looked right through him, even though he said hello as she passed. Not a flicker.

That night he tried to remember every detail of their conversation at Doktor Grunewald's. How she had looked and the way she had stared into his eyes. No girl had ever done that to him before. He wondered if he'd said something to her that had upset her or caused her to think twice about seeing him again.

He went to Anselmus for advice, although he suspected his uncle was not the best person to ask about anything concerning the fairer sex. 'Women are strange fickle creatures, my lad,' he said. 'You must resign yourself to this simple truth, unless you intend to spend the rest of your life in a remote monastery.'

Lukas nodded, but when his uncle was out, he asked Otka.

She smiled. 'This girl, she shy,' she whispered. 'Then she bold,' she shouted. 'Now she shy again,' she whispered. 'Maybe next week, she bold.' She roared with laughter at Lukas's bewildered face. He was no wiser.

When he went into the city centre one late afternoon a few days later, to purchase supplies for Anselmus, he saw Etienne in the main square. Lukas had expected gentle mockery when he asked Etienne's advice, but his friend was surprisingly kind to him. 'She does sound beautiful,' he said. 'No wonder you feel disappointed. I think she's embarrassed. She was forward when she met you. Now she feels she has to be aloof, so you won't think she's too bold. I'd just ignore her too. If she thinks you're desperate to get to know her, she'll lose interest.'

That made more sense than the advice anyone else had given him.

Lukas suggested they go to the Stone Table tavern, close by the square. He wanted to see his friend on his own. But Etienne insisted they go to the Three Violins. 'I know the villains in there,' he winked, 'so I feel safer.'

The others were gathered round their usual table, and Lukas decided he would join them for a little while, then go home. After all, he was carrying valuable materials from the apothecary. There was space at the table next to a fellow in early middle age who seemed to know them all. Lukas sat down there. The man had the dark complexion of someone from further south – Servia or Wallachia perhaps – and a little pointed beard. Lukas noticed his left ear was missing. Something about him made Lukas feel uneasy.

'This is Mister Hlava,' said Etienne. 'He joins us from time to time. We help him out with errands, little jobs . . .'

Lukas had learned not to ask Etienne's friends the standard questions on introduction, such as 'What do you do?' But on this occasion Etienne offered the information. 'Mister Hlava is a mechanical-instrument maker.'

Hlava turned away and began talking to Strom. Lukas became distracted by Jenka – admiring the way she dealt with her more obnoxious customers.

108

'Get me a mutton pie, wench,' said one rotund drunk as he grabbed her round the waist. 'I need sustenance before I go home to entertain my mistress.'

'Buy two pies,' said Jenka, prising his hand away. 'Then you may entertain her twice.'

Hlava noticed how Lukas's eyes followed the serving girl. He saw how his face tightened into a scowl when men patted her on the bottom or put an arm around her waist, and how he looked away when she flirted with other customers.

'What's her name?' he asked.

'Who?' said Lukas, embarrassed that his interest had been noticed. 'Jenka.' Hlava held his gaze. He felt the need to say more. 'She works here most days.'

Lukas and the newcomer fell into conversation. Hlava turned away from the others, saying he could hear much better on his right side. 'It's difficult to catch everything in a noisy tavern,' he said. 'You're a cut above, aren't you?' he went on quietly. 'I can tell by the way you speak. You've had an education – not like this lot!' He winked. 'I could use a boy like you – to help with some of my jobs. I pay generously – they'll all tell you.' He gestured around.

Hlava turned to address the rest of the group. They all leaned closer so they could hear him. 'I need some ivory, boys, and some good-quality malachite. Keep your ears and eyes open.' They all nodded.

As an afterthought he added, 'Oh, and I have something special for you all. Something that will make us a lot of money.'

Then he left for another rendezvous, without elaborating further.

'What happened to his ear?' said Lukas.

Etienne dropped his voice. The others clearly had a lot of respect for Hlava. 'There's a whole chapter to write about that. Some say he was savaged by a dog; he certainly doesn't like Belphegor. Others say a rival bit it off in a tavern fight. I've also heard he used to be employed in the court in Vienna. When he left he took several books that belonged to the Archduke. He's lucky he wasn't hanged for it. In fact, he's lucky he only lost one ear.

'Be careful with him,' urged Etienne as quietly as he could. 'He's a useful man to know, especially if you're short of a few pfennigs, and he seems to know some important people, but . . .' He shrugged, leaving the rest to Lukas's imagination.

Lukas had had enough of the Three Violins. He abandoned his beer and walked home.

# Chapter Sixteen

Don Jenaro Dorantes had been at the court for six weeks before he accepted that the stories he had heard about Rudolph were true. He had not expected to meet His Excellency the Holy Roman Emperor immediately. That was understood. He was an ambassador. His Excellency was the Emperor. Patience was part of his vocation. But six weeks was too long to keep anyone waiting – even an under-procurator from the court of the Duchy of Hessen-Rumpenheim – let alone an emissary from the Spanish Emperor.

When he first arrived, he sent out a request for an audience every morning via the court herald. Every evening he smarted with the humiliation of not having received a reply. Now he thought it prudent to request his audience every three or four days, just to remind His Majesty that he was still there and waiting.

After three weeks a reply came. 'His Majesty,' said a page, 'will see you in due course.'

That could mean anything from tomorrow to some time in the next century. But other members of the Spanish party had been gathering intelligence. When they met to discuss their findings the news was both good and bad. The Emperor, it was widely known, was a recluse who saw only those he chose to see. He spent a great deal of time alone, either in his Cabinet of Curiosities or his own chambers. Both places, it was whispered disapprovingly, were rumoured to be filled with paintings of a decidedly immodest character. But then, so were many of the open courtrooms of the palace, where Dorantes and his party were permitted to go.

Sometimes, it was said, Rudolph chose to see no one but his physicians. Even his mistress, who had reputedly borne him six children, did not see him for weeks on end. One of Dorantes's retinue gave a ribald laugh at that point. 'He obviously prefers to gaze upon his fleshy pictures,' he said with a smirk. The others, taking their cue from Dorantes, looked on with frosty disapproval.

Such works inflamed the humours. Dorantes had already taken to bathing in icy water and had scourged his back with a birch to purge himself of the excess of yellow bile such inflammation created.

'Our task here is too *delicate* for a written approach,' said Dorantes to his cohorts. 'We must persist in our attempts to meet the Emperor. I have it on the highest authority that he is a good Christian soul, and I am sure that once we are able to present our case to him, face to face, we will have no trouble in persuading him to return to the true path.'

Later, alone in his study, Dorantes considered his strategy. The physician Anselmus, the one who had been so interested in his sojourn in Peru – perhaps he would help him to talk to the Emperor. He could ask Anselmus about his inflamed humours too.

But he would have to approach him with caution. After all, he might be one of the heretics that the cheerless Doktor Krohl had talked about.

Dorantes called on Anselmus the next day and spoke

plainly of his desire to see the Emperor. 'I come with instructions from the Emperor of Spain,' he declared. 'He wishes me to talk to Rudolph personally on a matter of the utmost importance. I come to you, as you are so highly regarded both by His Majesty and the gentlemen of the court, to humbly ask your advice.'

Dorantes understood when to flatter and when to cajole. It was his job. He knew when to confide and when to conceal. He suspected Anselmus knew his purpose in Prague. He was uncertain, however, as to whether this peculiar man was friend or foe.

'Your Eminence,' said Anselmus, 'let us speak plainly. I have a fairly clear idea of your purpose. It is said around the Castle that you intend to persuade the Emperor to support the Pope and the work of the Inquisition in the suppression of heresy.' He searched the Spaniard's face for a clue.

Dorantes remained impassive. 'Are you a follower of the true faith?' he asked.

'Indeed I am,' said Anselmus, 'but here in Prague you will find there is a degree of tolerance not found in other parts of the Empire. Does it not say in John: *In my Father's house are many mansions?*'

Dorantes said nothing, but the expression on his face remained pleasingly open and he gestured for Anselmus to continue, which he did.

'Our Church of Rome has done much to discourage the natural curiosity of learned men. Despite my own adherence to the Church, that I cannot agree with. God gave us brains to think, not to accept everything our masters tell us.'

Dorantes nodded his head, as if in agreement.

Anselmus was surprised by such a positive response. He felt moved to say more.

'His Majesty has also done his utmost to ensure that his Catholic and Protestant subjects, and even his Jews, all live together in peace and harmony. Indeed, were we not at war with the Ottoman Muslims, I am sure he would also tolerate the followers of Allah.'

'But there are Muslims here in Prague,' said Dorantes. 'I have seen them in the market.'

'Indeed there are a bold few,' said Anselmus. 'I myself have met Muslim alchemists and natural philosophers. They have much to tell us about the workings of the world.'

Anselmus did not have the calling or the character of a diplomat. He found it difficult to conceal his feelings. 'I know at first hand of the activities of the Inquisition,' he told his visitor. 'Sometimes, in our persecution of our fellow creatures, I wonder if we are any better than the savages you spoke of, with their sacrificial knives.'

Dorantes suppressed his anger and shifted uneasily in his seat. He saw no value in pointing out that in their burnings the Inquisition was performing a holy duty, whereas the savages enacted their cruel rituals to pagan ends.

He now knew he was wasting his time. And he would definitely not be asking Anselmus about his humours. Still, it was his business to leave every door open. 'Good sir, there have been excesses, only a fool would deny it. But we do God's work, and sometimes only the severest punishments can save the world from Satan's legions.'

At that moment Lukas returned from an errand. He bowed, as he had been taught to when gentlemen of repute were present.

'Señor Dorantes is just leaving,' said Anselmus chirpily. 'Would you see him to the palace gate.'

Dorantes beamed at the sight of Lukas. 'So this is your nephew,' he said warmly. 'I remember the lad from that night we dined together. My foolish daughter talked of nothing else the following day. So, you are from Ghent? I know the town well from my days in the Low Countries.'

They walked down the stairs together and Dorantes stopped by the gate of the palace and beckoned Lukas closer. 'My daughter is very lonely here,' he said quietly. 'I am sure, as a relative of the great physician Anselmus Declercq, I can trust you to show her around the Castle. Perhaps also to escort her to the city so she can see the wonders of the town square. I have told her of the Astronomical Clock and the twin towers of Our Lady before Tyn.' Then he spoke even more softly. 'Celestina is taken with melancholy. She has been like this since her mother died. I'm sure the company of someone young like herself will bring some happiness back into her life – in the presence of her maid, of course.'

Lukas smiled brightly. Of course he would be delighted to escort Celestina around, he assured Dorantes. He would like nothing better. He walked back to his uncle's apartment thinking that fate was a funny thing and perhaps it was smiling upon him now. He felt nervous about meeting her again, of course, but he told himself that as long as he didn't suggest she try some of Anselmus's melancholy medicine, things would go well.

Three days later a letter appeared on the doormat. It was from Don Dorantes, thanking Anselmus for his hospitality and asking if he could spare his apprentice for an hour or two to show his daughter the Castle.

Anselmus was pleased. Lukas had met so few people of his own age in Prague. He knew about Etienne, whom Lukas had mentioned once or twice. That was permissible, though he worried a little about Lukas going to taverns, but the Ambassador's daughter would surely be a more suitable companion.

The Doranteses' quarters were a mere three minutes from Anselmus's rooms. Lukas walked there with some trepidation. He had not spoken to Celestina since Grunewald's party.

When he knocked on the door he heard the sound of excited barking. There was a scuffle and shouting and footsteps. The barking stopped and the door was opened by a stern young woman. She bowed, asked if he was Lukas and introduced herself: 'I am Perpetua – the Señorita's maid.'

She was not ugly – that was too strong a word – but her sturdy features had a sourness about them. Maybe it was the business of being maid to a girl only five years younger. Or perhaps Celestina was a difficult mistress.

'He's here,' she shouted into the next room. Celestina appeared, wearing a beautiful gown of silk and velvet – pale green in colour, with an intricately embroidered floral motif on the bodice and pleated sleeves. Lukas was about to compliment her on it when she said, 'Perpetua, please do not call me like that when I have a visitor. You are to come and find me and then say, "Señorita, your guest has arrived."'

She said this with weary, almost pleading, patience. Perpetua was probably new to the job. Lukas was glad

116

she had not spoken sharply to her. That would have disappointed him.

Then she turned to Lukas and offered him her hand to be kissed. 'Master Declercq,' she said with a smile and a curtsy, 'how kind of you to come and visit me.'

Her hand smelled of orchids. The scent, only recently applied, tasted bittersweet on his lips and smarted a little. She was as delicate as china and Lukas felt completely under her spell.

'May I offer you a glass of wine?' she said.

Lukas wanted to smile but stopped himself. She was pretending to be grown-up, just as he was. 'A glass of wine would be welcome,' he said.

Perpetua trundled off and returned with two glasses of wine. 'This is *vino de Jerez*,' said Celestina. 'We like to drink it in Spain. It reminds me of home.'

Lukas took a sip. It was sweet and strong. He liked it better than his uncle's wine. That was what you'd call 'an acquired taste'.

He looked around the apartment. It was sparsely furnished, with no decorations on the wall, no piles of books, no ornaments to make it feel like a home. A lace bobbin lay on one of the chairs. Perpetua stood in the background, hands clasped in front of her, a sharp look upon her face.

Barking started in another room. 'Oh, Chico,' she said. They let the dog out and he immediately leaped up at Lukas, desperately demanding his attention. Lukas liked little dogs and was happy to stroke him. Celestina beamed her approval.

'And are you comfortable here?' said Lukas.

'It will do,' said Celestina with a wan smile. 'As you

can see, there is little here to make it feel like home. My father insists on plain surroundings. He says that ornaments and adornments are vanities and distractions. I miss my home in Madrid. My mother adored her Moorish tiles and Italian tapestries, her portraits and oriental porcelains. I wish we could have brought some of her things with us.'

Lukas took another sip of his wine, feeling warm and a little bit bolder.

'Will you and your father be staying long in Prague?' he asked.

'I don't know,' said Celestina, and beckoned him to sit on a couch close to the window. 'He has come to speak to the Emperor, but I understand there are so many demands on His Majesty, so much imperial business, that he has not been able to find time to see my father yet.'

Lukas smiled. 'The Emperor has so much business,' he said, 'he often retreats from the court and will see no one, save for his physicians, for days on end.' Then he wondered if he'd said too much. Anselmus had warned him to be careful what he repeated to the Spaniards.

She nodded but said nothing more. They sat there for a while. Lukas was just beginning to wonder what else he could say when she clapped her hands. 'Come, Master Declercq, it is a beautiful day. Let us see what the Castle looks like in all this sunshine.'

It was one of those June days when the sun was hot enough to burn. Celestina wore a wide hat with a couple of feathers in the brim, and chastised Lukas for not wearing one himself. 'You'll get sunstroke!'

Lukas was pleased she cared.

They walked first to the West Gate – as Otka had done

with him. Perpetua came with them, of course. It was simply not done for the two of them to be alone – even outdoors. At first Lukas tried to include the maid in the conversation and explanations of parts of the Castle. But she took little interest in what he was saying. After a while Lukas almost forgot she was there.

Celestina seemed to hang on his every word as Lukas pointed out the locations of the Emperor's quarters and the menagerie in the Royal Gardens. And he could not resist telling her about the Cabinet of Curiosities. 'It's supposed to be a great secret,' he whispered as those brown eyes opened wide in surprise, 'but everyone seems to know about it. It's a marvellous collection of fantastical things.' He was boasting now. The wine and the sun had gone to his head. 'My uncle, he is the Emperor's curator. We often go there to work.'

He pointed out the Powder Tower, where alchemists laboured night and day, and she tutted. 'My father says it is a dark art and those who practise it are hell-bound.'

Lukas could well imagine Celestina's father sending alchemists to the stake. 'Do you think that too?' he said.

She seemed offended. 'Of course! I let my father guide me in the ways of the world. He is a wise man.'

Celestina was enchanted by the tiny houses of Golden Lane and shuddered when Lukas pointed out Daliborka Tower. He decided not to tell her about his visit there. It would make him appear foolish. Then they walked out of the East Gate and looked over Prague. 'It is a most impressive city,' she said, 'although not as large as Madrid. I would love to see it properly some time. If my father permits, will you take me?'

Lukas said he often went to buy goods for his uncle,

and he would be delighted to accompany her.

As they parted company she leaned towards him and said, 'The Cabinet of Curiosities – this I would love to know more about!' She took his arm and squeezed it. 'You must tell me, Master Declercq,' she whispered, anxious that Perpetua would not overhear. 'You might even take me there? Perhaps just the two of us.'

Lukas was thrilled by the idea of doing something so illicit with Celestina. But a venture like that would have to be planned very carefully.

# CHAPTER SEVENTEEN

The next time Lukas went to the Three Violins he was curious to see Hlava sitting with Strom and his gang. He was most generous, buying pitchers of beer, telling them he'd had a run of good fortune in a card game. Later in the evening he called for everyone to huddle close to hear something to their advantage.

'I have a great opportunity to make some money, for me and for you.' They all leaned closer. Hlava explained that he intended to pose as an alchemist and invite a wealthy crowd to watch him turn their coins into gold. Lukas thought it was a fine idea. He was beginning to appreciate what Etienne had always known. People were gullible – even clever, wealthy ones.

'And you, Lukas, shall be an essential part of this,' said Hlava. 'We need you, to ensure it will succeed.'

Lukas's amusement turned to alarm. He enjoyed being a spectator to their misdeeds, but not a participant. Besides, this was too public. There were so many things that could go wrong. As he muttered his reservations he sensed a rising hostility around the table, so he assured them he would consider the idea, which seemed to mollify them. He was relieved when the conversation turned to a spate of burglaries in the mansions around the Castle. 'The price you can get for a couple of candle-sticks, especially in the New Town!' said Oldrich. 'Enough to keep you drunk for a week.'

'But you have to be careful of the market,' said Dusan. 'The lords and ladies, they come round the stalls with the constables, looking for their belongings. You have to pick your moment to sell, or you'll find yourself with a hot iron through your tongue.' That was one of the punishments for robbery.

That seemed unlikely though. To go by their boasts, Etienne's mates were never caught. Lukas fleetingly wondered again if he could steal something too. It was difficult living on the apprentice wage his uncle gave him. He would like to buy new clothes. And it would be good to splash his money around with these men. It would make him feel like a grown-up – instead of the little brother they deigned to tolerate.

'I'll tell you what makes the most,' said Radek. 'A nice shiny timepiece. I had one you could pick up with one hand. Beautiful. Chimed on the hour. That paid the rent for a month. And I ate meat every day.'

Dusan nodded. 'Timepieces, they're the future. The smaller the better. I've seen one the size of an egg. All gold it was, and complicated, like a Chinese puzzle. That would fetch a pretty penny. Imagine that. Something that does the job of the town hall clock and it fits in the palm of your hand.'

'Nothing sells quicker than a timepiece,' said Oldrich. 'Mantelpiece to customer in a couple of hours.'

When Lukas left, Etienne walked along the riverside with him, back to the great bridge. 'Don't steal anything from the palace and bring it to that lot,' he advised. 'I could tell you're tempted.' He laughed. 'I can see it in your face.'

'But if you do take something,' he went on boldly, 'just

come to me. I'd be happy to help you get a good price. Strom and his mob are useful people to know, but you have to be careful with them. Don't go thinking they'll treat you fairly.'

He let what he had said sink in, then laughed again. 'We could make some real money here. Not just a few pfennigs telling fortunes.'

Lukas remembered the conversation they'd had soon after they first met, when Etienne had agreed to travel with him to Prague. He'd let Lukas know he expected favours in return – maybe this was one of them.

Lukas tried to steer the conversation in a new direction. 'And what do you think about Hlava's scheme?' he said, but Etienne just shrugged, then bade him farewell.

He walked home alone, hoping it would come to nothing. But now he had heard the details, how could he drop out?

Back at the Castle, Lukas was too restless to sleep. What Dusan and Oldrich had said about timepieces had caught his imagination. The Cabinet of Curiosities was full of them, from extraordinary marble and brass ones that would dominate a room to tiny ones no bigger than stag beetles, ticking away the seconds of the day inside their shiny golden coats.

Anselmus had told him Emperor Rudolph was especially fascinated by timepieces. He employed a whole workshop of horologists. Sometimes he joined them at their workbenches, to squint though a magnifying glass and assemble the minute mechanisms. He would spend hours lost in wonder, trying to match the perfection of his craftsmen.

Despite the Emperor's moods, Lukas admired him. He

liked the way he would sit among his humble artisans and try to learn their skills. He had a Christian modesty about him that was appealing in an all-powerful ruler. But that didn't stop Lukas wondering if he could steal something from him and sell it.

Lukas didn't go back to the Three Violins for a week after that. He sensed he was teetering on the brink of something disastrous and he knew he should resist. But he felt so restless during his evenings at the Castle. He spent most of the day with his uncle, and at night they rarely did anything other than read or play chess. Eventually, the lure of the Three Violins was too strong. Lukas convinced himself that if he was careful everything would be fine. They were seasoned crooks, these people. They would be careful too.

They welcomed him back like an old friend, but much to his dismay Hlava joined them soon afterward. He ordered beer for them all, then beckoned them to gather round.

'Our enterprise is close to fruition,' he said in a low voice. 'Word has gone out to the wealthier streets of Prague, among the alchemists of Golden Lane and natural philosophers of the University, that an alchemist from the far reaches of Astrakhan has come to demonstrate his art and search for a patron. A room has been hired in one of the more respectable taverns.'

They all listened intently, trying not to miss a word among the hubbub of the tavern. Then Hlava turned his gaze to Lukas. 'You, my young friend, you have a central role in this venture. I hope you will not disappoint me and your friends.'

Lukas's stomach turned over. They were all staring at him, their faces a mixture of hope and suspicion. 'You're not a spy, are you?' said Hlava, with a twinkle in his eye. 'A spy for the city constables, sent to inform on the more "enterprising" citizens of our city.'

Hlava was teasing him, but some of them began to look suspicious. This was an idea that had to be swiftly crushed.

'I'll do it,' said Lukas quietly. 'Who would not want to earn that kind of money in an afternoon?'

They all clapped him on the shoulder. Even Oldrich bought him a beer. Lukas tried to put his worries out of his mind and told himself this was the price he had to pay for their company. Sometimes he wondered if they only let him sit with them because they thought he would be useful to them one day. Well, he would do this and prove it. Besides, Lukas told himself, he was so much better off than they were. His life was quite luxurious compared to their daily grind of villainy and ale. Why should he not help them make a few crowns?

Barely a day after Lukas had committed himself, Anselmus mentioned he had heard that an alchemist from Astrakhan was visiting the city to demonstrate his skills. 'I shall have to go, of course. If he is as capable as he says, then I shall recommend him to the Emperor.'

Lukas nearly choked on his soup. 'But, Uncle, he sounds like one of those charlatans you told me about. Surely you will be wasting your time?'

Anselmus shrugged. 'Maybe so. But Ruzicka has told me he will be there. And if the Emperor's chief alchemist feels it is worth attending, it's not for me to look down my nose. Besides, my fellow physicians Tesarik and Vrzala will be there too. I really ought to go.'

Lukas had foolishly assumed his uncle would be too worldly-wise to be interested in a prank like this, and certainly too important to visit a town tavern to witness a demonstration. He felt awkward about letting his friends down, but it was the perfect excuse to get out of it.

The next time they were all in the Three Violins he gathered his courage. 'I've heard people from the Castle are coming. I can't do it – they'll know me.' There were angry noises around the table. Karel took out his knife and began to clean his nails.

'I'll tell you how to make an easy penny,' said Oldrich abruptly.

Lukas breathed out again, relieved that they were talking about something else.

'The University, the school of anatomy, pays twenty crowns a corpse. If you poke around the South Gate first thing on a cold morning, there's usually an old beggar died in the night. But you can't just march in with the stiff and plonk him down on the counter. You have to know the right people.'

Karel spoke up. 'They don't pay twenty for an old beggar. You get ten if you're lucky.' Then he looked straight at Lukas. 'To get twenty you have to bring them something fresh. Something . . . young.'

Lukas didn't know whether they were being serious, but a sliver of fear ran through his guts. He wanted to leave that instant and never come back. He looked at his glass of beer. It was almost full. Intuition told him not to rush out. Besides, at that moment he felt too frightened to move, let alone swallow anything.

Hlava put a friendly hand on his shoulder and dismissed his concerns with a reassuring smile. 'You have ideas above your station, young Lukas. No one takes any notice of a humble stable boy. Besides, in the demonstration you will be invisible to all,' he said. 'There will be no problems.'

It was too late to stop now. They were determined to carry it through and Lukas was a crucial part of it. There was a lot of money to be made, Hlava had promised them. Lukas had to play his role to perfection. If he let them down, he didn't like to think about what would happen to him.

# CHAPTER EIGHTEEN

'She's been babbling again,' said Anselmus the following evening. 'Babbling about the neighbours stealing things from her house. She's convinced someone has broken in and been moving her possessions about. I knew I should have insisted she come to live with me. She's not safe on her own, especially with her bad eyes. And that place she lives in is such a hovel.'

'At least it's warm,' said Lukas, who was finding it hard to keep his thoughts away from Hlava's forthcoming demonstration, which was now only three days away. His Auntie Elfriede was the least of his worries.

During breakfast the next day a note arrived from Dorantes, asking Anselmus if he could spare Lukas that morning to show Celestina and Perpetua around the city. 'You may go, of course,' said Anselmus, 'but I would like you to visit your aunt on the way, to take her some bread and see if she is well.'

Lukas couldn't believe his bad luck.

'Tidy yourself up a little too,' said Anselmus.

Lukas asked his uncle if he could have a bath and Otka boiled up some water. But when he came to dress, Lukas was perturbed to discover that none of his clothes were clean. They were all ingrained with dirt and sweat. Just recently he had neglected his laundry. He had so few clothes he grew tired of constantly washing them. When he asked if Otka could clean them, Anselmus told him frostily that she had quite enough to do already.

'I need some more clothes, Uncle,' he said truculently.

'Then you shall have to buy some,' said Anselmus tartly.

There was one tunic in his clothes chest which was just about presentable. It was a little threadbare, and had a hole in the elbow, but it would have to do.

Lukas arrived at the Doranteses' quarters clutching a loaf of bread. Celestina said she did not mind making a diversion into Prague by way of his aunt, but she did refer to him teasingly as 'the delivery boy'.

She also noticed the hole in his tunic. At first she hinted that Perpetua might like to mend it, but her maid gave her such a poisonous look she dropped the idea at once.

'Perhaps we will find a tunic for you in the city,' she suggested.

Lukas felt mortified. He had no money. 'My uncle disapproves of me spending money on clothes,' he lied.

Perpetua and Celestina exchanged surprised glances.

'Then I shall treat you,' she said. 'To thank you for showing us the city.'

When they reached Elfriede's house she peered from the door with her usual sour suspicion. Marushka emerged between her black skirts and mewled pitifully. The girls both stood back and crossed themselves.

Lukas handed over the loaf and enquired whether Elfriede was well. She looked towards Celestina and Perpetua and asked him if he was courting. Lukas squirmed with embarrassment, but neither of them was listening. They were talking rapidly to each other in Spanish. He said a hasty goodbye.

As they walked towards the Stone Bridge the girls started sniggering. Lukas felt excluded from their joke and asked Celestina what was so funny. She looked bashful. 'Perpetua –' she raised her eyebrows and tried to sound affronted – 'thinks your auntie looks like a witch! I've told her not to be so disrespectful!'

Lukas grew more despondent when they crossed the Vltava and into the Old Town, where the stench and filth of the narrow streets caused the girls to wrinkle their noses in distaste. Celestina said she was glad she had not brought her dog.

Lukas sulked and wondered what she had expected to encounter outside the Castle walls. When they arrived at the magnificent church of Our Lady before Tyn, the twin towers failed to elicit more than polite appreciation. 'We have much better churches in Madrid,' said Celestina. But they were both fascinated by the Town Hall's Astronomical Clock.

'Now, this we have nothing like,' said Celestina. Lukas took this as an opportunity to impress her with his knowledge and explained how the great golden dials and numerals showed the orbits of the Sun and Moon around the Earth and the signs of the Zodiac, and the varying lengths of night and day as the seasons changed. He was starting to explain that the numerals around the rim of the clock represented Old Bohemian, Present Day and Babylonian Time, when she began to talk to Perpetua in rapid Spanish and they both pointed and giggled at a tiny dog being carried by an elderly lady. She stopped to let them pet it, and Lukas realised they were no longer listening to him.

Celestina hadn't entirely lost interest. 'It is pleasing to

know the clock shows the natural order of the heavens,' she said to Lukas, who was eager to be included in the conversation again.

'There are many learned men at the palace, such as my uncle and Doktor Grunewald, who believe the sun is in fact at the centre of the heavens, and not the Earth,' he said.

Celestina shook her head sadly. 'It distresses me that such learned men can hold views contrary to the Holy Scriptures.'

Lukas didn't have a strong opinion either way so he let the matter drop.

They seemed to be enjoying themselves a little more now and watched in queasy fascination as a young man had a tooth drawn by a street surgeon. Then they were entertained by a hurdy-gurdy player, accompanied by a small monkey who went among the crowd collecting coins.

What they enjoyed most were the market stalls in the square. Perpetua bought some cheese and fruit, and both of them admired a selection of velvet and lace fabrics. 'I will make you a tunic,' said Celestina, and asked Lucas to choose a colour. He was embarrassed, but felt it would be rude to refuse and picked a dark blue velvet. They both approved of his good taste.

Loaded down with their purchases they returned to the Castle. The girls were in a buoyant mood and both of them curtsied as they thanked Lukas for a most enjoyable excursion. While Perpetua hurried up the stairs with their provisions, Celestina turned to look him straight in the eye and said, 'I shall send your tunic round as soon as I have finished it.'

Lukas felt pleased with himself. He wondered what he might be able to give Celestina in return.

Later that afternoon Anselmus announced he was to pay another visit to the Cabinet and asked Lukas if he would like to come. Lukas leaped at the chance. Back in the great chamber he let his eyes wander around the tables while Anselmus left him to search for a particular set of Chinese porcelain in the room next door. Just the day before, a trader had arrived with a beautiful luminous white vase, a dragon painted exquisitely on the side. What had fascinated Anselmus was that the dragon was depicted with fur and spots – like a leopard but with a lion-like mane.

'Dragons are a great fascination for the Emperor,' he said, raising his voice so Lukas could still hear him from the next room, 'and for myself too. They are reported in many civilisations other than our own – from Asia Minor, and even as far as the islands of Japan. Agamemnon knew of them. They occur in the Bible from Job to Revelation. Yet they do not seem to live now. This depiction is particularly interesting, for most dragons are shown as scaly, lizard-like creatures. I think the Emperor will be keen to acquire the vase. It will be something to show him when he returns from his country estate.'

Lukas smiled. He suspected that Anselmus wanted the vase too – and why not? Why should his uncle not also gain pleasure from collecting what he desired? As he thought this his eye alighted on a small silver pomander – made to be worn on a ribbon around the neck. It was shaped like an orange, and when Lukas picked it up he discovered it opened into hinged segments filled with sweet-smelling lavender. Some of the lavender fell on to the table and he hastily closed it again. In an instant he realised it would make a beautiful gift to win the favour of Celestina, or it might be something that he and Etienne could sell for a hefty fee. How wonderful it would be to have a little spare money to buy some fine breeches to go with the new tunic Celestina was making him.

He slipped it into his pocket and wandered off to look at a bizarre painting propped against the wall, showing sinister figures with human bodies and frog faces emerging from a river to seize a young woman sheltering under the shade of a tree.

Guiltily looking back at where the pomander had been, he noticed again the grains of lavender on the table. He began to tremble a little and knew at once he had to put the item back exactly where he'd found it.

Just as he slipped it back into place his uncle returned. 'Come now, Lukas, we must away. There are herbal remedies to prepare, and Doktor Grunewald and his assistants are coming to dine with us.'

As they passed one of the tables, Anselmus pointed to a beautiful polished agate bowl and said, 'Look, there's the Holy Grail! Well, that's what some say it is.' He clearly didn't think so. Lukas looked at it and saw it had a distinctive pattern in the stone that could be taken for writing, but he was not paying attention any more.

They walked out of the rooms and Anselmus locked the door behind him. 'You look troubled, my lad,' he said.

Lukas was flustered and began to blush. He was covered in a thin film of sweat. 'It is a picture I saw in the

Cabinet, Uncle,' he lied. 'A painting showing the tortures of the damned. It is most distressing.'

Anselmus ruffled his hair. 'But you're a good boy, so I'll not have you worrying about eternal damnation. You *are* a good boy, aren't you?' he teased.

'Yes, Uncle,' said Lukas, trying his best to feel convinced.

# CHAPTER NINETEEN

Anselmus Declercq sat at the back of an upstairs room in a respectable tavern in the centre of the city. It was a warm afternoon and the room was already uncomfortably full. Anselmus recognised one or two faces from the Castle, but most of the audience were wealthy merchants from the Old Town. Ruzicka had not appeared, nor any of the other eminent natural philosophers or physicians of the court. Anselmus felt a little foolish to have come but told himself he was doing his duty.

At the front of the room a space had been cleared. Behind it was a door to the landing beyond, where Lukas crouched to peer in through a crack in the frame. He spotted his uncle and was relieved to see he was not sitting near the front. That was good, at least.

Neither Strom nor Etienne had turned up. Hlava just shrugged. 'More spoils for the rest of us,' he said. Lukas wished he'd had the courage to stick with his instincts and turn this venture down, but now it was too late.

The others stood around the landing, biding their time. Hlava was delighted that he had managed to attract such a large crowd. He was wearing a magnificent purple robe with gold and silver stitching. A large white turban hid his missing ear, a thick black beard covered his face. They had all looked astonished when they saw the costume earlier in the day. 'Lesson one, my friends,' said Hlava. 'If you want people to think you have the means to create great wealth, you have to look the part.'

He stood between Radek and Dusan and slapped their broad backs. 'Wait behind the door. Stay hidden. I will call if I need to frighten anybody.' He chuckled. 'Now let us proceed!' He opened the door and the crowd immediately fell silent.

Peering over the heads of the audience Anselmus thought there was something familiar about the man. But when, speaking in a barely decipherable Russian accent, he introduced himself as Doktor Novakovich, he decided he did not.

'I have demonstration for you. I learn from the ancients to turn your lead, your tin, your zinc . . . to gold.'

He clapped his hands and Oldrich and Karel staggered into the room via a door at the back with a heavy, iron-bound chest laden with crucibles, tongs, bellows and other laboratory equipment. Built into it was a brick-lined charcoal brazier. Hlava's assistants were also dressed as visitors from the far reaches of the Muscovite dominions, and they too sported sumptuous beards.

'My gift is one that is much abused,' said Hlava. 'There are many trickeries, many . . .' he paused, as if grasping for a difficult word, 'charl . . . atans. So I ask for one of you –' he smiled broadly at the audience – 'to do my experiment.'

Anselmus saw one of the alchemists step forward. Hlava recognised his type at once. 'You, sir, are learned man. But I want man who know nothing of our calling. A man who has no knowledge of natural world.'

A suspicious murmur rumbled around the room as the alchemist started to return to his chair. But Hlava

136

surprised them all by asking him to stay.

'You, sir – you watch. You watch careful, for tricks.'

This seemed to please his audience. Then he picked a finely dressed fellow sitting in the front row of the audience. 'And what is your profession, sir?'

The man declared himself to be an importer of wines.

'And will you help?'

He stood up to an appreciative murmur. The audience was getting excited.

Hlava settled them down with an upheld hand.

'Now, I tell you what I do. We mix litharge –' he held up a small glass jar of powdered dark ore – 'and orpiment.' A jar of glittering crystals. Then he gestured to two other containers: 'Then borax, and salt.' All were handed to the alchemist to examine. He sniffed, tasted or shook each jar and nodded his approval.

Hlava turned to the merchant and handed him a small measuring vessel.

'You must mix one-third each for borax and salt, then half each for litharge and orpiment. Place here,' he said, pointing to the stout iron crucible atop his apparatus.

As he spoke, Oldrich and Karel began to light the small charcoal brazier built into the chest. Hlava announced he had other assistants too. 'I have a gift,' he said solemnly, 'for I can speak with angels.'

The atmosphere in the room changed at once. The alchemists began to scoff and the merchants laughed.

'I understand your disbelief,' said Hlava, who was completely unruffled by their contempt. 'All I ask is that you continue to watch my demonstration.'

The audience settled again. Hlava raised his hands and eyes to the ceiling and began to speak in an unknown tongue. Some wondered if this might be Enochian, the language of angels.

When he had finished his angelic discourse, Hlava turned his gaze to his audience.

'Now we must leave the room so our heavenly accomplices can do their work undisturbed.'

There was an outcry. Angry voices shouted, 'Impostor!', 'Fraud!' Hlava settled them again. 'We will all leave. And I will seal the room.' This seemed to reassure the crowd.

As he spoke, Oldrich and Karel set about marking the door behind them with wax seals. Then they proceeded to the two window handles. Hlava gestured to his audience, inviting them all to leave by the other door. He asked the merchant and alchemist to be the last to go and ensure no one was in the room. Out in the corridor Oldrich and Karel sealed that door too. 'Who will watch the windows?' asked Hlava. Two men volunteered.

'How long will it take?' said one of the audience.

'Ten minute,' Hlava assured them. 'Is very delicate procedure,' he explained. 'Vibration in the air, or noise . . . anything at all disturb the peace of room, and process not work.'

It seemed a reasonable enough explanation and the audience were happy to wait outside the tavern.

Inside the chest, Lukas was drenched in sweat from the heat of the fire. He could feel it burning his back and was desperate to emerge from his hiding place. He tried to stifle the cough that rose in his throat and cursed himself for being stupid enough to agree to this stunt. If anything went wrong, Anselmus would be there to witness his humiliation and collusion. At best, Lukas would be sent back to Ghent. But Hlava had managed to convince him that he was the only choice for the job. 'Karel is not heavy,' he had confided, 'but he is stupid. You will not let me down.'

He listened for the shuffle of feet as the crowd left the room, and counted, as he had been instructed, to one hundred. Then, once he was sure he was alone, he slipped the catch in the back of the chest and tumbled out. When he tried to stand up a terrible pain shot up his back. His legs, which had gone completely numb, collapsed beneath him. He lay on the floor praying for the strength to stand, although he realised how absurd it was to ask God to help him in his mischief.

After a short while, sensation returned to his legs and he carefully stood upright. In his pocket was a small leather bag containing gold filings, and he scattered the flakes in among the smouldering chemicals in the crucible. That was all he needed to do. He took a deep breath and folded his body back inside the chest. His shoulder, which had been pressed against the burning brazier, began to hurt terribly. He realised he had to change his position and shuffled out again. There was a commotion at the door. Hlava was announcing in a loud voice, 'I shall now break the seals and we may all re-enter the room.'

Lukas was barely back in the box when the door opened. Fortunately the audience, in their dash to view the crucible, and their excited chattering, was making enough noise to enable him to click the lock back in place before they arrived at the chest.

Hlava called for quiet. He lifted the lid off the crucible

and a great gasp rose from the crowd. There among the ore and crystals were melted flecks of gold. Hlava picked them out with a small metal implement, separating them on a silver plate.

Seizing on their enthusiasm, he called for silence and then spoke again. 'This process of producing gold works in many ways, and with many different concoctions, but the most effective is by including a little gold in the original mixture. I ask you gentlemen, those among you who have gold crowns to give, to contribute to my next experiment. I promise you I will return your donation fourfold.'

Immediately the crowd began to reach into their purses and pockets, anxious to profit from this miraculous process.

Oldrich and Karel stepped forward to record the donations. Karel, who could not write, placed the crowns in a leather bag. Oldrich recorded the names in his childlike hand.

By the time they had finished, they had collected more than one hundred gold crowns. Hlava instructed his audience to be seated. There would be no assistants or observers this time. As Oldrich and Karel fussed around the furnace he waited for his moment, and with a magician's sleight of hand he replaced the coins with brass forgeries concealed in a compartment in the chest. These he quickly covered with salt, lead, eggshell and dung. Then he ostentatiously tossed in two of his own coins to help maintain his audience's faith in him.

As the audience watched, entranced, Hlava mixed a strong acid and mercury in a crucible. It produced a hideous stench. The room filled with smoke and the

140

audience began to cough and splutter. Hlava slipped a glass tube of gunpowder into the fire. The sides of the chest were reinforced with heavy iron plates, protecting Hlava, his assistants and Lukas. But the front of the brazier wasn't. There was a loud explosion and red-hot coals shot out into the room.

Some of the audience were burned, others were choking so hard they were gasping for breath. There was a crush at the door as people tried to escape.

Inside the chest, Lukas was close to panic. Hlava had not told him about this. The explosion followed by the shrieking and cries of the crowd were frightening him half to death. Was the chest itself on fire? If he came out, Anselmus would see him. Had his uncle been hurt? What should he do?

He heard the catch click and strong arms hauled him from his hiding place. Oldrich and Karel dragged him away. Dusan and Radek, waiting behind the landing door, picked him up and all of them escaped down the back stairs and into the maze of streets and alleys that made up the Jewish Quarter.

In Lukas's mind the whole escape was a blur. He only began to think clearly when they arrived breathless at a house near the tavern. Hlava knew the occupant, who was pleased with the gold crown he received for his troubles.

As they removed their outfits and beards and changed into the street clothes they had left there beforehand, Hlava, Oldrich and Karel were in high spirits. The scam had worked. Lukas felt too stunned to trust himself to say the right thing. 'Weren't you worried about hurting anyone?' he wanted to say. But looking at the elated faces around him, he thought better of it.

Hlava gave Dusan and Radek a gold crown each and sent them on their way. When they were gone he counted out another ten gold crowns and told Oldrich to divide it between the rest of them as he thought fit. He and Karel kept four crowns each and gave Lukas two. 'But mine was the most difficult job,' Lukas protested. Karel fingered his knife and asked what he was going to do about it.

Lukas looked at Hlava, expecting him to agree. But Hlava just shrugged. 'You were hidden away, my boy,' he said. 'Oldrich and Karel were exposed to public view. They took the greater risk.'

Lukas headed for home in a foul mood. As he walked, his blistered back rubbed painfully against his shirt.

The closer he got to the Castle, the more he worried about what he would find when he got there. Had Anselmus seen him make his escape? Had he been hurt in the explosion? If his uncle was all right, he wondered if he should confess, and promise he would never do anything like that again.

Discovering the door unlocked, he opened it gingerly and peered in. Anselmus was sitting by the window, immersed in a book. He barely acknowledged Lukas's arrival.

When he got to his room and lay down on the bed, Lukas felt light-headed with relief and decided he would not tell his uncle anything about the day. The coins felt heavy in his pocket. Two gold crowns was more than he would earn in two months as Anselmus's apprentice.

When they talked over supper, Anselmus mentioned that he had gone to an alchemy demonstration in the Old

Town but had left before the climax. 'The man was obviously a crook,' he said dismissively. 'I couldn't be bothered to discover what happened next. No one ever made gold from litharge and orpiment.'

# CHAPTER TWENTY

Two days later, a parcel for Lukas Declercq was waiting on the doorstep when he returned from delivering food to his Aunt Elfriede. It was the blue tunic Celestina had promised to make him and it was magnificent. As he unwrapped it, he looked for a note from her. It fluttered out from the folds of the material and he eagerly opened it. There was just one word.

*Cabinet?*

Lukas had hoped she might forget. It had been very foolish of him to even tell her about it. He had to play this very carefully.

But that week everything fell into place. At breakfast one morning Anselmus announced he was taking his sister to buy supplies for her medicines and would return that evening. And, as far as Lukas knew, the Emperor was away at Brandys nad Labem, his favourite country estate. He wrote a little note to Celestina, sealed it with wax and slipped it under her door. She invited him round at once.

His knocking at the door brought the usual flurry of barking. This time Celestina opened it. 'My father has business in the city,' she whispered, 'but we must divert Perpetua!' She giggled. Lukas was thrilled to find her in such high spirits.

'I'll give her the day off,' said Celestina. 'I'll say I have a slight fever – ask her to go into town and get me some herbs and treat herself to some fabric. She's always saying she needs some velvet for a dress. That'll take her most of the day. Meet me back here in an hour.'

Lukas had prepared the ground. The Cabinet was rarely directly guarded because there was only one entrance and it required a key to open it. Only a handful of people possessed that key. The palace entrance was guarded, of course, but those who came and went with regularity were allowed in without a second glance. Fortunately Celestina's quarters were close to the great door that led to the Cabinet. All that was needed were the keys – and Lukas knew exactly where Anselmus kept them. They were behind a medical encyclopedia on a lofty bookshelf that ran across the top of one of the windows. It required a set of steps to get up there. Anselmus had never exactly shown Lukas, but he made no attempt to hide what he was doing when he retrieved or returned the keys.

The hour came. Otka was out. Lukas was alone. It took a couple of attempts to find the right volume, but the keys were there, up against the wall.

Lukas walked past the Emperor's palace entrance. He deliberately did not speak to the guard. He didn't want him to remember even seeing him. Then he sprinted up to the Doranteses' apartment.

Celestina opened the door and came straight out. They crept down the stairs, trying not to giggle in their daring. As they reached the corridor that led to the great door of the Cabinet she grabbed hold of his arm in her excitement. She would never do such a thing with Perpetua keeping an eye on them. Lukas liked the touch of her hand.

It was now mid-morning, and everyone else who lived in that part of the Castle was out and about on imperial business. Warm sunlight flooded the corridors and there was a pleasing sleepy silence about the place.

Lukas produced the keys as a stage magician produces a magic wand. He quickly slid one into the lock and turned the mechanism. The door creaked alarmingly as it opened a fraction. They both panicked. Lukas snatched the key out and they ran as quietly as they could back down the corridor. The guard at the palace entrance was only one floor below. What if he came up to investigate? Surely the noise they had made would travel down the stone staircase.

They stopped in an alcove, Celestina still holding tightly to his arm, and waited for their breathing to steady. 'There is a delivery late every morning,' she said. 'A donkey and cart come by with vegetables for the kitchens. He'll be here very soon. Let's wait.'

Just moments later they heard a distant clatter.

'He's coming,' she said.

With a rattle and clop, the cart clattered past the open door of the palace. The sound was so loud on the stairs Lukas thought he could have battered down the door with an axe and the guard would not hear him.

Within seconds they were inside, with the door locked behind them, while the donkey and his cart were still within smelling distance of the guard on the door. The inner door swung open with barely a squeak.

Celestina stared open-mouthed at the paintings on the walls.

'There's so much here,' she said. She was giggling in

the way people do when they're embarrassed.

'Let's go to the next gallery,' whispered Lukas. Being with her and these lurid paintings was making him feel uncomfortable. 'There are many other things to look at.'

They tiptoed down the central gallery, looking neither left nor right at the extraordinary cornucopia of treasures that surrounded them. In the next room – off at a right angle – was the Emperor's collection of relics. Lukas guessed this would interest Celestina.

'Look at this,' he said in a suitably respectful whisper. 'It's a nail from Noah's Ark!'

She dropped to her knees in reverent awe. 'What else is there?' she said, barely believing what she was seeing.

Lukas tried to remember what else Anselmus had shown him and walked over to the table opposite. He pointed to a long piece of ivory. 'This is a unicorn horn,' he whispered, 'and this is a feather from a phoenix.'

'How amazing,' said Celestina. 'But how do we know these things are really what they say they are?'

Lukas shrugged. He wasn't expecting to have to defend the veracity of these objects. 'I suppose the Emperor has experts who tell him if something is real or not. Look – here's a demon trapped inside a glass jar. Would you like to open it, to see if he's really in there?'

She shook her head fearfully. 'Let's get away from it.'

She picked up a beautiful silver lattice sphere enclosing a roughly-textured lump of something. 'Euuurgh!' she exclaimed. 'How odd – to surround something so ugly in such a beautiful casing. What is it?'

Anselmus had told Lukas and he was keen to show off his knowledge. 'It's a bezoar from a unicorn. That's a stone that forms in the gut of an animal. Humans have them too. They're used as a cure for poisons.'

She started looking further afield. It was then that Lukas's eyes fell on a timepiece, placed randomly between a tortoiseshell and a string of lustrous amber beads. It was an extraordinary thing. The octagonal case would fit in the palm of his hand and was full of wondrous detail. The dial was decorated with a geometric pattern and held a single hand in the shape of a mermaid's tail, to point to the hours. Gold-plated beading surrounded the face in a floral design like a raspberry thicket. At the top was a little key for winding the mechanism, and a gold ring and silk ribbon so that the watch could be hung around the neck like a pendant.

Lukas had never seen anything quite so exquisite. He thought of Etienne's proposal. In one mad, impulsive moment he picked up the timepiece and slipped it into his tunic pocket.

Celestina had her back to him, but she soon turned and whispered, 'Look at this lovely drawing of a hare.' It was fantastically lifelike. Lukas peered at the signature at the bottom: 'A. Dürer'.

'It's beautiful,' he said. 'I wish I could draw like that.'

'All of this . . .' She gestured at the room. 'I have never seen anything so strange. What would anyone want with such a bizarre collection?'

'Uncle Anselmus says the Emperor is trying to fathom the meaning of creation. He thinks if he can gather up every extraordinary thing he can lay his hands on, it will all fall into place.'

They reached the end of the hall and turned into

another long room. Here, away from direct sunlight, were portraits of Rudolph and his family. One of them caught Lukas's eye. It was someone from the Emperor's family – the likeness was obvious. But when he looked again, the portrait had changed to one of Rudolph and his brother.

Lukas shuddered with fear. At once he was keenly aware that their trespassing was a grave transgression and wondered whether Rudolph might, by some magical means, be spying on them from afar. He suddenly felt so frightened it was all he could do to still his trembling hands.

'You're white as a ghost,' said Celestina.

'That picture changes,' said Lukas. 'You look at it and it's one of Rudolph's brothers. You look at it again, and it's Rudolph and another brother. What sort of sorcery is that?'

She looked, then walked down the room and looked again. She giggled impishly. 'I've seen one of these in Madrid. It's clever, isn't it?'

She took his hand and led him up to the picture. 'Look,' she said, as if explaining something to a five-year-old. 'The surface is made of three-cornered wooden strips. Like triangles.'

It was. The closer he got, the clearer he could see the sharp angle of the strips. 'One side lies flat. Then you paint one picture on the left-hand side and the other picture on the right. It appears to change when you look at it from different places in the room.'

Lukas began to blush. But before he could say anything they were startled to hear the sound of a bell, a long melancholy chime that hung in the air and slowly shimmered into silence. 'It must be a clock,' whispered Lukas. 'It's chiming the hour too early.' But the chimes carried on, without the regularity of a timepiece. Lukas was desperate to leave. The watch sat there in his tunic, weighing heavily on his chest and his conscience. He wondered if it showed among the folds of clothing.

Before he could stop her Celestina was walking towards the source of the noise. 'Come back,' he whispered, but she was too far ahead to hear him. The long room turned again at a right angle. He caught up with her as she was looking around the corner into the next chamber. She quickly pulled back and began to breathe deeply, as if in shock. Lukas gingerly peered around the corner.

Close to the far wall, sitting on a plush red chair, was a familiar figure. He was half turned away from them, but Lukas recognised him at once. It was Rudolph. In one hand was a large golden bell. In the other hand he held an ivory pole as long as a man. As he rang the bell he muttered incantations to himself. Lukas could hear snatches of Latin. From what he understood, he thought the Emperor was trying to talk to the dead. Placed on the floor in front of him was the delicate agate bowl that Anselmus had told him was supposed to be the Holy Grail.

Celestina was terrified. 'We must go,' she hissed. They both hurried back to the entrance, expecting to see one of the Emperor's courtiers at any moment. But no one else was there. Rudolph, it seemed, had gone there alone. 'The donkey should be back soon,' whispered Celestina. 'We can leave then.'

They crouched down close to the door by one of the larger cases. Standing upright made them both feel too vulnerable, too conspicuous.

'Who was *that*?' she asked.

Lukas told her.

'You told me he was away from the Castle,' she said.

Lukas shrugged helplessly. That was what he had heard.

'And what was he doing?'

'I think he was trying to talk to the dead,' Lukas explained. 'My father was burned at the stake for far less,' he said, suddenly indignant.

She looked aghast. Lukas realised too late he had told her something best kept secret.

They stood by the entrance, ears straining, not catching each other's eye. When the donkey cart passed they made a swift escape, and she ran down the corridor away from him without another word.


'It is a peculiar collection, Father,' said Celestina later that day. 'Full of lewdness and the infatuations of a disordered mind. There are beautiful things and repellent things too.'

She felt haunted by her visit and had already begun to ask herself whether everything she had seen and heard had actually happened.

'And the boy,' said Dorantes. 'Can we expect him to help us?'

'Not directly,' said Celestina. 'His mind is corrupted by heretical thoughts.'

She wondered whether or not to tell him about Lukas's father, but something held her back.

Dorantes's face wrinkled in distaste. 'Just like his uncle. It is this city that poisons men's minds. I have no doubt if we stay much longer we too will fall prey to this freethinking malady.'

Already, when he was alone, in the dead of night, Dorantes had begun to doubt the wisdom of his own country's expulsion of its Jews by the Inquisition. He could see how the Jews lived here without baleful consequence and how they benefited the city. He fought to crush such feelings and convince himself that his uncertainties would be quelled as soon as he returned to Spain.

Celestina was staring at him, wondering what he was thinking. He smiled. 'I can't believe you have grown up so quickly,' he said. 'I still think of you as the little girl I left in the Low Countries. But you are a shrewd young woman with wisdom beyond your years. And you are proving to be invaluable in my mission.'

These parental intimacies embarrassed her. 'I don't think we will ever enlist the boy to our cause,' she said, 'but perhaps we can still make use of him.

'He thinks me pretty,' she smirked, 'and will do anything I ask of him.'

Dorantes's voice took on a stern edge. 'Beware of vanity, my child. It is the Devil's playground. *When pride cometh, then cometh shame* . . . You know the words of Proverbs chapter eleven, verse two.'

Celestina blushed, but her shame was mixed with indignation. Her father was a difficult man to fathom – unlike Lukas, whom she could read like a book.

'Now, you must tell me more of the contents of the Cabinet,' said Dorantes. 'I need to know in what the Emperor takes delight, so I may use this intelligence to influence him and his courtiers. If I can speak to him face to face, I am convinced I will be able to persuade him to support our work to suppress the heretics.'

'The Cabinet is a bewildering collection of religious relics, magical talismans and extraordinary natural objects,' said Celestina, and reeled off as many items as she could remember.

As he listened Dorantes felt a flash of hatred for the custodians of this bizarre repository. It was men like Anselmus Declercq and his portly friend Grunewald, with their lax orthodoxies and wanton curiosity, who fed the madness of the Emperor and corrupted his proper understanding of the world.

'And there is a section of the Cabinet,' she said with a flash of inspiration, 'full of treasures from the New World. There are paintings of the flora and fauna, preserved bodies of animals and the ornaments and trinkets of the savages.'

'Now I know how to obtain an audience,' he said. His hand rested on her shoulder. 'Well done, my child. You have the makings of a fine diplomat, and you have done me a great service. It is a pity you were not born a boy. Now I must away, but let me remind you of Proverbs twenty-five, fifteen: *By long forbearing is a prince persuaded, and a soft tongue breaketh the bone.*'

Celestina envied her father's ability to always find a suitable quote from the Bible. It was a skill many a cleric would admire. But she shuddered a little at the violence implied in his words.

She also shuddered at the terrible risk he had asked her to take. She had not told him she had glimpsed the Emperor. It was a moment that would give her sleepless nights, and she did not want her father to know how close they had been to disaster. But she had enjoyed this little task he had set her. Perhaps he would ask her to do more for him now. It was certainly more interesting than whiling away her days with Perpetua, reading or working at making lace in their dreary quarters.

# CHAPTER TWENTY-ONE

'Señor,' said Rudolph, and held out a hand for Dorantes to kiss, 'we thank you for your extraordinary gift. It will take pride of place in our collection of treasures from the New World. It is indeed an exquisite piece.'

On the table in front of them lay Dorantes's Inca sacrificial knife, which had been the key to this long-awaited meeting.

Dorantes was surprised to hear the Emperor speaking so eloquently. From the reports of his colleagues he had assumed Rudolph would have the character of a surly, monosyllabic youth.

'And what news is there of our uncle Philip? We were educated at his court as a young man,' said Rudolph. 'We hold your sovereign in great esteem.'

To Dorantes, this seemed a perfect opportunity to mention the purpose of his visit.

'His Majesty is well, Your Excellency,' he said, 'and sends his fondest affection . . .' He paused. '. . . but he is also distressed. He hears that in your great realm there are many troubles. And that Christians live side by side with Jews and heretics, even in the greatest city of the Empire. He commands me to tell you, and I in turn humbly beseech you, to put the authority of your crown to the service of the Inquisition and the Jesuit colleges recently established in Prague.'

Dorantes searched Rudolph's face for a reaction to his

words, but the Emperor remained inscrutable. The only emotion the ambassador detected was faint boredom. He carried on with his much-rehearsed script.

'His Majesty hears that sorcery and deviation sweep the land . . .'

Rudolph cut him off. 'Your Eminence,' he said impatiently, 'these are not issues that interest us.'

He turned his back on Dorantes and stared out of the window, breathing deeply, trying to control his anger.

Dorantes stood there feeling foolish. Although he was desperate to leave, he had waited too long for this moment. He searched his mind, wondering what else he could say to prolong this audience and further his mission.

Rudolph came to his rescue. 'Let us talk no more of these matters,' he said, turning back to his visitor. 'Come, we shall take you to our Cabinet. You may be able to tell us more about the articles we possess from the wondrous region from which you have so recently returned.'

Dorantes remembered the words he had spoken to his daughter about soft tongues breaking bones, and nodded graciously. 'You do me a great honour, Your Excellency.'

During that afternoon Rudolph showed him many of his cherished possessions, including the luminous white vase Anselmus had brought him with a depiction of a dragon with fur. 'Our good Doktor Declercq is a man of great learning, both ancient and modern.' The Emperor beamed. 'His mind is open to all the wonders of the world. He does not let dogmatism and zealotry cloud his perception.'

Dorantes ignored the implied criticism. Instead he tried to impress Rudolph with his own knowledge.

'These are coca leaves, Your Majesty,' he said, pointing to a skilfully executed watercolour of Peruvian plant life. 'The natives chew on them when they are tired, and the leaf gives them energy. I too have tried the leaves. They have a bitter taste, but the effect is similar to imbibing the crushed and stewed seed of the Ottoman coffee bush.'

The Emperor seemed fascinated by these observations. But whenever Dorantes tried again to raise the concerns of his uncle Philip of Spain, Rudolph would divert him by pointing to yet another marvellous artefact in his magnificent collection.


Dorantes returned to his quarters feeling overwhelmed by the burden of the task before him. His fellow courtiers were waiting for him. He breathed deeply and thought carefully about what he had to say.

'His Majesty has the vestiges of a good Christian soul,' he said dismissively, 'but I can find not a glimmer of interest in our mission.'

'Your Eminence,' said Elias Aguilar, Dorantes's second in command, 'how can he be a good Christian, if he will not support our work? Impeding the spread of heresy is our monarch's greatest desire and has the blessing and full support of the Holy Father. Can it be that he is not a believer in the one true faith?'

'He is a believer,' said Dorantes wearily. 'Of that I am sure. But his mind has been disordered by the heresy that surrounds him. He does not consider it important that all his subjects are true to the Church of Rome.

'Besides, he has left himself foolishly dependent on the Protestant nobles of this land for arms and money in his battle against the Turks. He is held to ransom by this obligation.'

'It is a shame that his brother Maximilian does not rule in his stead,' said Aguilar. 'He would be far more sympathetic to the wishes of our crown and the Holy See. I hear he gives three hours a day to his devotions. The Emperor in this realm is elected by his peers. I wonder if we should advise our own Majesty to redirect our efforts towards usurping this ridiculous buffoon?'

Rudolph's habit of not seeing diplomats for months on end had instilled in the Spanish party a deep-seated loathing of their host. Spending their days among the heretics and the natural philosophers of the Castle had not improved their mood. They were proud men with an inborn sense of their own importance, and they did not take kindly to being kept waiting like minor functionaries at a town-hall assembly. Now they could see that Dorantes's mission had no hope of success, their anger was unrestrained.

'His Majesty has achieved little in his war against the Turks,' said Aguilar. 'Even now, they menace Vienna and civil war simmers between his Balkan allies. Heretics and Jews, even Muslims, live freely in many of his lands, with no fear of the Inquisition. The foul sin of alchemy is practised even within the palace walls. And still this man professes his love for our King! He has done everything a ruler should not do to keep the love and respect of his court and people.'

Such treasonous talk would warrant execution if overheard by any courtier with a scintilla of loyalty to the Emperor, yet Dorantes noticed how every man in the room snorted and harrumphed their approval and support. He sat for a while before responding in a quiet, measured tone.

'I will send word to our Majesty. I will suggest that we change the purpose of our mission and begin to build support for one of the other archdukes. I understand that there is little love between the Emperor and his brothers, which can only aid our cause.'

'We must chose our candidate well,' said Aguilar. 'The Archduke Matthias is his natural successor, but he too has proven to be open to an understanding with the Protestant nobles. Maximilian would be a worthy heir to the Holy Roman Empire. He will have the will to crush the heretics and infidels that swamp these lands. And the Archduke Ferdinand may also serve our purpose.'

Dorantes thought Aguilar was overreaching himself and tried to re-establish his authority with a bold proposal. 'And while we wait,' he declared, 'we must try to undermine those servants of Satan who besmirch the judgement of the Emperor. I can think of no finer place to start than his heretic physicians.'

Aguilar volunteered, considering them an easy target. 'We must strike at them by any means, oblique or direct. Perhaps we might enlist the Inquisition in our task. They still have jurisdiction in matters of witchcraft. Accusations could be made. I have contacts in the city,' he said. 'I will see to it at once.'

159

# CHAPTER TWENTY-TWO

As he hurried from his uncle's quarters on another visit to the apothecary, Lukas looked up at the rear of the great Cathedral looming before him. The pillars rose to sharp points on the columns supporting the chancel walls and he was struck for a moment by their resemblance to the pointed hoods of the Inquisition. The gargoyles looked down on him with their cold stone eyes.

Lukas's trip to the Cabinet with Celestina had not brought the reward he expected. She was avoiding him again. But that was the least of his worries. It had been five days now since their visit, and he had begun to bitterly regret stealing the timepiece. His guilt was like a demon squatting on his shoulders – an almost physical presence weighing him down. He could no longer under-stand what had made him do it.

He had hidden the timepiece behind some books in his bedroom. Otka tidied his room every day, but he was sure she would not find it there. Any pleasure he got from taking it out of its hiding place and looking at it had quickly evaporated.

He had swiftly rejected the idea of selling it. The piece was so exquisite he could imagine wearing it next to his heart for the rest of his life. He wanted to keep it. Then he wondered if he should give it to Celestina. That would win her heart, no doubt. But did she deserve such a prize? And how could he be sure she would not betray him? Or show it to someone else?

That afternoon Lukas could not settle to his studies. Neither could he do anything right for his uncle. Each medicine he made was too sweet or too bitter; the ingredients he fetched were wrong. Anselmus grew so vexed with him, he sent him to bed with stale bread and cold bratwurst.

Otka could do nothing to please Anselmus either. He had invited Grunewald and some other friends for that evening and had instructed her to bake them a pie. But early in the preparation she had noticed the flour had spoiled and had had to throw a whole jar of it away. Anselmus had accused her of keeping it carelessly. She had been most affronted and, although she had cooked a stew instead, she left that evening without saying goodbye.

Lukas spent a fitful night drifting in and out of restless sleep as he listened to the laughter and excited conversation of Anselmus's guests. Some time in the night he began to dream. He was alone in a great laboratory, standing in front of a long mirror, dressed in the black gown of the condemned at a heretic burning. Torches were flickering on high stone walls. Alembics and stills and cauldrons and phials bubbled and steamed, and there was a choking stench of sulphur.

But the smell did not come from the smouldering matter thickening in the crucibles. Behind him, in the mirror, he could see a pair of glowing red eyes in the darkness. Too terrified to move, he watched a shape take form in the gloom. He saw two horns atop a goat-like head on the scarlet body of a great brute of a man. It was the Evil One, come to claim him.

161

The apparition raised a hand and from the open palm flowed a ray of swirling light. In an instant Lukas found himself unable to move. The figure faded into a haze of smoke. Now he was looking out at the room from the exact spot where the mirror stood. He was caught between glass and mercury. Trapped inside the mirror until Judgement Day, when the Devil would return to gather his soul.

In the morning Lukas felt groggy and in ill humour. 'What is up with you, boy?' said Anselmus. 'I shall have to bleed you if your temper remains so bilious.'

'I'm sorry, Uncle,' snapped Lukas. 'I was, as you observed last night, very tired. Now I have slept badly.'

'Bleeding,' Anselmus said sharply. 'The perfect remedy for imbalanced humours, by cutting or by leeches.' A while later he said, 'Perhaps we have been feeding you the wrong victuals. Salad followed by fruit . . . that's what's caused your sourness. Moistness and coldness can ruin the digestion and set the humours out of kilter.'

They passed the rest of the day in sulky silence. Otka's arrival did not help. She was still angry with Anselmus, and a poisonous atmosphere hung over the whole apartment. That evening Anselmus went to see Grunewald and Lukas hoped that would put him in a better mood. But his uncle returned immediately. That very hour Grunewald had been taken violently ill and was in no state to receive visitors.

Next morning Anselmus sent Lukas to the apothecary to fetch supplies. It was a relief to get away from the stifling atmosphere of their chambers.

As he walked down to the Stone Bridge he began to fret again about the watch. It was too unusual, would be too easily recognised. Now his every waking hour was entangled, like brambles around a tree, with the thought of what would happen to him when he was discovered.

Stealing from a market stall got you a whipping or even a branding. Stealing from the Emperor would mean death. And who would make a more infamous thief than the apprentice of one of Rudolph's most trusted physicians? They would make an example of him. If he was lucky he would have his head cut off. That was quick, at least. But being broken on the wheel was hideous and it could take several days to die.

Then there was the matter of Anselmus. He would be disgusted with his protégé. And he would be ruined too. His reputation would not survive such a disgrace.

'Think straight, Lukas,' he muttered to himself. 'Let us look at this in the scientific manner.' That's what his uncle would encourage him to do. Examine the known facts and then act upon them.

He could destroy it.

He could cast it to the floor and smash it to pieces beneath his boot heel. Bury it in the garden. Throw it into the Vltava. But how could he do that to something so beautiful? He thought of the hundreds of hours the instrument makers had laboured, fashioning the tiny cogs, flywheels, springs and screws, and the thousands of hours the goldsmiths had put into the intricate design. To destroy it would be a worse sin than stealing it.

Sell it?

Perhaps this was the best idea after all. Etienne would help. There was a good chance he would get a handsome price for it and, even if Lukas only got half of it, he would be left with more money than he could earn in several years of his apprenticeship. What a temptation that was. He would even be able to rent his own apartment.

But how could he explain his newfound wealth to his uncle?

Or he could just put it back.

Why didn't he think of that before?

The donkey and his cart would have come and gone. He would have to wait until tomorrow.

Lukas returned to his uncle's quarters feeling a great sense of relief. His problem was solved. Anselmus was not home and Lukas began to feel impatient for his midday meal.

Then there was a commotion at the door. Anselmus burst in. 'Lukas – Lukas, are you home? Come quickly! Something terrible has happened . . .'

Lukas felt so sick with fear he almost retched. He had been found out. He rose unsteadily to his feet and opened the door. Trying to arrange his features in an approximation of surprise he said, 'Why, Uncle, what has happened?'

'It's my poor sister,' he said. 'They have arrested her – accused her of witchcraft. She is held in the New Town jail. She was in the market and she collapsed, muttering something about flying. And then she started to talk about how she was burning. I have just been to see her. I tried to persuade the jailer to let her go. It's just the imaginings of a lonely old woman, I told him. She is doing no harm. I even offered him five crowns, but he told me that the Inquisition had already been summoned. "She said she was flying," he said. "Flying and then tormented by the fires of hell. She must be a witch. The burning is a foretaste of what is to come."

'They are to take her to Daliborka Tower . . .' He could speak no more and let out a great desperate wail.

Lukas felt sad. As much as he disliked his aunt, she did not deserve the attention of the Inquisition. He wondered how someone as frail as her would stand up to them.

There was a loud knock at the door.

'Go and see who it is,' said Anselmus. 'Tell them I'm not in.'

An imperial herald stood at the door holding a small scroll. 'A message for Anselmus Declercq,' he announced to Lukas, 'from His Imperial Highness.'

'Thank you,' said Lukas. 'I will give it to him.'

The man looked affronted. 'Messages from the Emperor are to be delivered straight to their intended recipient,' he said sternly. 'I must see him in person.'

'Please come in,' said Lukas, feeling silly.

Anselmus looked up from the table where he had buried his face in his hands. Lukas could see tears streaming down his cheeks.

'A message from His Imperial Highness,' announced the herald, taking no account of Anselmus's condition.

Anselmus pulled himself together. 'And does His Majesty require an immediate response?' he said.

'I am to wait,' said the man.

Anselmus took the parchment and hurriedly broke the red wax seal that held it as a scroll. Lukas searched his face for clues, but all his uncle did was give a little nod.

'Return shortly,' he said to the herald, who left the chambers without another word.

Lukas looked at his uncle in silence.

'You may return to your studies,' he said. 'We shall

have to discuss Aunt Elfriede later.'

Lukas went back to his room and opened his herbal encyclopedia. He was consumed with curiosity about what was going on. He could hear scuttling and scratching and wondered if Anselmus was looking for the keys to the Cabinet. He hoped he had put them back in exactly the right place and, in a sudden moment of panic, prayed that his uncle had not left a hair or some other indicator in place over the keys, so he could tell if anyone had moved them.

Anselmus was gone fifteen minutes and returned, his face drawn and white with anxiety.

'Uncle, whatever is the matter?' said Lukas.

'The Emperor has gone to his country estate and has sent for his pendant watch, which he left in the Cabinet. But I've just been there and it's gone.'

Lukas's stomach lurched and he feigned disbelief. 'How can that be?'

Anselmus ignored him. 'He left it there the last time he visited. He was admiring a set of amber beads on the table. It is well known that amber has great healing properties when worn next to the skin.'

Lukas pictured the gemstones with a queasy jolt of recognition. They had been right next to the timepiece when he had taken it.

'Now he tells me he took off his pendant watch there. It was probably knocking against the table as it hung from his neck – I've seen it happen before. And then he forgot it. His letter instructs me to collect it and give it to the herald. It is his favourite timepiece. I have gone and looked in exactly the spot he describes. I have found the beads – and the tortoiseshell he said was also there – but there is no timepiece. It has gone.'

'But surely he could be mistaken,' said Lukas. 'Perhaps the watch is somewhere else.'

Anselmus wiped his eyes. 'The Emperor lacks much in the working of his mind, but he has an excellent memory and is rarely wrong in such matters.'

Lukas couldn't believe his ill fortune. It was not even part of the collection, something that might be forgotten among ten thousand other trinkets and baubles. It was the Emperor's favourite timepiece. How could he return it now? He cursed himself bitterly for having taken it.

Anselmus demanded they both return immediately to the Cabinet. 'You may see what I have overlooked,' he said desperately. Lukas was trying to think of an excuse, something that would allow him to go to his room and retrieve the watch in order to slip it back on to a table in there, but his mind had gone completely blank.

As he hesitated, his uncle grabbed his arm and hurried him to the Cabinet. They searched, Anselmus fretting pitifully all the while. 'If the watch has gone, then the Emperor will blame me. For no one else among his curators has been into the Cabinet since his departure to his summer lodge. Fischer and Tesarik are both there with him. Vrzala is in Hradec and Grunewald has not been there for months. No one else has the keys to the Cabinet. All fingers will point at me. I shall be ruined.'

Lukas felt terrible. It hadn't even occurred to his uncle to accuse him.

'And there are worse things than ruin. If the Emperor decides I have betrayed his trust, then I shall be taken to Daliborka Tower and tortured. They may execute me. I can't face the thought of being broken on the wheel. I would rather kill myself.'

'Uncle, you mustn't say such things. You will imperil your soul.'

They searched for an hour in the gathering gloom, Lukas still trying to think of how he could spirit the watch back to the Cabinet. The herald came and rapped on the door, demanding that he be given what he had come for. Anselmus begged him to wait another hour. The overcast day shed little light on the vast array of treasures before them.

Anselmus, in his frantic searching, was muttering desperately: 'I shall be ruined, tortured and ruined.'

Lukas had begun to think of the words he would use to explain what he had done. When he could bear it no longer he said, 'Uncle, I have something to tell you, but please let me tell you away from here, in our rooms.'

Anselmus looked at him with a piercing glare. He understood at once what Lukas was going to say. 'The Devil is a great seducer,' he spat. 'Satan has leaped on you as hunger does on a hot loaf.' Then he took several deep breaths.

'Where is it?' The words were forced out between teeth clamped together in simmering rage.

'I will show you. But, please, can we return to your chambers?'

The herald was waiting by the door. 'We will present you with your item presently,' said Anselmus with as much of a smile as he could muster.

As soon as they returned home Anselmus said, 'Give it to me now.'

Lukas went to his bookshelf and held out the time-

168

piece, knowing that would be the last time he would ever see it. Anselmus inspected it for damage, complaining, 'Lord, I've not been a wicked man. Why are you punishing me so?'

He hurriedly wrapped it in thick velvet and placed it in a small wooden casket. 'Give that to the herald, then come back here immediately.'

Lukas ran as fast as he could to the Cabinet corridor and handed over the container. When he emerged from the palace entrance he was torn as to what to do next. Flee, while he could, and seek out Etienne and his gang for board and lodging, or return to face the burning wrath of his uncle.

# CHAPTER
# TWENTY-THREE

Lukas paused at his uncle's door, still paralysed with indecision. What if he had him arrested? What if he had him sent to the executioner's block? What would Etienne do in his shoes? He would know Anselmus could not betray him, because it would bring ruin upon himself. Lukas pushed down the door handle and braced himself.

There was no shouting and raging. It was far worse. Anselmus had composed himself. His anger was stone cold and all the more terrible in its chilling certainty.

'By your return to my quarters, I see you have rightly guessed that I am not going to report your act of larceny. It would destroy my own reputation, and I have spent too long, and worked too hard, establishing that.'

He paused and Lukas saw his chance to speak. 'Uncle, I am so –'

'Do not speak to me, Lukas Declercq,' he said with menacing authority. 'The palace executioner will not kill you, but you are dead to me. Your life here is over. In honour of your widowed mother and my poor dead brother, I will allow you a week to find yourself a job and living quarters away from the Castle. I will even pay a month's wages to send you on your way.

'I had my doubts from the start, but I wanted to give you a chance. I was too weak. Even when you failed to return money I gave you to buy goods from the apothecary, I indulged you.'

He pointed to the portrait of Thomas Declercq. 'You have failed your father and you have failed me. Look at the poor man and ask yourself, "How can *I*, the son of such a noble father, have stooped so low?" I hear the tanner down the road from my sister's house is looking for a boy. I suggest you go there at once.'

'I shall go immediately, Uncle.' Lukas's brain was reeling. A part of him hoped his uncle would still forgive him. That seemed unlikely, given Anselmus's parting words: 'A job treating animal hides with dog excrement will suit you down to the ground.'

Lukas ran down the road away from the palace, hardly believing what had just happened to him. He looked to the sky with indignant disbelief. 'Why have you thrown *this* at me?' he asked the heavens. But he also felt a creeping sense of wretched contrition. There was no one else to blame. His own vanity and stupidity had cost him his life at the Castle.

As he reached the riverside road close to the western gatehouse of the great Stone Bridge, Lukas resolved he would not go to the tannery. He understood enough about what they did in those places to know that although he deserved it, he could not face a job like that.

He headed straight on into the centre of Prague. But luck had thoroughly deserted him that day. He tried the market stallholders, the merchants, even the riverside sawmill works, but no one had a job for him. Etienne and his friends were nowhere to be seen.

Lukas bought a flagon of ale and a gristly stew in a tavern off the Old Town Square and felt very sorry for himself. As he drank his ale he began to feel his uncle was doing him an injustice. He had been planning to put the

171

timepiece back. He knew he had done wrong. In another day no one would have known anything about it.

He returned at dusk, with the Castle glowing pink in the last of the sun, its sharp edges and pointed towers stark against the fading blue and first stars of the evening sky. This he was being cast out of, to live with the carrion birds in the city below. He bit his lip to stop himself from sobbing.

Anselmus was sitting at the table, his half-eaten supper left before him. Otka stood behind him, her hands on his shoulders, and glared at Lukas. Anselmus had told her.

'Uncle,' he said, 'may I speak with you alone?'

'You may not.'

'Uncle,' pleaded Lukas, 'I wish to explain myself. Please allow me to do so without –'

Anselmus interrupted. 'And why should I spare you the humiliation of pleading for your position in front of my loyal and decent servant?'

Lukas began to explain himself. 'I realised I had done wrong. I was going to put the timepiece back tomorrow.' He expected Anselmus to tell him to shut up, but his uncle sat there in silence. 'If the herald had not come, no one would have known. I would still have my apprenticeship and you would still have your apprentice. Have I not been useful to you, Uncle?' he pleaded. 'Have I not been a good pupil?'

Anselmus spoke in the cold, measured tones he had used earlier in the day. 'An apprentice must be more than a diligent scholar and a quick learner. He must have the trust of his master. You are a boy with no common decency, Lukas. How can I trust you again?'

Something in Lukas snapped. 'You are a fine one to

172

talk about decency,' he said, emboldened by the ale he had drunk. 'I've seen you with Otka.'

Anselmus went white with rage. 'What sort of vile beast has my brother raised?' he spluttered. 'There is nothing improper about our relationship. But since you have had the impertinence to raise it, I shall tell you that Otka is my daughter. She is a simple girl, and very young for her years. She works for me here so I can protect her.'

Lukas wanted the ground to open up and swallow him, as it was supposed to do if you raised the Devil and he carried you back to hell.

'Taking you into my home has been a grave mistake,' said Anselmus. 'You will leave here by sundown tomorrow. Your contract with me is ended. I do not wish to set eyes upon you again, or hear you speak another word, for the rest of my life.'

# CHAPTER TWENTY-FOUR

The next morning Lukas got up, determined to go to the tannery. He was a day away from begging on the streets.

'Where are you going?' said Anselmus coldly, as Lukas prepared to leave.

'The tannery,' said Lukas. 'Yesterday they told me the master was away –' he lied so easily these days – 'and that I should come back today.'

'You can go later,' said Anselmus. 'For now I have a final job for you. My sister has been brought to Daliborka Tower. The cells are cold and damp when the braziers are unlit. Go and fetch a shawl from her house. And be quick. I have spoken with the guards, but they will change in an hour. The new ones might not be so kind.'

Lukas hurried down to Elfriede's place. Her house was cold – even in summer it needed a fire to keep off the damp of the river. The smell inside had changed too. In Elfriede's absence, things were already going mouldy. Lukas looked into the gloomy galley kitchen to see if there was anything he could throw away. He gathered up some meat and a couple of lemons and opened the window to let out the cloud of flies that infested the place.

Marushka the cat leaped in at once and prowled around his ankles, begging for food. He gave her some of the meat and bent down to stroke her. 'You need a new home, my girl,' he said. 'Someone else to make a fuss of you.'

It was good to have the window open. Elfriede still had opaque oiled paper in her frames rather than glass and Lukas could see much better in natural light. Yet even with the window open there was still an odd smell. He looked around. There in the corner of the kitchen a pile of barley stalks caught his eye. Some of them had already been crushed for flour. Lukas could smell something fishy about them. Something rotten and fishy. He looked closer and saw black spores in among the grains.

This reminded him of something that had happened far, far back in his childhood. His father had been involved. And the town physician. Why was he remembering it now? That smell had kindled an ungraspable memory.

He hurried back with the shawl, trying desperately to remember why it was so important.

'Uncle,' he said on his return, 'there's something I need to tell you.'

'There's nothing you have to say that will interest me,' Anselmus snapped. 'Now, take the shawl to the tower at once, assuming you can prevent yourself from stealing it. Ask for Kamil, and be sure you give it to him. He has an elderly mother too, the same age as your aunt. He has a kind heart.'

Kamil, Lukas discovered, was the same guard who had brought him food and spoken to him so gently when he had been held prisoner in the tower.

Back at his uncle's quarters he felt even more determined to speak to him about Aunt Elfriede's rotten flour. But when he tried again, Anselmus turned his back.

'Uncle, please listen.'

Anselmus opened the door for him to leave.

Lukas stormed out, slamming the door violently. As he hurried down the stairs he muttered that they could burn his aunt at the stake. He didn't care.

As he roamed the Castle, trying to calm down, fragments of memory came back to Lukas. That smell, the black dots in the grain – it was to do with a horrible sickness. It was a strange illness – with attacks of the flux, and a terrible burning under the skin, but also bizarre visions.

He could remember no more, but he returned to his uncle's quarters determined to be heard.

'Uncle, please listen to me.'

Anselmus started to shout him down, but Lukas continued talking.

'I have something to tell you that might help Aunt Elfriede.'

Anselmus stopped and stared at him. His eyes were burning with resentment.

'In Ghent we had something like it. I remember a bit about it. But I was very young.'

'Like what?' Anselmus snapped.

'Horrible nightmares, but when you're awake. Like what Aunt Elfriede was talking about. And burning under the skin.'

'And what happened?'

'I can't remember. I just . . . when I was at Auntie's house there was a strange smell in the kitchen – rotten fish. But there was no fish about.'

'So what? She lives very close to the river. It doesn't mean anything.'

'Uncle, please come with me to have a look. There's barley in the kitchen with black mould on it. I'm sure that has got something to do with it. I remember exactly the same thing in Ghent. People accused of witchcraft – it was awful. But the town physician was a very learned man. He said something, something to the magistrates . . . I can't remember any more.'

Anselmus nodded his head. Then he reached for a couple of hefty volumes and handed one of them, a medical encyclopedia, to Lukas.

'Look up "Devil's Fire" in there,' he said.

Anselmus had a botanical compendium and was searching though the entry for barley.

'Did the ears look like this?' he said, showing Lukas a beautifully drawn illumination of barley stalks with blackened grains.

'Uncle, come and see for yourself.' Lukas hurriedly turned a few pages. 'Look here in Devil's Fire.' He pointed to the encyclopedia entry. There, among other symptoms of lunacy, were flights of fancy and burning under the skin. It said it might be due to poisoning, but was vague about the causes.

'Come,' said Anselmus, and they hurried to the house. Halfway down the hill Anselmus returned for a jar. 'I want to take the grain away. I need to see what's happening to it.'

As they walked back, Anselmus said, 'You have disappointed me greatly, Lukas, but I am grateful to you for your help. I shall have something good to remember you by, after you have gone.'

Lukas didn't know what to say to that. But he was keen to know what his uncle planned to do. 'Might I ask what will happen now?' he said meekly.

'I shall examine the grain, and prepare a case to present to His Highness. The Emperor does not usually involve himself in charges of witchcraft. Such cases are invariably left to the Inquisition and the town magistrates. But I shall use my position. He values me, and when he returns we shall have to see if I can persuade him to intervene. I hope I catch him when his mind is steady. He has recently been in the darkest of humours.'

'Do you know when he is coming back?'

'Perhaps in a week. He is rarely away from the Castle, so I cannot imagine he will remain longer at his lodge, unless the weather stays as fine as it has been. We must pray for rain.'

'And when will they start to question Auntie?' asked Lukas.

'It could be a week, it could be a day. Perhaps I should tell her to admit to everything they accuse her of to spare her from torture. Then perhaps the Emperor will intervene before sentence is carried out.'

Anselmus fell into silence. Then he said, 'You may stay for now. You have been useful. But you will go once this has been resolved.'

Otka had been watching the goings-on with uncharacteristic interest. When Anselmus and Lukas left the room, she examined the barley ears they had brought back. There were black spores in them – just like the ones she had found in the flour she had had to throw away.

Anselmus was in luck. Rudolph returned two days later and summoned his favourite physician at once for a routine medical inspection. Anselmus broke every rule of palace etiquette, trusting the Emperor would forgive him on this occasion.

Anselmus came back very late from his audience. He looked drawn.

Lukas feared the worst. But what he heard came as a shock.

'His Majesty has said he will suspend the Inquisition proceedings while further investigations are carried out. Unfortunately these investigations involve a dangerous experiment. He has decreed that three of his best natural philosophers, and the Grand Inquisitor, should serve as witnesses while someone partakes of the infected grains. If they exhibit similar symptoms, then Aunt Elfriede will go free. If they do not, then the Inquisition will proceed with their questioning.

'Of course I volunteered to take the poison. But His Majesty would not hear of it. I begged, but he said he was not prepared to lose his best physician, and besides, the Inquisition would say that I was acting out the symptoms in order to save my sister.'

'Then I shall do it,' said Lukas. 'It will be my penance for stealing the timepiece.'

Anselmus shook his head. 'No, I cannot permit it. Besides, we do not know the amount Elfriede ingested. She may have had but a little. And you may have too much and die.'

'Uncle Anselmus,' pleaded Lukas, 'who else will put themselves forward for such a dangerous trial? Please, I must do it. It is the only way I can atone for my misdeed.'

# CHAPTER TWENTY-FIVE

The trial was held in one of the Powder Tower's laboratories. Perhaps Rudolph had a cruel sense of humour, Lukas thought. 'It is an experiment.' Anselmus shrugged. 'What better place for it than here?'

The experiment was to be overseen by the Emperor's chief alchemist, Bedrich Ruzicka, a Father Brozek of the Catholic Church, and palace physician Doktor Krohl. If and when things started to happen, the Emperor Rudolph and the Grand Inquisitor would be summoned to observe.

The laboratory was full of extraordinary implements, all dedicated to the task of turning ordinary metals to gold. The heavy smell of chemicals caught in the back of Lukas's throat and burned his sinuses. Fires glowed in every grate, despite the heat of day, and Lukas immediately began to feel hot and flustered.

'We are to record everything as it happens,' said Anselmus. He and Doktor Krohl had both brought their quill pens and paper. Lukas was pleased to note that his uncle was being quite civil, although the warmth he had previously displayed towards him was still absent. Krohl was his usual detached self. Lukas wondered fleetingly if his rivalry with Anselmus would affect his judgement.

His uncle had told him that what he would see and feel would be all in his mind. Lukas was queasily anxious and tried to reassure himself by thinking that he had coped with more frightening things recently.

Lukas was disconcerted to see the room filling up. It seemed as if the palace's entire collection of alchemists, natural philosophers, clerics and every shade of learned man had come to witness his ordeal.

'We have a chair for you,' said Anselmus. 'Please be seated.'

He turned to the crowd and announced, 'I shall now prove to you all, by the scientific method, that the cause of my sister's strange behaviour is entirely due to her ingestion of mouldy grain, which affected her mind.' He continued: 'I shall begin by offering my apprentice a small amount of this grain, used to make bread, which we found in her home.'

He held up an ear of barley and walked around his audience, pointing out the spherical black flecks of mould within the seeds. Lukas felt like a magician's assistant about to be sawn in half.

It tasted horrible of course – like rotting fish – and it was all Lukas could do to swallow it without being sick. His uncle had thoughtfully provided a pitcher of beer to wash it down, which Lukas was happy to drink.

After that things got boring, and within half an hour most of the crowd had left. Father Brozek, the Grand Inquisitor's representative, said, 'Anselmus Declercq, this whole performance is a circus designed to save your sister from the attentions of the Inquisition. I move we end this travesty at once.'

Anselmus looked at Brozek coldly and declared, 'You may call me "Your Eminence". That is my rightful title. I am physician to the Holy Roman Emperor.'

Much to Lukas's surprise, Krohl came to Anselmus's aid. 'It is well known that poisons take several hours to work their evil on a body – sometimes days. We must be patient, Father.'

Anselmus looked grateful for his rival's support. Lukas wondered if he even felt a little guilty about the unkind things he had said about him.

Bedrich Ruzicka agreed. 'You must expect this experiment to last for several days.'

Father Brozek let out a contemptuous sigh and shifted restlessly on his chair.

Another hour passed. The remaining onlookers drifted away and all three observers took out books to read. They tapped their feet and drummed their fingers. The noises were starting to irritate Lukas. He also began to notice that many of the scratches and marks on the laboratory walls resembled angry faces. The light from the window hurt his eyes.

'Uncle,' he said, 'I need to pee.' He was beginning to wish he had not drunk so much of the beer. Strangely, he also found himself desperately thirsty. Perhaps it was the heat from the furnaces.

As he stood up Lukas seemed to rise above his chair and immediately felt light-headed. Walking out of the room he had the strangest sensation that the stones on the floor were made of a soft springy substance, like dry moss.

A wooden bucket kept in a side room served as a urinal. It was useful to the work of the laboratory, as urine was an ingredient in some of the alchemists' concoctions.

As Lukas emptied his bladder he was amused to see a

throng of grinning faces in the bubbles his urine produced in the half-full receptacle. He began to laugh and returned to the room with a benign smile on his face.

'Are you all right?' said Anselmus. 'You were gone a long time.'

'I'm sorry,' beamed Lukas, who thought he had been gone for only a minute. 'I'm fine. I do feel a little strange though.'

'Good,' said Anselmus.

Lukas felt sleepy and closed his eyes for an instant. When he opened them the whole room had changed. It seemed to have lost its depth and its dimensions were now strangely flattened – like a child's toy theatre where the actors are paper cut-outs on sticks.

'Can I have some water to drink?' Lukas asked his uncle.

Anselmus turned to his judges. 'See how he slurs his words. And look at his eyes. The pupils are greatly enlarged.'

They all gathered round to peer and at once Lukas was terrified. All three of them had taken on the appearance of wolves, and their growling, snarling, slavering mouths were butting him and crowding him. Anselmus, standing to the side, had turned into a timid sheep. Lukas expected him to bleat in protest, but he just stayed silent. Perhaps he didn't want the wolves to see him.

Lukas's skin began to itch and the dryness in his throat became unbearable. In the grates the alchemists' fires were burning unnaturally vivid violet, turquoise and lavender. Lukas looked at his judges, now returned to their seats. Their faces were glowing like coals in the fire.

Lukas was unbearably hot. 'Uncle, water, please!' He

snatched a brimming tumbler and drank half of it, pouring the rest over his smouldering body.

'My skin is burning,' he said. 'Please, please, bring me more water.'

'Trickery!' snapped the priest. 'I have seen better acting in a nativity play.'

But Krohl and Ruzicka weren't so sure. 'Look how his body is covered in sweat,' said Krohl. He came forward and held a hand to Lukas's forehead. 'He has a high fever.'

Anselmus said, 'We must summon the Emperor. And the Grand Inquisitor.'

Father Brozek was sceptical. 'I hardly think so. His Imperial Highness and the Grand Inquisitor should not be troubled to witness this play-acting.'

Anselmus snapped. 'Father Brozek, you are not familiar, I see, with the concept of a scientific experiment. It is based on observation rather than received wisdom. It relies on direct experience. Most especially, those who conduct the research are not trying to reach an answer they have already decided on. The result of the experiment is based on the observable facts rather than the prejudices and blinkered perceptions of closed minds.'

'I would remind you,' threatened Brozek, 'that your sister is in our custody.'

Anselmus was not intimidated. 'There are three observers, Father Brozek. I am grateful to God, and to the Emperor, that there are three. Two of them have come here with open minds.'

Lukas was reacting badly to this open hostility. Now he was a tiny flailing lizard surrounded by giant black crows, who were alternately pecking at each other then trying to impale him with their beaks. As he writhed in his chair another sensation took hold. He felt as if he was travelling at great speed. This was a novel experience. Until that moment the fastest Lukas had ever been was running down a hill, or dropping from a high over-hanging branch into a river. Now, although he was stationary within the room, he seemed to be moving at such a speed he clung tightly to the arms of his chair so as not to fall off.

When he opened his eyes, Rudolph himself was peering at him. But in his altered state Lukas perceived the Emperor as a great rhinoceros – an inquisitive, benign rhinoceros. Lukas started to laugh and reached out a hand to pat him on his huge head.

'See how he mocks us,' said another voice from far away. It was the Grand Inquisitor. He and Father Brozek both approached to observe him closer. Lukas looked over and saw two gigantic spiders lumbering towards him on spindly, hairy legs. He shrank back in horror and began screaming.

'See how Satan produces foul illusions,' said the Inquisitor.

'See how he recoils from the servants of Christ,' said Father Brozek.

'He is clearly in the grip of demonic possession,' said the Inquisitor.

Now Lukas's head was spinning and the grey walls of the laboratory were glowing in violent blues and greens. Overcome by a terrible urge to be sick, he leaned forward and spewed copiously over the Grand Inquisitor.

Lukas perceived the resulting howl of outrage as a vast stream of rats scurrying from the Inquisitor's mouth. He fell from his seat and cowered in a ball as their tiny scratching paws raced over him.

'I have seen enough,' said the besplattered Inquisitor. 'Satan clearly has designs on the Declercq family. First the sister, now the nephew. Surely it is only a matter of time before our physician here falls victim to demonic possession. I demand that they all be chained and put to the torture.'

'You *have* seen enough,' said the Emperor quietly. 'You will leave now. As will Father Brozek.'

Lukas looked up to see both the cleric and the Inquisitor had turned into giant buzzing wasps. The others in the room were waving them out with great oversized hands.

When they had left, Lukas's perception of the room changed altogether. The burning feeling had gone. Now everything was smooth cool marble. He called again for water. When he drank it was as if his whole body was like a desiccated sponge filling with liquid. It was the most delicious, delightful sensation he had ever experienced.

The Emperor turned to his witnesses. 'We have learned much from our Spanish friend Don Dorantes on this matter. The Incas of the New World make concoctions from plants for their own pagan rituals and these produce strange visions. It seems to us that we are witnessing a similar phenomenon.'

Krohl spoke. 'The boy has been poisoned, Your Highness. It is good that he has voided his stomach. I suggest we administer a remedy before the remaining poison causes further damage to his mind and body.'

'What would you recommend?' said Rudolph, with

186

his usual interest in these matters.

'I have a bezoar in my medical cabinet,' said Krohl, 'from the gut of a bull. It is the perfect remedy. I shall go at once and grind a sample of it into a palatable potion.'

The Emperor nodded. 'Declercq –' he turned to Anselmus – 'fetch the rhinoceros horn goblet from our Cabinet. We have it on good authority that it is the best vessel for drinking medicine to avert the effect of poison.'

Anselmus bowed low. 'It is a great honour you do us, Your Highness.'

Lukas's sleep was long, deep and dreamless. When he stirred he realised he was back in his room in Anselmus's chambers. The light hurt his eyes.

His uncle was sitting at his bedside. 'Elfriede is released and has returned to her house,' he said. 'I have been there with Otka and we have scrubbed and swept the place clean, especially in the kitchen. You must rest until you are strong enough to get up. Then you may continue your studies.'

Lukas felt as though his brain had been sucked out of his eye sockets and then squeezed back into his head through his ears. But even in this pitiful state he realised he had been given a reprieve.

When he was strong enough to sit up and eat, Anselmus brought him a bowl of soup. 'I want to tell you about Otka,' he said. 'Her mother was my housekeeper when I first came here. She's dead now. Otka was born out of wedlock. We quarrelled when she was with child and she went away to have the baby in Brno. She came back a year later with Otka. We worked out a story. She had married a soldier who had been killed fighting the

Turks. It made it all respectable. Then she remarried –
you met her husband, Otka's stepfather, in the Powder
Tower – and they lived on Golden Lane. He knows
nothing of all this and he must *never* know.' He put a
hand on Lukas's shoulder. 'Do you understand?'

Lukas burned with shame but he was too groggy to
think of any suitable words to say.

# Chapter Twenty-Six

Three days later, on a fine late-summer afternoon, there came extraordinary news. Philip II, King of Spain and ruler of the greatest empire in the world, was dead. His successor was his son, also named Philip.

The news came as a hammer blow to Dorantes and his cohorts. They met at once at Dorantes's quarters to review their position. Celestina's dog was barking constantly. It seemed very agitated and would not shut up. The noise made their fraught meeting unusually bad-tempered.

The new king was a pious man, with no serious vices. They all agreed on that. Unfortunately, as it was widely said, that was his only virtue. He was known to be uninterested in affairs of state and happy to let a handful of favourites rule for him. These were not men the ambassadors admired.

As the Spanish party cursed their luck, Aguilar raised another problem.

'It grieves me to say it, but I feel we must take matters here into our own hands. Rudolph is a blight on his Empire and the Church. I believe it is God's will that we implement his removal as soon as possible. With His Majesty King Philip no longer here to give the world and the one true faith the leadership it needs, we cannot sit back and let the most powerful position in Europe continue to be occupied by a heretic and a madman . . .

They say he even dabbles in necromancy.'

'They say many things,' said Dorantes wearily. 'We must be careful not to give too much credence to what *they* say.'

A silence descended on the room while the others considered Dorantes's stinging retort. But even as he said it, Dorantes had wondered if it was true. There was so much there in the Cabinet that could serve as a conduit to the dark side. Even his own sacrificial knife was tainted with unspeakable wickedness. Such things were a magnet to Satan's servants – drawing the lower hierarchy of demons and infernal spirits to the Earthly plane.

And, from clandestine conversations with disaffected courtiers, the Spanish party had gained the opinion that Rudolph displayed every attribute a ruler was not supposed to possess. He was changeable, frivolous, irresolute; he produced as much exasperation in his fellow courtiers as he did in the visiting ambassadors who waited for months or even years to see him. These were all classic conditions for court conspiracies.

'But what of the people?' said Dorantes. 'Do they clamour for change?'

Aguilar shook his head. 'They too seem corrupted by freethinking and are altogether too forgiving of heresy. And Rudolph is not a cruel and overbearing tyrant. While the people are free to trade as they wish and have bread on their tables, they care not a jot for the Emperor's behaviour. Only if the Turk threatens their city will they rise against him.'

'We must begin at once canvassing support for a new emperor,' said Dorantes.

Aguilar crossed himself, muttered a short prayer, then

spoke in a low voice. 'That process will take years, and who knows how we may fare? If we are discovered, then our actions may threaten the entire alliance and leave us facing the executioner's blade. Nonetheless, I believe it is God's will that we take matters into our own hands. The Emperor is frequently ill. Perhaps, perhaps we could . . . help him on his way?'

'Don Aguilar, you overreach yourself,' said Dorantes. 'Your scheme to discredit the physicians came to nought and now you place your mortal soul in peril. You are relieved of your duties. Go to your quarters and await my instructions.'

Don Valdez, another of the ambassadors, stood up. 'Forgive me, Your Excellency, but I believe Don Aguilar to be right. Rudolph's affection for our dear departed King was well known. Perhaps it kept him in some contact with the Church. He has no relationship at all with our new ruler. Who knows how much further he will stray from the true path?'

There were mutterings of agreement around the room.

Dorantes spoke again, trying to keep his temper. It was obvious that Aguilar had the support of everyone else present.

'If we are implicated in the murder of the Holy Roman Emperor, it could set the two greatest powers in Europe at each other's throats. Think of it, gentlemen – the two principal champions of the Roman Catholic Church consumed by war? See how Satan's Protestant allies . . . in England –' he spat the word – 'in the German princi-palities, in the Nordic lands . . . how they would flourish as we tore each other apart.'

Don Aguilar was still firmly seated. He had no intention

191

of withdrawing to his quarters. Feigning a humility he did not feel, he spoke again. 'Forgive me, Don Dorantes. I spoke only for the good of my country and the love of my God. Rudolph has been a disaster. While his empire falls into squabbling and strife and the Turks threaten to overwhelm our Christian lands, he spends his days lost in his Cabinet of trinkets, contemplating the infernal. I believe it is our duty as Christians to bring his reign to an end.

'If you will allow me, I would like to introduce you to two friends of mine.' He left the room, returning a minute later with two men. The barking reached a frenzy and Dorantes ordered Chico to be placed in the room furthest away.

One of the arrivals they all knew. It was the Grand Inquisitor. The other was a small man of eastern European appearance. There was something odd about him. It took a few seconds to realise what it was. One of his ears was missing.

The Inquisitor gave an almost imperceptible nod, as if his status relinquished the need for courtesy. The smaller man, eager to please, smiled to all and bowed low.

Dorantes had gone white with rage. 'How dare you bring this stranger into our midst. Do you know this man?' He pointed at the stranger. 'How can you begin to think he should be a party to our strategy?'

Don Aguilar was calm and ingratiating. 'Your Excellency, the Grand Inquisitor will vouch for this man's integrity with his life. As will I. He has assisted us before on our mission. It was he I enlisted to poison and discredit our enemies at court, and their accomplices. He is a firm and steadfast ally and a believer in the one true faith and he has a solution to our problem.'

Dorantes was not encouraged. The plot with the poisoned grain had been cunningly executed, but it had failed in its purpose.

An uncomfortable silence had fallen on the room. The stranger glanced at Don Aguilar, who nodded at him to continue.

# CHAPTER
# TWENTY-SEVEN

Hrusosky Hlava had taken many risks in his pursuit of wealth and comfort. It had occurred to him as he approached the Castle that day that this might be the most dangerous one yet. But he knew his worth, and he was determined to sell his services for the highest fee he could muster.

Now they were waiting to hear what he had to say.

'His Imperial Highness has a fascination with extra-ordinary mechanical devices,' began Hlava. 'The more uncommon, and the more beautifully embellished, the greater his desire to own them. Furthermore, the more gaudy the claim made for such a device, the more he will be desirous to see it. In his search for power over life and death he is ready to believe anything, no matter how fantastical or ridiculous. His Highness has learned little from previous experience. Many times he has been disap-pointed, but this does not quench his thirst for novelty and sensation.'

'Your accomplice wearies us with his discourse, Monsignor Mach,' said Dorantes to the Inquisitor. He deliberately chose not to address Hlava directly, to show his anger at the arrival of this outsider.

Hlava was not a man to let an insult get in the way of business. He bowed low and replied directly, making it plain he was neither hurt nor intimidated by the reproach. 'Your Excellency, I apologise. I will tell you immediately of my suggestion.'

He looked at Dorantes for permission to continue. Dorantes nodded curtly.

'My plan is to present the Emperor with a gift that he will not be able to resist.'

Dorantes coughed in an irritated manner.

'I will create a beautiful machine. Once it is set in motion, His Highness will fall into a deep sleep, from which he will not awake.'

'You dare to waste our time with fairytales!' snapped Dorantes. He could barely contain his anger.

Mach intervened. 'Your Excellency,' he spoke directly to Dorantes, 'Mister Hlava has told me of his plan in detail. I suggest it will be greatly to your benefit to hear what he has to say.'

Hlava licked his lips and began to outline his scheme. Gradually the anger and scepticism ebbed from every face. He finished on a flourish: 'And in the morning His Highness will be dead and his courtiers will suspect nothing, although some might surmise that the Devil came to claim his soul during a night of necromancy.'

'And do you have such a machine?' said Dorantes expectantly.

'I do not. But if you provide me with sufficient resources, then I shall make one.'

'And what will your fee be?'

'Three thousand ducats should be sufficient.'

'Two,' said Dorantes.

Hlava shook his head. 'Your Excellency, it is a grave thing you ask me to do.'

Dorantes mulled it over. It was a huge sum, but if Hlava was able to do what he claimed, it would be worth it.

'Two thousand ducats is a ransom worthy of a prince,' said Dorantes. 'It will utterly deplete my resources.'

'Two it is,' said Hlava. He couldn't believe they were prepared to pay him that much.

'And how long will it take?' said Dorantes.

'I will have it ready by the end of the month.'

'And who is to present this machine to the Emperor? Surely whoever does this will cast suspicion on himself?'

Hlava nodded. 'You are most wise, Your Excellency.'

'I do not need you to tell me I am wise,' said Dorantes. He was not going to let this sinister little man patronise him.

Hlava nodded and smiled his ingratiating smile.

'I have a friend who will play the part of a traveller who purchased the machine in Asia Minor. I will prepare instructions for the use of it – with a clear command that it will work only in the presence of a single soul. I am sure the Emperor will not be able to resist such a prospect. My friend will need to be rewarded, of course.'

'I'm sure you can see to that yourself, with the generous fee we are prepared to pay you,' said Dorantes. He was affronted that Hlava was fishing for even more money. 'And can we be sure we can trust your friend?'

'I will use only the most reliable gentleman. Of that you have my assurance. He will know nothing of our intentions.'

'You must keep me informed of your progress,' said Dorantes. 'You may have one thousand ducats to cover your immediate purchases, and the remainder when the Emperor is no longer with us.'

# CHAPTER TWENTY-EIGHT

Hlava was surprisingly calm about the enormity of his task. He felt he knew the Emperor's character well. Although he had never met him, he knew people who had. In the past he had mixed with some of the stargazers of the court and had even been with them to the top of the Astronomical Clock to observe the heavens. Now many of his acquaintances were former alchemists or natural philosophers who had fallen foul of Rudolph. One of them had written to the Emperor to say he had invented a perpetual-motion machine. He was summoned to the Castle and seen immediately – which caused no end of ill feeling among the ambassadors, diplomats and emissaries who had been waiting months for an audience.

But the meeting was a short one. The machine, a complex contraption featuring a ball rolling down a series of tilting planes, failed to perform as expected. Rudolph was so angry at having his expectations raised and time wasted that he had the man sent to Daliborka Tower. They let him go after a month, without torturing him, although he witnessed other wretches undergo great suffering and his every waking hour was spent in dread, wondering when it would be his turn on the rack. Hlava told himself that all would be well with his scheme if he had no contact at all with Rudolph's court.

He returned to his home, just north of the Old Town

Square, close by the Jewish Quarter, and went straight to his workshop, which was crammed with the paraphernalia of the alchemist and inventor. Hlava's trade was making automata – little dolls that moved their eyes, dancing monkeys that bashed tambourines and did somersaults. Here and there were the hides of cats and dogs – fur for the animals he created. Levers, cogs and sundry other mechanisms lay on his workbench. Once he had fashioned great complex mechanical creatures, who could play the violin or write the future with pen and parchment. But such creations were too time-consuming and the commissions too infrequent. These days Hlava's main customers were local toyshops. But there were always much easier ways of making money.

He knew exactly what to do for Dorantes. And he would not even have to make the expensive purchases the foolish Spaniards had funded him so generously for. In the basement below his workshop, concealed beneath dust sheets, were two magnificent machines stolen the previous year from a maker of scientific instruments in Plzen. They had caught his eye when he walked past a shop-window display close to the University there.

In the small hours of one hot August night, Hlava had returned to Plzen with Oldrich and Karel, and a cart with well-oiled wheels. They disturbed the nightwatchman and had to kill him. Oldrich had the bright idea of taking the body with them. They had strangled him, so there was no blood. 'If he's gone, they might think he's made off with the very things we're taking,' he said with a chuckle.

The watchman was weighted with a millstone and dumped in the river. It took several months for his bloated, unrecognisable body to break free of the rope that held it and float to the surface. By then everyone had forgotten about him.

The instruments had been worth the trouble. One was a brass torquetum. This astronomical measuring instrument was the size of a small low table, with three variable circular measuring planes. At its base was a compass and a plumb line and on each plane elaborate floral patterns were woven between the intricate calibrations.

The other was an astronomical clock. It was an even more magnificent work of art and science than the torquetum. Four overlapping dials displayed the hours and minutes of the day, together with the phases of the Moon, the signs of the Zodiac, the times of sunrise and sunset and a calendar that could calculate days and dates up to the year 3,000. The entire instrument was housed in an ebony and glass case that allowed the inner workings of hundreds of gleaming overlapping brass cogs, flywheels and levers to be seen.

Hlava began a dramatic reconstruction. The ebony wood that made up the casing of the clock was skilfully removed and replaced with polished golden oak, inlaid with green Indian marble shaped to form alchemical symbols. Arabic inscriptions were carved into the wood and inlaid with carnelian. That gave it a nice mystical feel.

The torquetum was more difficult to alter, but he managed to lay a tiny mother-of-pearl band around the sides of each of its three variable planes.

The torquetum was set atop the clock, which in turn was to be mounted upon a solid iron strongbox surrounded by polished oak. Into this, Hlava carefully placed a hefty clockwork mechanism positioned to operate a set of bellows, and a chiming glass bowl which gave out a strange singing note when rubbed with a leather cloth. This too was operated by mechanical means and would give the machine an additional air of magic as well as covering the sound of the bellows.

Inside the strongbox there was also space for a large leather bag – the sort that could be used to carry water. This would contain a deadly vapour he would need to prepare. It was a curious by-product of alchemical research, known to a few of his acquaintances. If the *lana philosophica* – the philosopher's wool, which some call *ninx album*, or zincum – was mixed with pearls, or even limestone, and then heated, a vapour of sorts was produced, odourless and colourless and undetectable to human senses. Inhalation led directly to death. Being without form or smell it was quite perfect for the discreet disposal of unwanted emperors.

'There,' he said to himself. 'You wind the mechanism to start the machine; that turns the flywheel, which pumps the bellows. The glass bowl starts to sing and vapour seeps from the underside of the machine, and that . . . will be that.'

He finished the work within a week, then settled down by the window with the oldest, most withered parchment he could find and began to write a detailed set of instructions. Each page was then left in the early autumn sunshine, which allowed it to fade most convincingly.

# CHAPTER TWENTY-NINE

Strom and Etienne had spent the morning offloading trinkets in the market. When Hlava found them they were whiling away a pleasant afternoon in the Three Violins.

'I have a job for you, my friends,' he whispered to them, after looking around to check no one else was in earshot. 'I want you to take something to the Emperor. It is a machine of great ingenuity. One that can stop time.' He gave a wink.

'Hlava, you stinking dog's arse,' said Strom, who had drunk more than his usual for that time of day. 'You can do a job like that yourself. Then I can come and admire *your* head on a spike on the Stone Bridge, because that's what's going to happen to me if I do it.' He snorted, as if it was a bad joke. 'The Emperor!'

Hlava tutted. 'Such intemperate language, my friend. Would you not like to hear more of my plan?'

Strom gave him a grudging nod, but Etienne was all ears. Hlava would not normally tolerate such rudeness so cheerfully so this must be important.

'You are to tell the Emperor's curators you are merchants travelling from Asia Minor with treasures for the courts of Europe. Your journey is almost at an end, but you still have the most wondrous device of all, one reputed to stop time. I will provide such a machine and you will deliver it. You may sell it for a considerable sum and have it sent to the court. Not only will you keep the sum you sell it for, but I will also give you two hundred ducats for your troubles.'

'Ducats?' said Strom, spluttering out a mouthful of beer in his astonishment. Now he was tempted. That was enough to buy a house. 'Hlava, if this goes wrong, and I do end up on the Stone Bridge, then I'll get Radek and Dusan to hang your entrails round my severed neck.'

'It will not go wrong, my friend. I will see to it. I have a name at the Castle: Anselmus Declercq. He is the Emperor's chief curator. Write to him and tell him what you have. Be sure he meets you at a place you will not need to return to ever again. And when it is done, you and I will all be richer.'

Etienne looked on in amusement, but declared himself out. He had to be somewhere else anyway. He had to go.

'So be it,' said Hlava, 'but no one else must hear of this.' He knew this was a job Strom could do alone, but he always liked Etienne to be involved in his schemes. He was reliable and intelligent – which was more than you could say for most of the others.

As he left them talking, Etienne tried to remember where he had heard that name Declercq. It seemed familiar, but he could not place it. His instinct told him to have nothing to do with Hlava's scheme, although he could see why Strom was tempted. He remembered with a wry smile how he had intended to work as a translator here in Prague – instead of all this mischief. For now he was enjoying himself living on the wrong side of the law, but maybe it was time to consider that more carefully.

As curator of the Cabinet, Anselmus Declercq was often

approached by merchants and craftsmen who had something strange and wonderful for the Emperor. It was one of his jobs to investigate which of these items were worth acquiring. Now a merchant travelling to Asia Minor had written to him with details of an extraordinary device that was certain to attract Rudolph's interest. The merchant let it be known that he was intending to sell his machine to the murderous Mehmed the Third, in Constantinople, but he wanted to know if his great enemy would like to buy it instead. Strom thought this was a more effective pitch than the one Hlava had thought up.

Anselmus took the bait. He arranged to meet this fellow the next morning, just after breakfast at an inn in the Old Town. When he arrived, Anselmus was immediately impressed by the beauty of the machine. 'And what does it do?' he asked.

Strom was evasive. 'I don't know. I came across it in the basement of an abandoned monastery, Your Eminence. There are instructions – at least I suppose they are instructions . . .' He pulled out a drawer at the side of the device and gave the faded parchments to Anselmus. They were written in Latin.

Anselmus read quickly. He understood enough to know that the apparatus was some sort of temporal device. It claimed to be able to 'stop time' – something Anselmus immediately rejected as impossible. But he was still interested. It was a beautiful machine made in glittering gold and silver with gemstones, and inlaid with ivory embellished with alchemical symbols. He was sure the Emperor would be delighted to have it in his collection.

To look at, he could see it was a mixture of a torquetum and an astronomical clock. In fact it was the mechanical equivalent of those bizarre mythical creatures that he sometimes saw at fairs and in the cabinets of the more gullible collectors – the gryphons, dragons, mermaids and unicorns that were clumsily stuck together by barber surgeons from the remains of other animals.

'And how much do you want for this device?' he asked.

'Four hundred ducats,' said Strom.

Anselmus was wary of Strom. There was a shifty nervousness about him and he was undoubtedly not a merchant, especially with the facial tattoos he could see peeping out from either side of the hood he had wrapped tightly around his head. Neither had he found such a device in a monastery.

'Sir,' said Anselmus, 'this machine is clearly not able to do what it claims . . . but it is still very beautiful. I should like to buy it for that reason alone, although I can offer you only two hundred ducats.'

He was expecting the fellow to haggle and had already decided he would pay up to three hundred ducats. He was surprised when Strom said, 'Done,' and thrust out his hand to shake on the deal. The man seemed anxious to be rid of it and on his way.

'I shall send some soldiers from the Castle to carry it back. They will pay you the money when they collect it.'

'Do so immediately,' said Strom. 'I must be away by midday.'

As Anselmus walked back to the Castle he kept chuckling to himself. Travelling to the court of Mehmet the Third, indeed. That man would have been slain at the border, or taken as a galley slave. But Anselmus knew something strange and wonderful when he saw it. This was the best bargain he had ever purchased and he was sure the Emperor would be fascinated by such a bizarre contraption.

Anselmus mentioned the machine to Rudolph when he and Lukas visited him for his weekly examination that morning. The Emperor was especially despondent that day, and the news cheered him immensely. 'Have it delivered as soon as it arrives, my dear Declercq,' he said. 'I shall read the instructions with great interest. What I would give to be able to stop time . . .'

Anselmus expected the Emperor to see this contraption as he himself had – as an amusing fraud. He was surprised to hear him express such open enthusiasm. Perhaps the Emperor believed it might work because he so desperately wanted it to.

# CHAPTER THIRTY

Rudolph sat in his Cabinet later that afternoon and surveyed the strange machine before him. It was exactly as Declercq had described it – a cross between an astronomical clock and a torquetum. There was a large handle on the lower section. On a whim he turned it a quarter. As the cranking handle clicked, the machine whirred into life and for a few seconds Rudolph heard a haunting singing sound – like a wine glass when you run a wet finger around its brim.

The Emperor smiled a rare smile, decided he would try it out and sat down to read the tattered instructions.

They made some sense, he supposed, as he skimmed through them.

> *Behold and wonder. You have before you an instrument that will grant you prodigious power. For should you wish it, this machine will still the world, prevent the Moon from falling to the rim of the Earth and the stars from turning in their celestial orbits.*
>
> *For this is a machine that can impede the passage of time.*
>
> *. . . The apparatus is to be aligned exactly north. The Horizon, Equatorial and Ecliptic discs of the torquetum are to be positioned with their pointing arms south, east and west, and*

*the perpendiculum straight down towards the
centre of the Earth . . .*

*. . . The device is powerful enough to work only
in a small room and in the presence of a single
soul. Great care should be taken to seal doors
and windows lest the essence of time seep either
in or out of the room and disturb the equilibrium
of the outside world . . .*

*Such an experiment should start only at
midnight – on the final chime of a church clock . . .*

Rudolph knew he must try it, even though everything
he had learned of science and the occult told him
the machine was a fraudulent nonsense. But the
thought of being able to sit in a small room while the
machinations of the court, the clamouring attentions of
scores of ambassadors, the squabbling of his brothers
and the dreadful melancholy that weighed on him like
a lead suit of armour all hung in the air like flecks
of dust – that would ease his troubled soul like nothing
else.

He called to his equerry and instructed him to find
men to move the machine to a small study in his quarters, seal the windows with wax and bring tapestries and
carpets to cover the door. A supply of food and drink and
a chamber pot were also to be provided. The room
would need to be prepared and made ready by the
following evening.

The Emperor looked at the instructions again and
decided that their complexity called for a learned assistant. If the apparatus did work, what would it matter if
there were two people in the room rather than one?

Especially if the room was small. Anselmus Declercq would be just the man for the job.

Anselmus was in a good mood that evening. Rudolph had sent him round some quality provisions to thank him for his latest acquisition. As they feasted on venison and drank a fine bottle of red wine from the Emperor's vineyard, Lukas gingerly asked him about the strange machine he had mentioned to the Emperor that morning. He was still wary of aggravating his uncle and measured every word before it left his mouth.

'It is a transparent fraud,' he laughed, 'reputed to stop time. But it is a very beautiful machine and worth much more than the two hundred ducats I parted with. As for the so-called merchant who was selling it, he looked nothing less than a street thug. He had a tattoo on his face, although he was trying to hide it with a hood.'

Lukas felt deeply alarmed. Even among the villains of Prague, facial tattoos were uncommon. He understood it was essential to keep his life in the Castle separate from Strom and Etienne and the gang. These were two worlds that should never meet. If Strom had sold the piece there would be something nefarious about it. He didn't want his uncle to get into trouble and make a fool of himself with the Emperor.

'Was he quite a tall, solid man?' said Lukas.

'He was.'

'Did he have tattoos that were like two interweaving lines along the sides of his face?'

'He could have. I could only see a little.' Anselmus was beginning to sound alarmed. 'Do you know him?' he asked brusquely.

208

His uncle's prickly anxiety persuaded Lukas he should not tell him he knew Strom well. So he tried to warn him indirectly.

'I've seen him around the town. He always looks as if he's up to no good.'

'I'm perfectly aware of that,' Anselmus replied curtly.

As soon as he could reasonably excuse himself, Lukas went to the Three Violins. He had to find out what Strom had been up to. There had been too many near-disasters recently. If something happened to his uncle, what would become of him? He had seen what life outside the Castle would be like. Then he cursed his own selfishness. He needed to find out to protect his uncle, not just himself. The wine he'd drunk with the meal had gone to his head and Lukas had to force himself to think clearly about what he needed to say.

Strom asked if he'd seen anything interesting lying around the palace – anything worth picking up. It was a question they never tired of, although Lukas always said no and protested that he didn't clean the imperial quarters or anywhere where you'd see things worth stealing. He was strictly stables and courtyards.

Then Lukas swallowed hard and made his pitch. 'I was doing my rounds today when I saw one of the Castle philosophers with a group of soldiers. They were carting this great heavy thing in through the palace gates,' he said. 'He called me over to give them a hand. I didn't mind. He always stops to talk to me anyway – most of them wouldn't. He was in a particularly good mood, and when I asked him why, he said he'd just bought a fantastic machine from a merchant in town – paid him a quarter of what it was worth.'

A fleeting look of alarm passed over Strom's face. 'Oh yes?' he said casually. 'Good deal he got, by the sound of it.'

'Yes. He paid two hundred ducats. Said it was worth nearer a thousand! I can't imagine what I'd do with that sort of money.'

Strom tried to remain calm, but Lukas could see a suppressed rage boiling up behind his eyes as he paused, then asked, 'And what sort of machine was it?'

Lukas had found out all he needed to know. The less he said about it now, the better. But Strom made him nervous and he was frightened and confused about what he should do with his newfound knowledge. He blurted out, 'I don't know – something about a time machine. It sounded ridiculous.'

'Time machine?' spluttered Strom, and laughed scornfully. Belphegor picked up his master's annoyance and let out a menacing growl. Strom shook his head to indicate the conversation was too stupid to continue. He left soon afterwards, Belphegor following at his heels.

As Strom walked through the dark streets he cursed his impetuosity. He had gone into this enterprise with no thought of the consequences. Now he had a nagging feeling that what he had done would have serious repercussions. Lukas knew the man who had bought Hlava's machine off him. That was too close to home. Questions could be asked.

Why was Hlava so keen for the Emperor to have that machine? What if Declercq and Lukas put two and two together and the palace guards came looking for him? He had a nagging suspicion that Lukas knew it was him who had sold it. Otherwise, why would he have mentioned it? He really didn't want to kill Lukas to cover his tracks. He had grown to like him.

Back at the Three Violins, Lukas drank up his beer and headed for home. He felt uneasy. Had he said too much? Strom was unpredictable at the best of times. But something was going on and Anselmus was caught up in the middle of it.

As Lukas turned the corner close to the grand stairway that led to the Castle, a beggar was singing a carnival song on a street corner:

*How lovely is youth*
*Yet it slips away*
*Who knows what tomorrow may bring*
*So be happy while you may.*

Hrusosky Hlava was woken by a loud banging at the door. He cursed himself for not having spent money on a bodyguard. There was always someone, somewhere, who had a reason to kill him. Hlava told few people where he lived. He listened in the silence between the thumps. Then he heard a hoarse whisper. 'Hlava, it's me, Strom. Open the door.'

He hurried down the stairs and drew back the five bolts, lifted the two wooden planks and turned the keys to the three locks.

'That creature isn't coming in my house,' said Hlava, pointing to the dog. Strom ordered Belphegor to sit and wait.

'You know that boy Lukas?' he said, as Hlava closed the door behind him.

Hlava looked blank. He had acquaintances all over the city. He had no talent for remembering names.

'He's the one you got to hide in the chest when you did the gold crowns robbery . . .'

'Yes?'

'He knows the fellow at the Castle who bought the machine.'

'What? But he's just a stable boy, isn't he? Or some other low servant. That was Anselmus Declercq. He's one of the Emperor's physicians. How can the lad know *him*?'

Strom shook his head. 'I don't know. He said he talks to him sometimes . . . and Declercq told him about the machine he'd just bought. I think Lukas knows I sold it. So what's the point of that thing? You didn't want to sell it for profit, that's for sure.'

Hlava made no reply.

'You said I should sell it to him for any price,' Strom continued, 'just as long as it got to the Castle and the Emperor. So what's it for?'

'It is of no concern to you, Strom. I told you I expected complete discretion, and I have paid you well. If the boy knows it was you who sold the machine, you must dispose of him before he tells anyone.'

Strom grabbed Hlava by his gown, lifted him clean off the floor and drew his face close to his. Before Strom could utter the threats he intended to make, Hlava had whipped out a stiletto knife and plunged it into the back of his neck.

Nothing killed a man quicker.

# CHAPTER THIRTY-ONE

Hlava slept fitfully and woke early, feeling annoyed with himself. A shrewder man, he rebuked himself, would have had Strom kill Lukas and *then* killed him. Now Hlava had a corpse in the kitchen and the boy to dispose of. He chewed over his breakfast bread and made himself a rare brew of coffee. It was a luxury he indulged in infrequently, but today he needed a lively mind.

Wearily mopping away the pool of blood Strom had made on his stone floor, Hlava was conscious of his victim's cold, sightless eyes. 'You, my old friend, are going for a swim tonight,' he said to the stiff white corpse.

Then he made a mid-morning visit to the house of the Grand Inquisitor. When he left, in the early afternoon, he had a definite spring in his step. Everything was back on course. It was going to be all right.

He hurried to the Three Violins. Oldrich and Karel were drinking there. Beckoning them close he said, 'That lad, the one who helped us with the alchemy job . . .'

'Lukas,' said Oldrich. 'The stroppy one, who complained about his cut?'

'That's him,' said Hlava. 'Can you tell him that Jenka wants to see him at her house? It's close to the Old Town Square, behind Our Lady before Tyn. There's a sign of a golden cup above the door. Tell him she asked for him. Don't say it was me.' He winked, then gave them each a silver crown and went on his way.

They gave each other a knowing smirk. Hlava was up to no good, but they didn't care. Lukas, the jumped-up stable boy who thought he was better than them, was going to have an interesting evening.

Lukas came into the Three Violins around six o'clock, hoping to find Etienne. It had been a brilliant autumn afternoon and the air still held the warmth of the day. When he saw the back of Oldrich's bald crown and noticed that only Karel was sitting with him he decided to go back to the Castle. But Karel spotted him and called over, 'Hey, Lukas. We have a message for you.'

When he was close enough, Oldrich leaned down and said in a low voice, 'Jenka was asking for you. Says she needs your help with something.'

Karel began to laugh suggestively. But Oldrich kicked him under the table. 'Can you go to her house?' he said.

'I don't know where she lives,' said Lukas. He was bemused. What would Jenka want with him? Still, he wasn't going to turn down the chance to help a pretty girl.

Oldrich described an address in the Old Town, as Hlava had instructed. It was twenty minutes' walk from the Three Violins.

Lukas hurried off, deep in thought. It had been an odd day. He still hadn't worked out a way of warning his uncle about the machine without revealing he knew the 'merchant' who had sold it to him. If Anselmus realised he knew people 'like that', Lukas fretted, he'd never let him go out on his own again. Perhaps he could ask him why he thought he had got it for much less than it was worth. But wouldn't that make him suspicious? Lukas could imagine how angry Anselmus would be if he thought his nephew was questioning his judgement.

It was only when he reached the house Oldrich had told him about – the one with a golden cup above the front door – that he began to feel uneasy. He had expected Jenka to live in a humble dwelling, like the ones on Golden Lane. This was rather grand. Maybe she was a servant who lived and worked here during the day, then worked some evenings at the Three Violins?

He banged on the door and was startled to find it opened by a man whose face he recognised at once. It was the Grand Inquisitor.

Lukas's first instinct was to run, but he felt rooted to the spot with fear. 'I've come to see Jenka,' he blurted.

The Inquisitor gave him a pleasant smile but showed no sign of recognising him. He waved Lukas in and bade him sit down on a spindly chair in the hall. The house was as grand inside as it was out, with heavy carpets and tapestries and finely carved furniture.

'Jenka will be down in a minute,' said the Inquisitor. 'It is a hot day. I'm sure you are thirsty.' He called for a servant and within a minute an elderly man had brought him a drink.

Lukas *was* thirsty. The sun had baked the ground hard and there was a great deal of dust on the streets of Prague. He gulped down the strong-tasting liquid before he had even thought about what it might be. It had a sweetness about it, like a fruit punch, but there was a bitterness too which he only noticed as he drained the final few drops.

At once Lukas began to feel drowsy, and what happened next occurred like a long, strange dream. First

he could see the elderly man leering at him and cackling.
Then there were other people in the hall. He had a sack
thrust over his head and shoulders. It smelled strongly of
hay. Someone had pinned him down and was tying his
wrists to the arms of the chair. When he lazily kicked out
with his feet he found he had no strength in them at all.
After that all was a blank.

# CHAPTER THIRTY-TWO

It was a slow evening at the Three Violins. Karel had gone home and Oldrich was getting bored with his own company. His bald crown had gone a painful-looking pink in the sunshine, and he was so drunk he could barely stand.

Etienne arrived with Radek and Dusan. 'Seen Strom?' they asked Oldrich. He shook his head. 'Has Lukas been in?' said Etienne. Oldrich babbled a story about Lukas going to Jenka's. They pushed him off his chair. 'Go home, you drunken fool,' said Radek.

Etienne was uneasy. He was supposed to have met Strom at midday in the Unicorn tavern, to pick up some goods to sell on the market. When he had not turned up Etienne had gone to the Blue Star and the Spider but there was no sign of him there either. He even went to his home. The woman he lived with complained that he had been out all night and subjected Etienne to a ten-minute tirade about how she wasn't going to put up with him any longer. Then Etienne had seen a dog he was sure was Belphegor wandering disconsolately in the Old Town Square. He shared his fears with Radek and Dusan. They agreed. Something was up.

Radek and Dusan loomed over Oldrich and dragged him to his feet.

'What's this about Lukas and Jenka?' said Etienne, trying to get some sense out of him.

'Ohhh, I dunnow,' slurred Oldrich. 'Hlava said to tell him she'd asked him to go to her house.' Then he clasped his hand to his mouth. He had promised not to mention Hlava.

'Do you know where that house might be?' said Etienne.

Oldrich shook his head. 'Big secret.'

'Not to me it isn't,' said Dusan, and placed both his hands on Oldrich's shoulders, close to his throat.

Oldrich didn't need much persuading. He made some grrrring and grunting noises to show he was thinking. 'Something about a cup, back of Tyn, sign of a golden cup . . . near the square . . . can't remember any more.'

They left him slumped face down on the table.

As they walked to the Old Town Square, Etienne tried to piece all the disparate facts together. Strom was missing. He was working for Hlava on something big. Now Lukas had been sent somewhere by Hlava, who had told a lie to get him to go there.

Etienne wondered how much he could tell Dusan and Radek and decided that this was not the time for discretion. He caught up with them. 'A couple of days ago,' he began, 'Hlava asked Strom and me to do a really risky job for him – I know it was dangerous because he offered us a fortune to do it. We had to sell something to the palace. Some sort of machine. I wanted nothing to do with it, but Strom said he'd do it.

'Then I overheard Lukas talking to Strom last night in the Three Violins. Lukas said something about someone selling a strange machine to the palace. Strom looked really uneasy. It has to be the same one. He left soon after and no one's seen him since.'

Radek looked puzzled. 'But how would Lukas know about that? He's just a stable boy!'

Etienne considered his reply. He couldn't tell them the actual truth. It would put both him and Lukas in a bad light.

'I dunno. He works around the Castle on all sorts of things. I don't know who he's friends with or what he might hear about. Maybe he had to carry the thing up to the Emperor's quarters?'

'He's a clever man is Hlava, but he's dangerous,' said Dusan. 'We've been too greedy, letting him use us like this. Now it's come back to bite us.'

'It's him that needs biting,' said Radek, 'right in the bastard's neck. Time we chose our friends a bit more carefully.'

Intuition told Etienne that Strom was in trouble. He had known him for six months now, and Strom was someone who turned up when he agreed to meet. And Lukas – this cock and bull story about Jenka – that didn't make sense either. What had happened there? Was Hlava covering his tracks? Strom and Lukas both knew about this machine. And so did he. Would he be next?

The three of them split up when they reached the square, concentrating on the streets close to the great church of Our Lady before Tyn. There were so many house signs: scales, snakes, cats, dogs, even lobsters. It was Radek who found the one with the golden cup above the entrance.

Etienne approached the door, grateful he was not alone. Being the sort of size and characters they were, Dusan and Radek were not afraid to rush in where angels feared to tread. They banged on the door with their fists.

A little voice asked who was there.

'Delivery – two cases of wine,' said Dusan, sounding as respectable as he could. The door opened an inch and they were in. A little old man stood quaking in the hall. Etienne addressed him politely. 'We're looking for a friend of ours.'

'Go away,' said the man. 'How dare you come into my master's home like this. Go now, before I call the guards.'

'Call them,' said Dusan.

'My master is not to be trifled with,' said the man.

'Call the guards,' said Dusan.

'Guards, come quickly,' said the old man. But his voice lacked conviction and they all knew there would be no thunder of feet into the hall. He was here on his own.

'No visitors at all this evening?' said Etienne. 'Did someone ask for Jenka?'

The man denied it, but he was beginning to tremble with fear.

'What are you going to do to me?' he pleaded.

Radek looked him in the eye and said, 'We're going to tie you up and then set the house on fire.'

'I don't know the lad. I haven't seen him before.'

No one had mentioned a lad.

'What's happened to him? Where did they take him?' snarled Radek.

The man knew he was defeated. He tried to make a dash for the door, but Radek stopped him with insolent ease.

Dusan stood behind him and pinned him tight to his side with one massive arm while holding his head rigid with his huge hand. Radek put his face up right against the old man's. 'Tell me what happened to your visitor, or I'll bite your nose off.'

'What the master will do to me will be far worse,' said the old man, finding his courage.

'I doubt it,' said Radek. 'Now where is the lad?' He stretched his mouth out over the man's nose and slowly began to close his jaw. Gripping the nose firmly in his teeth he began to rock slowly from side to side, all the while making angry growling noises.

'On four,' said Dusan, and he and Etienne began to count 'One . . . two . . . three . . .' as the rocking gathered momentum.

'I'LL TELL YOU,' screamed the old man. 'They're in the New Town, by the city walls. The house of the Two Suns, close by the West Gate.'

'And what are they doing there?'

'I don't know,' he pleaded.

'Then let's go and find out,' said Dusan.

'It's a ten-minute walk from here,' said the old man. He'd stopped trembling now. He thought his ordeal was over.

'Probably fifteen with you,' said Radek.

The man looked puzzled.

'You're coming with us.'

Radek and Dusan told the old man exactly what they would do to him if he tried to call for help. Dusan showed him the sharp knife he carried and assured him he would slit his throat in the beat of a gull's wing. The man got paler and paler and his legs gave way beneath him.

Dusan hauled him to his feet. 'They're not at the house of the Two Suns, are they?' he said.

The man shook his head. 'They're in the forest near Dablicky. Out past the North Gate.'

'What the devil are they doing out there?' said Etienne.

The man said nothing. Radek lurched towards him, mouth open.

'It's a sabbat,' said the man in a tiny, terrified voice.

'A *what*?!' said Etienne. 'You mean, with witches and everything?'

He nodded.

'Have *you* been to one of these?' said Radek.

The old man nodded.

'And what are they going to do to Lukas?' said Etienne.

The man shook his head.

All four of them left the house at once, Radek in front, the old man in the middle, Etienne and Dusan close behind.

# CHAPTER THIRTY-THREE

When Lukas came to his senses it was dark. He tried to move but realised he was still tied to the chair. He was outside, somewhere in the countryside, and there was a very strong smell of woodsmoke. The scene that greeted him was as bizarre as anything he had seen when he took the poisoned bread mould in Anselmus's experiment. He was in a forest clearing. There was a great bonfire burning at the centre, and he could hear the rattling and scraping of a tambourine and viol. Silhouettes of tall trees loomed above him against the blue-black of the night sky. The stars seemed especially bright. All around the fire were people chanting and dancing. They were naked, save for garlands of flowers and the masks they wore – animals, Devils, blank carnival faces. Some were young and lithe, some old and saggy with pot bellies wobbling before them. All were daubed with strange blue and red markings.

Only one figure was clothed. He wore long white robes and carried a flaming torch. On his chest was a necklace of holly, and over his head was a great mask in the shape of a goat's head.

Fear made Lukas's heart beat hard and cleared his groggy head. What on earth was he doing here? He began to shiver in the night air.

As his eyes grew used to the dark, more details of this bizarre scene became apparent. Around the fire were grotesque objects: skulls, daggers, and even a severed head.

Some of the revellers sat outside the dancing circle. A few had black cats sitting on their laps, and one woman had a large black rat. A tethered owl sat on a perch, staring impassively into the bonfire.

To the left of him there was another fire, underneath a small cauldron. Someone was pouring ingredients into it while consulting a book.

The more he became aware of his surroundings, the more frightened he felt. Lukas had heard about witches' sabbats – everyone had. But his father, and his uncle, had encouraged him to believe that such events were entirely imaginary. His father, especially, had told him that the whole idea of witches was dreamed up by the Church as a means of frightening their flock into fearful obedience. Yet here was a scene straight from *Malleus Maleficarum* – a book his father had told him was disgraceful nonsense.

Something was happening. The figure with the goat's head had seated himself on a large wooden chair. Several of the younger women present were arranging themselves at his feet. He raised a hand and the music stopped. The dancers stood stock-still. 'Bring me the victim,' said the goat-man.

Lukas was overcome with panic and strained at his bonds. But no one came over to him. Instead a wax figure the size of a doll was handed to the robed man. 'Behold, the Holy Roman Emperor,' intoned the man, and held the doll up. Lukas could see it was clothed in court finery and wore a tiny crown. He also thought he recognised that voice. The man started babbling in a strange language Lukas did not understand, although he did recognise the names of some of the demons Satan was supposed to send to Earth to aid evildoers.

The music started again and the dancers began to sing a strange dirge-like melody. As the song reached its climax the goat-man began to thrust pins into the figure. Every time he did this the dancers would let out a horrific shriek, as if they themselves were being pierced to the innards. Another pin went through the doll's heart and the little figure was thrown into the fire. All the dancers gave a final shriek and fell to the ground.

The man in the goat mask was standing up now, in front of his chair. He cast his torch into the blaze and picked up a hideous-looking dagger. It had a very sharp blade and a silver handle shaped like an elongated goat's head, its two horns making up the hand-guard.

'Bring the sacrificial goblet,' called out the goat-man. One of his minions brought forward a chalice stolen from a church.

'Now bring forth the offering,' he commanded.

This time they did come for Lukas.

He was lifted to his feet. Two of the biggest men there pinned him from either side. He was completely helpless.

The dancers began to chant, but the goat-man stilled them with a wave of his hand.

'OH, DARK LORD,' he called out to the sky, 'TAKE THIS, OUR HUMBLE OFFERING, THAT WE MAY GROW STRONGER!'

He raised the dagger and rested the point on Lukas's throat. One of the young women moved closer with the chalice, ready to catch the blood that was to be spilt.

Others crowded round her. Even through their masks, Lukas could see their eyes were wide with a frenzied, unnatural excitement.

In his terror Lukas struggled to escape, but the two men held him tight as a vice. He closed his eyes and clenched his teeth as the mob began to chant. His heart was thumping in his chest.

A loud crack rang out over the chanting, and Lukas opened his eyes. The goat-man lay on the ground. His mask had fallen off and a hole in the side of his head was oozing blood. His close-cropped white hair looked very familiar. In the second he saw him, Lukas thought he looked just like the Grand Inquisitor.

A second later there was a great explosion in the fire and burning sticks flew everywhere.

The revellers were seized by panic and scattered in all directions. Lukas was cast to the ground.

Dusan had thrown a gunpowder pouch on to the flames.

Etienne emerged from the darkness. 'Quick,' he said, as he slashed at Lukas's bonds with a knife. 'Before they gather their wits and come back to look for us.'

The old man was with them too, held tight by Radek. As soon as Lukas was free, Radek gave the man an almighty thump with a length of wood and the four of them ran into the forest, only stopping when their legs could take them no further.

# CHAPTER THIRTY-FOUR

Anselmus was pleased to receive a late-evening summons to the Emperor's quarters; it flattered his vanity that Rudolph should ask for him. But the physician was anxious too. Rudolph had been in an especially black mood over the last week. Courtiers who had displeased him had been sent from his presence with a hailstorm of abuse. Anselmus was worried about Lukas too. He'd gone out earlier that day and should have been home by now.

When Anselmus arrived at the Emperor's quarters, one of the equerries showed him into a small room. The time machine was set up in the middle. The Emperor was there too, sitting on a padded chair, reading the instructions. There were dark rings around his eyes. He looked as if he had not slept for days.

'My dear Declercq,' he said wearily, 'these scribblings are somewhat complex. We should like you to assist us.'

Anselmus set the machine up exactly as the instructions described. He pointed out – trying to keep the scepticism from his voice – that they did state that only one person should be present. The Emperor was uninterested. 'It is a small room,' he said impatiently. 'We are sure it will work in here for you and us, or not work at all.'

So be it, thought Anselmus. It will make no difference. They waited for the Castle clock to strike midnight and Anselmus wound the handle. It made a satisfying clicking noise – exactly like a large clock mechanism – and after a few seconds the device began to emit a pleasing ringing sound.

They sat there, waiting to see what would happen. After a while Anselmus looked out of the window. As far as he could make out, people still walked across the bridge, and ripples from the river still caught in flickering torchlight. He thought to draw this to Rudolph's attention, but when he saw how serene the Emperor looked, sitting with his eyes closed and a beatific smile on his face, he didn't have the heart to tell him.

'Ah, Declercq,' said Rudolph sleepily, 'we have not felt so completely at peace since we were a small child. It pleases us greatly to know that outside these four walls there is nothing happening to threaten our person or the peace of our realm.'

Anselmus nodded, but he was finding it difficult to collect his thoughts. He could feel a thick, muggy headache coming on. He was desperate for a breath of cool night air, but he did not feel it was his place to suggest this to the Emperor. Besides, the instructions clearly stated that windows and doors should be sealed.

Another five minutes passed. Now both of them were drowsy. Anselmus, in fact, felt as though he was at the bottom of the sea. The Emperor slumped back in his chair, his mouth wide open. The last thing Anselmus heard before he lost consciousness was the Castle clock striking the quarter-hour.

Lukas and his rescuers heard the clock too. They were seated by the road close to the North Gate, straining for breath. As it was after midnight the city gates had been locked until dawn. They found a barn and bedded down.

'This reminds me too much of that night back in Momalle,' whispered Lukas to Etienne. Dusan and Radek were both snoring loudly. 'I hope we don't get any more visitors.

'That man you shot when you rescued me,' he added, as the bizarre details of the night came back to him. 'I'm sure it was the Grand Inquisitor.'

Etienne didn't seem surprised. 'I can't think of a better alias – the Witchfinder was a witch himself!' He seemed to admire the man's deceit.

'Strom has vanished,' said Etienne, 'and Oldrich says Hlava told him to send you down to a house close to the square. What's going on, Lukas?'

'Hlava had me sent there?' exclaimed Lukas. 'What a fool I was to swallow that story about Jenka!'

'Why d'you think they wanted to kill you?' asked Etienne.

Lukas shook his head. 'I don't know for certain, but last night I asked Strom if he'd sold something to one of Rudolph's courtiers. He denied it, but I could tell he had, and he seemed very agitated that I knew. My uncle – Anselmus – he told me he'd bought a strange machine from someone in the town who had tattoos on his face. I thought it sounded like Strom. But why is Hlava mixed up in it too?'

'What sort of machine?' said Etienne.

'Something about time – I can't quite remember. It sounded ridiculous.'

'I was there when Hlava came to talk to Strom about selling it,' said Etienne. 'He wasn't interested, but Hlava talked him round. I don't think it's a straightforward deception. There's something odd about that machine.'

Lukas felt sick. 'If Hlava made it, then I definitely have to warn my uncle,' he whispered. 'I found out about it and he tried to have me killed; Strom knew about it and he's missing. What is it about that thing that's worth killing your accomplices for? You know about it too,' he added as an afterthought. 'Make sure you watch your back with Hlava.'

Etienne shrugged. 'He trusts me. I'm too valuable to him.'

For a moment Lukas thought Etienne looked a little afraid.

'I've got to get back to the Castle as soon as possible,' said Lukas. 'My uncle bought that machine for the Emperor and I think it's going to get him into terrible trouble.'

As they settled down to sleep Etienne turned and said, 'I've had enough of this life, Lukas. I'm sure Strom's dead. You nearly ended up with a knife in your throat. Oldrich and Karel betrayed you for a few coins. When this is over, I'm going to start trying to make an honest living on the market.'

What Etienne said troubled Lukas greatly. As he drifted off to sleep he knew in his bones that his friend would find it impossible to get away from the life he had chosen. He was too well known now in the Prague underworld. The merchants would soon get to hear of his reputation. They would not trust him. Only men of bad character would seek out his services.

# CHAPTER THIRTY-FIVE

The potion that had rendered him unconscious the previous evening still lingered in Lukas's body and he slept heavily. He woke later than intended and left his companions still snoring. By the time he reached the city gates the morning sun had already brought a warmth to the day. In the square the market was busy with customers.

Lukas ran as fast as he could to the Castle. His uncle rarely left his quarters before ten so Lukas was alarmed to discover he was not at home. He went to Anselmus's friend Doktor Grunewald's chambers and banged on his door. Grunewald looked most displeased to see him.

'What has happened?' said Lukas. 'Do you know where my uncle is?'

'What has happened?' echoed Grunewald coldly. 'I'll put ten gold crowns on your having something to do with it.'

Grunewald used to be so pleasant with him. Lukas supposed Anselmus had confided in his friend when he discovered his nephew had stolen the timepiece from the Cabinet.

Grunewald reluctantly ushered him in. The man looked sick with worry. 'I was disturbed early this morning – before first light – by cries in the Castle court-yard,' he said in a clipped, angry voice. 'I looked out to see several of the guards struggling with Anselmus. Now

I hear he has been sent to Daliborka Tower, accused of trying to kill His Excellency. That cannot be true. No one is more devoted to the well-being of the Emperor.'

He looked at Lukas with an accusatory glare. 'Is this your doing? Is your misbehaviour bringing further grief to your uncle?'

'He's accused of plotting to kill the Emperor?' Lukas could not believe his ears. 'Your Eminence. I am desperate to assist my uncle as best I can,' he blurted, 'but I have only hearsay and supposition to help me –'

'You have caused enough trouble to last a lifetime,' interrupted Grunewald.

There was a loud banging at the door. 'Only the palace guard knock like that,' said Grunewald. 'I'm surprised they did not arrest you at the Castle gates. Anselmus's acquaintances are being questioned. Is it you they seek? I shall be happy to present you to them.' He turned towards the door.

'Please,' Lukas begged, grabbing the physician's arm. 'I have information that could help my uncle. If they take me, then I will not be able to do so.'

Grunewald paused and frowned. Then he beckoned Lukas to another room in his quarters. 'Go quickly into my bedchamber and hide,' he whispered. 'When they have gone you must tell me everything.' Lukas dived under the bed and listened.

He heard the door creak open. 'Your Eminence,' said a commanding voice, 'we search for Lukas Declercq, apprentice to the assassin Anselmus Declercq. Do you know of his whereabouts?'

Grunewald shook his head and assured the guards he would let them know if he saw the boy. Lukas heard the door close and the physician came at once to the bedroom.

'Now tell me what you know,' he said brusquely.

Lukas's head was spinning. 'I know of people in the taverns,' he said, 'who have sold Anselmus a strange machine. I think this machine might have caused the trouble.'

'These people – did you tell them about your uncle?' Grunewald was simmering with suppressed anger.

'No! Never!' Now Lukas was angry. 'I have done selfish, stupid things, but I would never betray my uncle. I knew nothing of this until it was too late to warn him,' he pleaded. 'This has nothing to do with me and I need to find out more. What can I do? I've got to get my uncle out of the tower.'

'For now, I choose to believe you,' said Grunewald. 'Who sold the machine to your uncle?'

'Strom, he's called, but I think he's dead. I'm sure the man who made it murdered him. His name is Hrusosky Hlava.'

Grunewald looked appalled. 'And how do you know such people?'

'I go to a tavern in Mala Strana. I overhear things.'

'You must find this man Hlava and bring his whereabouts to the attention of the guards. Perhaps this will help your uncle,' said Grunewald. 'I have done what I could. I went at first light to the tower. When they would not let me see Anselmus, I protested until the officer of the watch accused me of being an accomplice. He even threatened to arrest me. Everyone is certain something terrible has occurred. Now you must go. If you are found here, my life will be ruined.'

'But I won't make it past the guards,' pleaded Lukas.

'Come,' said Grunewald, grabbing a bunch of keys and a small lantern. 'I will help you get out of the Castle.'

They hurried out. Instead of taking the main stairway, which led out into the square behind the Cathedral, Grunewald took Lukas down a narrow staircase at the rear of the building. Thin arrow strips let in light and air for the first fifty or sixty steps, but these stopped as the staircase continued below ground. It rapidly became too dark to see ahead, and Grunewald began to fumble with his firebox, striking sparks to light his lantern candle.

A strong smell of damp and mould wafted up from below. 'Quickly,' urged Grunewald, who was already out of breath, as they continued their descent into the bowels of the building. 'There is a tunnel down here, recently built, which takes floodwater away from the Castle. You can follow it down to the banks of the Vltava.'

They had reached a large vaulted chamber with a slippery flagstone floor. Lukas could not tell how tall the room was as the light from the candle was too dim to reach the ceiling. At the far end was the entrance to a tunnel. From what little Lukas could see in the dim light, the brickwork was new and of a high standard. It was a good size; only the tallest man would not be able to stand upright.

'I am sorry, but you will have to make the journey without light,' said Grunewald. 'I need my lantern to return to the staircase.'

He patted Lukas on the shoulder and gave him a handful of gold and silver crowns from his purse. 'Prove to me you have some worth, Lukas. I wish you luck.'

Grunewald dashed off towards the stairwell. The

lantern light receded until Lukas was in complete darkness. As Grunewald's footsteps faded he was left in eerie silence, save for the occasional dripping of water and the squeaking and scurrying of rats.

At his house near the Old Town Square, Hlava went through the events of the last few days in his mind, too restless to settle. When Strom told him that the boy Lukas had realised it was he who had sold the machine to the palace, he knew they both had to go. Monsignor Mach had agreed to dispose of Lukas. He seemed to find the whole business quite amusing. Hlava wondered what sort of fate the Inquisitor had arranged for the boy. He hoped he had done a proper job.

Then there was Etienne. Hlava had tried to enlist him in the plot. That had been careless of him. He should have approached Strom alone. If the scheme to kill the Emperor succeeded, there would be an almighty upheaval. There would be arrests and torture and who knows what would come out. Etienne would have to go too. It was a shame. He was a clever boy.

Now some fool messenger had come from the Spaniards demanding an urgent meeting. He did not say what had happened, but he was deeply agitated – enough to make Hlava suspect something had gone wrong. How many of *them* would he have to silence to prevent anyone betraying him under torture? This was all becoming very untidy.

He hurried to the Three Violins. He had to recruit someone to help him, and he thought Oldrich and Karel would be best. They'd done enough of his dirty work over the years. If the price was right they'd betray their

235

own mothers. They'd certainly know where to find Etienne.

He hurried over. They were there in the tavern. He'd given them enough money to keep them drunk for a week when he'd got them to send Lukas off to 'Jenka's' house.

Unfortunately for Hlava, Dusan and Radek were there too. He saw them all sitting at a table and immediately turned around before they noticed him. From what he could see, the two big men were very angry. Oldrich and Karel looked terrified. Hlava knew it in his bones – they had found out about him sending Lukas to his death. Hlava suspected his two accomplices might end the day floating face down in the Vltava.

As he hurried back to the Stone Bridge he spotted Etienne walking towards him. He smiled to himself. Fortune still favoured him. If he was careful and quick, the problem could be easily dealt with. The boy seemed lost in thought. Hlava hid in a doorway and when Etienne walked past he sprang out to greet him with a hug. Etienne had not forgotten Lukas's warning. Quick on his feet, he deftly sidestepped his assassin. He brushed away the arm that tried to embrace him, but felt a sudden pain in his hand as he made contact with Hlava's stiletto knife, which clattered to the cobbled street.

Etienne drew his own knife to defend himself, but a passer-by, thinking he was trying to rob Hlava, grabbed his arm. Etienne and Hlava both looked at the knife on the road.

Hlava thought to pick it up and finish the job, but this interloper was a big burly man and now people were watching. 'Be gone, you rogue,' said Hlava. 'Trying to take the purse of an honest merchant.'

Etienne pleaded in turn. 'This fellow has just attacked me.'

The man looked bewildered.

'Look,' said Etienne, holding up his bleeding hand. 'And there's his knife on the ground.'

They both turned around to see Hlava vanish into the crowd.

Lukas stood frozen in the pitch darkness, fighting the fear that rose in his guts. He was entangled in a sticky web of his own making. Everything he had – his uncle, the comforts of the Castle, his future – was crumbling to dust. And most of it was his fault.

The chime of the Cathedral clock, which drifted faintly down through the catacombs of the Castle, had already sounded two of its quarter-hours. Only when he heard the midday chimes did he find the courage to enter the tunnel. With one hand on the wall at his side, and the other held out in front of his face, Lukas lurched blindly into the darkness. It was cold and he was shivering. He could sense the tunnel gradient growing steeper as it led down the hill towards the river. Several times he lost his footing and fell hard on his haunches. Looking round he could see no light at all, neither in front nor behind. Lukas told himself he was lucky. This was, at least, only a floodwater passage rather than one of the Castle's wastewater drains. His instinct told him to protect his face and he had to constantly battle against a fear that he would walk into a wall or low joist.

Something ran past his ankles and Lukas let out a frightened cry. It must be a rat. At least it didn't bite him.

He lost track of how long he had been down there and sat down on the damp floor. He had been bad, he knew that, and he had been punished for it. But he had tried to mend his ways. Fighting back his tears he prayed to the God he no longer believed in to help him. And his uncle. The thought of Anselmus held prisoner spurred him on. He had to get out of this mess and find Hlava. Only that would save his uncle from the torturers.

Gathering his courage, Lukas stumbled on. The gradient had levelled off now to a slight slope and moving forward was easier. He sensed a cool breeze on his face. Ahead he could see a dim glow. Picking up speed, he hurried towards it. It was a ventilation shaft. Way above his head – perhaps the height of a four-storey building – was a circle of light.

A series of iron hoops driven into the wall led up to the surface. Lukas took a deep breath and began to pull himself upward. The hoops were slippery with moisture, and the higher he climbed the more frightened he felt, but he kept his eyes firmly on the light and when he spotted a bird swooping close to the top of the shaft, he knew he was nearly there.

The shaft was at the end of a luxuriant walled garden attached to one of the villas at the foot of the Castle. There was a gardener close to the house. When the man turned his back Lukas crept from the tunnel and shinned up a tree overhanging the garden wall. Dropping down to the cobbled street outside, he headed at once for the bridge. He did not know what he was going to do, but thought he would start by looking for Etienne around the Old Town Square. Then the two of them could look for Hlava.

# CHAPTER THIRTY-SIX

Dorantes had several paid informants among Rudolph's inner court and a garbled account of the night's events had filtered through to him that morning. The Emperor was still alive. The heretic Anselmus Declercq had been with him, but now he had been sent to Daliborka Tower. That was good news at least. The authorities had realised something nefarious was afoot, but Declercq was the chief suspect.

Dorantes had been deeply uneasy ever since this plan had first been suggested. How could he have let a man like Hlava become his accomplice? He had been a fool to trust him, and the Grand Inquisitor. Now Dorantes would be held to account by the Spanish court. He would have to justify his extravagant expenditure of one thousand ducats on this harebrained venture. He would demand it back – some of it at least. Dorantes had sent one of his subordinates to the Old Town with a message summoning Hlava. The man returned an hour later. 'He refuses,' he said. 'He asks that you meet him instead in the Stone Table tavern. He will be there at two in the afternoon.'

Perhaps it had been rash of Dorantes to expect the architect of this failed assassination to come to the Castle. He could understand Hlava's reluctance.

He then summoned Don Aguilar and told him what had happened. He asked him to come with him into the city. He was certainly not going alone. Aguilar had got him into this mess. Now he could help him out.

Aguilar accepted at once, but he also had a word of caution. 'Your Eminence, there is much at stake here. The Castle is in turmoil. Rumour and suspicion are endemic. We must be careful that our activities arouse no suspicion. Might I suggest we disguise our purpose?'

'I shall ask my daughter to accompany us,' said Dorantes. 'She longs to spend time away from the Castle. We shall accompany her into the city, and she and her maid can entertain themselves in the market square while we meet with Hlava.'

The two men armed themselves discreetly with pistols and daggers and Dorantes called for his daughter. As he predicted, Celestina and Perpetua were delighted to come with them.

Across the bridge, Lukas kept to the shadows of side streets and alleys as he made his way to the Old Town Square. Although no one looked twice at him, he felt uncomfortably conspicuous out in the open. All the while he searched for Hlava, hoping to see his enemy before being spotted himself. The thought of coming face to face with the man terrified Lukas. What would he do? He was sure he couldn't beat him in a fight. He didn't think Hlava would kill him in the street – although he couldn't be sure. He was beginning to understand how ruthless he was.

Lukas bought himself a pie and hid in the shadows to eat it. Some time soon Etienne was bound to cross his path. His old friend, he was sure, would help him find

Hlava and somewhere to hide. If Etienne didn't turn up, Lukas would have to go to the Three Violins that evening. Some of the gang would almost certainly be there. What would he say to Oldrich and Karel? Had they known what they were doing when they sent him to that house?

Constantly checking ahead and behind, Lukas neared the square. As he paused in a doorway he was alarmed to see Celestina, with her father, Perpetua and another one of the Spaniards, walk straight past him. The two men were deep in serious conversation, while Celestina talked excitedly with her maid. None of them saw him. Instinct told him not to approach them.

Lukas crouched down and waited for his heartbeat to settle. He was startled by a wet, slobbery sensation. Belphegor was licking the pie crumbs from his greasy hand. Lukas made another visit to the pie shop for him. Then boy and dog settled in the shadows of a boarded-up shop doorway overlooking the square. The sun turned in the sky as the afternoon wore on, and soon both were dozing in a warm pool of light.

Dorantes and Aguilar told the girls they had business to attend to and said they would meet them at the steps of Our Lady before Tyn later that afternoon. Then they went to the Stone Table and sat in an alcove on the far side of the room, opposite the door. It was the perfect spot for a discreet conversation.

An hour passed. Hlava was late! How dare he be so impudent! Then they began to worry. Perhaps he had been arrested. Perhaps their plot had been discovered. When they heard the chimes of the Astronomical Clock they got up to leave. At that moment Hlava walked through the door.

Although he smiled as he sat down, Hlava seemed agitated and would not catch their eye. 'And what news is there of the Emperor?' he asked.

Dorantes spoke in a low whisper. 'He was found insensible in his chambers. There was someone else with him – one of his physicians. The heretic Declercq. Both men have recovered, although Declercq has been sent to Daliborka Tower.'

Hlava said nothing. His face was impassive. His mind, though, was racing.

Dorantes had more to say. 'The money I gave you – the one thousand ducats – I demand you give some of it back, at least five hundred. Your scheme has failed. For now we are lucky not to have been discovered. Who knows how tongues will wag if this goes further and the torture begins?'

Hlava smiled. 'And I was going to ask you for the rest of my fee.'

Aguilar stood up, outraged by Hlava's audacity. 'You will pay us back the money we have asked for and you will not get a pfennig more.' Dorantes bade him sit down. He was being indiscreet.

Hlava looked disappointed, even a little hurt. He said, 'I undertook this venture at considerable risk. My plan was perfect. I built a beautiful machine worth well over my original thousand ducats and delivered it to the Emperor. The vapour would have done its work with one person – as my instructions clearly stated. Sharing it between the two of them weakened its effect. I kept my side of the arrangement. I advise you to pay me, Señor

Dorantes. You will find I am a poor choice of enemy. I will see you tomorrow. Be here for three o'clock, though I may be late.'

Hlava got up and left. He knew in his heart that the Spaniards were not going to pay him and it was all he could do not to slay them on the spot.

# CHAPTER THIRTY-SEVEN

Celestina Dorantes had not visited the city since that day with Lukas Declercq. It was a beautiful autumn afternoon and she and Perpetua were enjoying exploring the shops. Celestina had grown so bored of her lace-making and the four walls of her quarters. She missed Lukas. He had been amusing company. Now he had served his purpose her father had forbidden her to see him.

They went looking for silk and silver thread and also to see what they might find for supper. Having made this trip many times, Perpetua was not greatly concerned for her mistress's safety, especially at this time of day. The men would be meeting them soon, and they would all return to the Castle well before dusk.

It was Celestina's great ill fortune that she and Perpetua were walking past the Town Hall and back towards the market stalls of the square, just as Hrusosky Hlava was returning to his home. He recognised Celestina at once, of course. Who would not remember a girl who looked like that? She had been there, somewhere in the background, on the few occasions he had visited Dorantes at his Castle quarters. He weighed up the consequences of his actions and decided in an instant what to do.

He bowed low when he saw her, and gave a little nod of his head to Perpetua. Celestina recognised him too. 'My dear, I am so glad to have seen you,' he said. 'I have come direct from the Castle. I hear there are assassins at large – men in the pay of heretics who are determined to kill the Spanish ambassadors at court and all their associates. You must come at once to a safe place and I will arrange for soldiers from the Castle to escort you home.'

'My father is close by, sir,' said Celestina, who had no reason to trust this man. 'We will find him and tell him.'

'There is not a moment to lose,' said Hlava. 'They may be watching you even now.'

'But where would you take us, sir?' asked Celestina.

'Come,' he said and grabbed her arm tightly.

Dorantes and Aguilar had stayed a few more minutes in the Stone Table, pondering their next move. They would have to speak to the Grand Inquisitor, they decided. Monsignor Gerwald Mach lived on the other side of the square. He had introduced them to Hlava; he would know how best to handle him. They turned into the square to see Hlava on the other side, his hand on Celestina's arm. She seemed to be struggling to get away.

'Unhand my daughter!' shouted Dorantes.

Hlava paid him no heed and began to hurry the girl towards a narrow side street.

Perpetua leaped upon him, beating his head with her clenched fists, but he swept her away with his other hand, knocking her to the floor, and drew a pistol. Celestina screamed and bit his hand. He clubbed her with the pistol, then moved his hand around her neck. The few passers-by close to the scene stood motionless, too frightened to intervene.

Hlava pointed the pistol at Perpetua's head, but she had fallen hard and lay writhing in pain, clutching her ankle. She was no longer a threat. Instead he turned to

Dorantes and Aguilar, who were now running towards him. He fired, and Dorantes dropped to the ground, clutching his chest. There were screams among the crowd, who scattered like frightened lambs before a wolf.

Aguilar momentarily stopped to help Dorantes, who waved him away. 'Save my daughter,' he gasped. Aguilar ran on, only for Hlava to draw another pistol from his belt and fire a shot which hit him in the forehead. He fell straight back, as though his head had hit an invisible wooden beam, and lay face up on the ground, his dead eyes staring at the sky.

Dorantes struggled to sit up, but his arms would not support his weight. Hlava dragged Celestina into the narrow passage, thinking fast. There was a house close to here where he could hide – he had provided the owner with favours in the past – and send word to the Spanish party for ransom. Then he would have to leave the city.

First, though, Dorantes must be silenced. It would be best for Hlava if the other Spaniards did not know who they were dealing with. Warily he walked out again into the Old Town Square, which was now all but deserted. Everyone had fled or was hiding behind stalls and carts. He dragged Celestina with him, one arm clutched so tightly around her throat she could barely breathe, let alone cry out. Approaching the wounded Dorantes, he paused to wrench Aguilar's pistol from the dead man's hand.

'Let my daughter go,' pleaded Dorantes.

'I wouldn't worry about her, Your Eminence,' said Hlava. 'You are in far greater trouble.' He pointed Aguilar's pistol at Dorantes's head.

Dorantes gazed with anguish at the terrified face of his daughter, while muttering a final prayer for his soul. None of them noticed the rapid patter of feet as a huge brown dog launched itself at Hlava. It knocked him and Celestina to the ground and the pistol fell from his hand. Hitting the cobbled square, it discharged its round, which lodged agonisingly in Hlava's left shoulder.

Lukas, who was so exhausted he had managed to sleep through the previous commotion, now woke with a start. Belphegor was no longer by his side. He looked over and saw the dog on the ground with a bundle of clothes. The bundle got up. It was Hlava and Celestina. Two others lay close by. One was still, the other – Dorantes – was moving. Lukas watched the scene unfold, frozen in horror.

Hlava was not finished yet. He still had Celestina tight by the throat and he turned her body between himself and the slobbering, snarling hound. He cursed his own weakness. He should have killed the wretched cur when he'd done away with Strom.

Belphegor knew that the little man was his intended prey, not the wriggling frightened girl. He held back, ears up, growling angrily.

As Hlava held Celestina in front of him, movement at the edge of the square caught his eye. A detachment of the Castle guard, returning to the palace, had come to investigate the disturbance.

Seeing the guards gave Lukas the courage he needed. He began to run towards Hlava and Celestina. He was unarmed and he hadn't the first idea what he was going to do, but he could not just stand by and watch.

At the same time Dorantes mustered his strength and called out, 'Guards, come quickly.'

Seeing a squad of soldiers racing towards him, Hlava panicked. He pulled Celestina through the nearest doorway – the entrance to the great tower which held the Astronomical Clock. Those inside immediately sprang to their feet, and he found himself surrounded. His weakened hand sought out the dagger on his belt and, despite the shooting pain from his wounded shoulder, he held it at Celestina's throat. His meaning was clear.

Hlava could feel dampness on his sleeve, which was now drenched with blood. He could sense himself weakening. Should he slit her throat now, and be done with it? Dorantes deserved no less. He had got him into this situation.

Belphegor bounded through the open door, growling and dribbling, his body crouched low as if to pounce. Lukas was right behind him. Everyone backed away in terror. Hlava saw Lukas too and cursed him to the lowest depths of hell.

'Wait,' Lukas shouted. 'Stop! Listen to me!' He was desperate to get Hlava to believe he was not a hunted man. 'It's not you they want – it's Strom.'

Celestina looked at Lukas with baffled astonishment. Then she began to swear at Hlava in Spanish. He did not register what either of them was saying. He was working on pure instinct now, and instinct told him to go up. Higher. It was the only way to get away from the dog. He had been in this building several times before to stargaze. The door to the stairwell was close by. He kicked it open and dragged Celestina through.

Inside the tower well it was clammy and cold. Hlava began to shiver a little as he dragged Celestina up an ascending series of rickety wooden ramps. He released his grip and threw her in front of him. At knifepoint she hurried up the ramps with him, until Belphegor caught up with them again and he once again deployed her as a shield. The snarling hound came several steps behind, Lukas clutching his collar and the soldiers following.

The ramps were not made for this many people. There was a sudden splintering as two of the wooden planks split their mooring to the wall and the handrail came apart. The soldiers on the ramp fumbled desperately for a secure hold. One of them plunged to the base of the tower, his scream scoring the air as he fell. Those coming behind stopped in their tracks behind the broken ramp, not daring to go further.

Lukas looked at the frightened, hesitant soldiers behind him. It was just him and Belphegor now.

When Hlava reached the top he slammed the wooden door that led out to the enclosed platform. He and Celestina were both gasping for breath. The platform was surrounded by open arches and a fierce wind howled around their feet. Hlava was finding it difficult to focus. There was a ladder leading to the spire atop the tower. 'Up,' he ordered Celestina, and waved his dagger in her face.

The door burst open and Belphegor and Lukas spilled on to the platform. Hlava grabbed Celestina again and held his dagger firmly to her throat. He pulled her out through one of the arches and on to the balcony that ran around the platform. The parapet was precariously low and Celestina almost fainted as she caught a glimpse of the square in the dizzy drop beneath.

Lukas held Belphegor tightly by the collar, hoping he would not leap up and send all of them to their death.

Hlava looked at Lukas with boiling rage. 'Why aren't you dead?' he said through gritted teeth.

'Hlava – listen to me. The soldiers are hunting Strom, not you,' Lukas lied.

Celestina unleashed another blistering tirade. Hlava tightened his grip around her neck, but there was a glimmer of hope in his eyes.

Down in the square an officer with the soldiers shouted up. He recognised Hlava from his visits to the Castle as a guest of the Spanish ambassador. 'Give yourself up, sir, for the love of God.'

Hlava laughed. Lukas was a poor liar. He could see it in his stupid, pleading face. He also knew that what he had done merited nothing less than the wheel. He would kill the girl with the last of his strength and then throw himself from the top of the tower. He tightened his grip around Celestina's throat, lifting her neck taut for the killing stroke. 'The Devil take you all,' he said, and readied his dagger.

There was a strange whistling sound, like air being torn apart. Celestina screamed in pain and Hlava stood bolt upright, a look of agonised surprise on his face. He swayed on the parapet and his dagger clattered to the floor. Feeling herself falling backwards, Celestina screamed again. Lukas leaped forward and grabbed her wrist with his free hand, almost tottering over the parapet. If he had not had Belphegor's extra weight to anchor him in this terrifying tug of war the three of them would have fallen into the void.

Hlava's limp arm fell away and Lukas pulled Celestina towards him. As Hlava's legs buckled and he toppled over, Lukas could see the tip of the crossbow bolt that had penetrated his chest. It had pierced Celestina's back too, and a small bloody stain began to spread over her dress.

Lukas lowered her carefully to the floor and cradled her in his arms as she started to sob. An officer and a soldier hurried on to the platform. The officer signalled to the two crossbow archers he had sent to the Tyn church tower directly opposite. Lukas helped Celestina to her feet, then peered over the edge of the parapet. Hlava lay, impaled and twitching, on the metal spike of a pointed tower at the base of the clock.

# CHAPTER THIRTY-EIGHT

The officer turned to Lukas and told him he had orders to bring him back to the Castle. He was courteous, there was to be no manhandling, but there were questions to be asked.

Lukas held open his arms to show he was willing to come without a struggle. For now he was too happy to be alive to appreciate the consequences of what had just happened.

Lukas emerged into the square, with Celestina holding tightly to his arm. Unsteady on her feet and weak with shock, she still managed to dash to her father's side. He was conscious. Perpetua held his hand and he was wrapped in a cloak belonging to one of the soldiers. Four of them used it as a makeshift stretcher to lift him up and the whole party headed back to the Castle. One of the bigger soldiers picked up Aguilar's body and draped it over his shoulders.

Lukas walked alongside the Spaniards. 'You have saved my daughter's life,' Dorantes managed to say as he struggled to breathe. 'I thank you.' His face was a ghastly white and beads of sweat lined his brow.

'What else could I do?' said Lukas distractedly. The excitement of the moment had passed. Now he was wondering, with Hlava dead, how he could possibly save Anselmus.

Celestina squeezed his arm. Her strength was

returning. 'Lukas, you are the hero of the hour. Why do you look so troubled?'

Lukas spilled out his fears. 'My uncle is imprisoned in Daliborka Tower, accused of trying to murder the Emperor. Hlava – the man who was killed just now – I think he's behind it. What can I do now he's dead?'

Dorantes was in great pain. 'You have an impossible task . . .' he said through gritted teeth. 'Pray for guidance.'

Celestina struggled for a comforting word. She knew Hlava had been an accomplice to her father. Now she was beginning to wonder what role *he* had played in these dreadful events. 'You must tell them all you know,' she said plainly, then regretted it as she caught her father's reproachful eye.

Lukas noticed. Now, away from the terror and the tumult of the chase up the tower, he was beginning to think more clearly. Why had Dorantes and Celestina been there with Hlava? The rest of the journey home passed in grim silence.

As soon as Lukas reached the Castle he was seized. He could see Celestina watching him until he was out of view. He wondered again how much of the conspiracy she and her father were aware of.

The guards took him straight to Daliborka Tower, where he was thrown into a small wooden cell. Sitting in there, his back resting against the wall, was his uncle. 'I was hoping you might rescue me,' said Anselmus in a sad little voice.

'Uncle, what happened?' whispered Lukas.

'I hope this has nothing to do with you,' said Anselmus, suddenly angry.

'Why are you in here?' Lukas asked his uncle.

'The Emperor and I tried that time machine I told you of. When I brought it to life it sent the two of us into a deep sleep. I woke with a violent headache and a horrible metallic taste in my mouth. The Emperor had fallen off his seat and was lying face down on the floor. I went over to him at once. He was still breathing, although his skin had gone white.

'The room had a horrible stale smell about it. I could hardly breathe. So I flung open the windows and my head began to clear. I wondered at once what the machine had done to us. Then His Highness began to cough and splutter.

'"Your Excellency," I said, "that machine – it poisoned us. It rendered us both unconscious."

'"But we felt so peaceful," he said. "We could have slept for a week."'

Lukas had never heard his uncle mimic the Emperor before. And he had never spoken of him with such contempt.

'He looked like a sad little boy, and tears were falling down his cheeks. So I said he should let me take the machine to my quarters and examine it. And I foolishly confessed that I might have been at fault bringing it to the palace. There is clearly something in its mechanism that made us both very unwell.

'And what does he do to his loyal servant?' Anselmus had gone almost puce with indignation. 'He roars for his palace guard and three of them rush in. "This man has placed our life in grave danger," he says. Me – his *physician*! And I had done my best to discourage him from believing that infernal machine would work at all. Then

254

he says, "Take him to Daliborka Tower." And here I am. And that's the thanks I get for twenty years of loyal service. If I ever get out of here, I am never going to work for that . . . *imbecile* . . . ever again.'

Doktor Grunewald was summoned to attend to the injured. Celestina had a flesh wound from the arrow and a bump on the head where Hlava hit her with his pistol, Perpetua a twisted ankle. Dorantes was dying.

Dorantes had hoped he would survive his injury. He was doing God's work, after all. Surely it was not unreasonable of him to hope for a miracle. Now he contemplated his death with remorse. He thought back to the time in his life when he had been happiest – close to the sea in the Low Countries with his family, before Peru. He thought of the simple things in life and how they were often the most beautiful: the flowers in a hedgerow or foamy waves on a shallow beach.

In his final hours he came to realise that nothing was more precious than life itself. He thought especially of Anselmus Declercq, imprisoned and facing torture, and his nephew Lukas, also sent to the Tower. Anselmus had been gracious to him, and the boy had brought some happiness into his daughter's life. And she had told him Lukas had saved her from falling from the tower.

Despite his pain, and the awful gurgling of his lungs as he tried to breathe, his mind was as clear as bright autumn sunshine. He thought of all he had strived to do at the Castle and whether it had been right. The certainties that had moulded his life now seemed flawed. Despite their beliefs, these people, his enemies, were good at heart. It would be wrong to leave them to the torturers. Perhaps he could redeem himself a little, if he could help them.

Celestina asked for a priest. Father Johannes Pistorius, confessor to the Emperor himself, arrived at Dorantes's bedside.

'I understand the physician Anselmus Declercq is held,' he whispered to Pistorius before the priest began the ritual of last rites. 'And his nephew. Accused of attempting to kill the Emperor. Please tell the court they are innocent. The Emperor's machine was devised by an . . . acquaintance . . . of mine –' he could barely bring himself to speak the name – '. . . Hrusosky Hlava. It was he who perished this afternoon in the fall from the tower . . . and it was I who plotted with him to kill the Emperor. Just he and I. No one else.'

Pistorius went through his devotions as Dorantes faded in and out of consciousness. He was puzzled by Dorantes's admission. But Doktor Grunewald understood. Together with what Lukas had told him that morning, the story made perfect sense.

As soon as Dorantes ceased to breathe, Grunewald took Pistorius to one side. Shortly after, they both hurried to the Emperor's quarters.

Anselmus and Lukas spent what was left of the day contemplating the burning braziers in the dungeon and wondering how long they would be able to withstand the attentions of the torturers – especially when they had nothing to confess.

Lukas told his uncle all he knew, carefully missing out his own connection to the culprits. But when he had exhausted the tale of his adventure in the city centre, and

Hlava's lurid fate, they fell into an uneasy silence. Anselmus shook his head. 'Only this Hlava could have saved us. And now he's dead.' There was something else he wanted to say. 'Lukas, I always wanted a son, someone to whom I could pass on my craft, but God gave me a daughter – kind and dutiful, but one with no interest in reading and writing, or even conversation. So when you came I tried to raise you as my son. You have kept me company, good company, and been a worthy student, and although you did a terrible wrong you redeemed yourself when you took poison to save my sister. But you know, what upsets me, what I really can't forget, is that you repaid my taking you to the Cabinet, a place so few have been privileged to see, by stealing the timepiece. We went three or four times. When did you take it? What was I doing at that time? It haunts me.'

Lukas felt compelled to tell his uncle the truth. 'I went there myself, with Celestina. It was another wicked thing I should never have done, but I wanted her to like me.'

He expected Anselmus to be angry. Instead he looked sad. Lukas wanted to cry. 'I'm sorry, Uncle. You have been so kind to me and I have not deserved it.'

'Did she encourage you to take it?' He sounded hopeful – plainly he wanted to feel Lukas had been tempted.

But Lukas had lied enough. 'No. She would have been horrified to see me steal from the Cabinet. I took it while she was distracted by something else.'

Anselmus put a hand on his shoulder. 'I blame myself for your ill behaviour. I should have known you would want to find company your own age . . . have a life away from your stuffy old uncle. I should have made more of an effort to find you some suitable friends.'

Then he said, 'I took Otka's mother to the Cabinet too, in secret, when I was a young man. To try to impress her. It worked.'

Lukas raised a smile. They settled down to wait the worst, but at least they were at peace with each other.

The long-awaited banging at the door and footsteps on the stairs eventually came, and they feared their ordeal was about to begin. But instead the door to their cell was unlocked and they were released into the bracing freshness of an autumn evening to make their own way back to their quarters at the top of the Emperor's palace.

# Chapter Thirty-Nine

They climbed the stone staircase in a daze and as they opened the heavy wooden door Otka rushed up to greet them both with a tearful hug. She was so relieved to see Anselmus she forgot she was no longer friends with Lukas. Grunewald came to congratulate them on their release. Anselmus asked him to join them for supper and opened a bottle of his finest vintage wine.

Grunewald told them of Dorantes's confession and how he and Pistorius had spoken at once to the Emperor. He thought it best not to mention Lukas's own admission to him. After all, the boy had not let him down.

Anselmus was lost for words. 'What a fool I was,' was all he said.

'It is a febrile time,' said Grunewald. 'The strangest tales circulate around the Castle. I heard just now that the Grand Inquisitor has been found dead in the forest near Dablicky. They say he was kidnapped by Devil worshippers and sacrificed to the Evil One. It is a terrible fate – even for such a detestable man.'

As they ate their evening meal there was a gentle tapping at the door. It was Celestina and Perpetua. Celestina was almost too distressed to talk. The Spanish envoys had all been arrested, she told them. There were too many for Daliborka Tower and they were being held in a cellar beneath the palace. Back at their quarters, there were just distraught wives, children and servants, waiting anxiously to see what would happen next.

For her, something even worse had happened. Her father had been denied a Christian burial. The imperial executioner had come to decapitate the body and then cut it into four quarters. Dorantes's head was to be displayed on the Stone Bridge tower alongside the common criminals. The rest of him was to be buried in unconsecrated ground. 'Why must they violate his body like this?' she sobbed.

Anselmus answered plainly that this was the way with enemies who had committed grave crimes against the Emperor. He also advised that she should leave the Castle immediately. 'I've never been a great admirer of punishing the child for the sins of the father,' he said, 'but it would be prudent for you and your maid to flee, before someone decides to take their revenge on you.'

'But I have nowhere to go. I heard my father's confession. I am so sorry. He acted without authority. The Spanish court will disown him – and me also. I cannot even go home.'

'Then you must leave the city. I have a friend in Zidice. You may stay there. Go and pack. Tomorrow morning Lukas will go with you and your maid to hire a horse and carriage. You must take only what you can carry. I will give you a letter of introduction. Then, when the dust has settled and we see what has happened to the other members of the Spanish party, we will send word.'

Celestina looked dumbstruck. 'But why should your friend help me?'

Anselmus gave her a tight little smile. 'I will send a purse sufficient to cover your board and lodgings. Come back tomorrow morning at sunrise.'

She and Perpetua left with a flustered curtsy.

Lukas was speechless too. He had still not got over his infatuation with Celestina, but she had caused them all so much trouble. He thought about how much he had shown and told her and wondered guiltily what she had then told her father to use against them.

'Why are you being so helpful to her?' asked Lukas.

Anselmus gave him an impish grin. 'As a punishment! They came here detesting our philosophy, our quest for knowledge and our "heresies". Think what this will do to that girl. Grunewald here tried to save her father, you saved her life, now I am helping her! We represent everything she has been taught to despise. Perhaps this will make her question her actions and those of her father. If that makes her a better character, then that is good. She is still young. She can be redeemed.'

Grunewald gave a hearty laugh. 'And if she cannot see the error in her thinking, then she will lie awake at night wondering why Satan's accomplices saved her life and were kind to her when she was alone in the world. That will certainly torment her!'

They drank the rest of their wine and stared at the twinkling torchlight in the city below. After a while Anselmus said quietly, 'I have done my best to heal his mind. And serving him has allowed me to indulge my interests in the world. But I can no longer attend a man who has betrayed me like this. I no longer wish to be a servant of the Emperor.'

Grunewald urged caution. 'My dear friend, you will never hold such a position again. You will never reside in such splendour. Do not give these things away so hastily.'

Lukas listened sadly to their conversation. He did not

want to give this life up either.

'I am utterly certain of it,' said Anselmus. He sat at his desk and began to draft a letter of resignation.

Grunewald let him write for a while. Then he said, 'I am concerned that His Highness will see your actions as treasonable. Perhaps –' he looked at Lukas and Otka – 'perhaps all of you will be seen as traitors for leaving. His Highness is of such unsound mind I can no longer imagine what he will think.'

Anselmus stared out of his window for a long time. Then he tore up the letter. 'Maybe I will stay another few months . . .'

There was a forceful knock at the door. 'What now?' said Anselmus in despair. Lukas tensed, expecting the worst. It was an officer of the guard, with another soldier, who was staggering under the weight of the large box he carried in his arms. 'I have a message from the Emperor,' he said, and handed Anselmus a scroll. The soldier placed the box on the floor and they both left.

Otka and Lukas studied Anselmus's face for clues as he hurriedly scanned the message. He looked alarmed and then relieved.

'He wants me to go,' he explained. 'He thanks me for my many years' loyal service and wants me to take up the vacant post of chief physician at the hospital in Plzen. The box contains a generous contribution towards the upkeep and establishment of my new household.'

Lukas feared his uncle would feel further betrayal. But he seemed happy to accept this new position.

Grunewald came over to him and shook his hand. 'You have been a dear friend to me, Declercq. I shall miss you immensely.' Then he returned to his quarters.

'Grunewald has long coveted the view from my rooms,' said Anselmus. 'He would be most welcome to them.'

'So you don't mind going?' was all Lukas could think to say.

Anselmus smiled. 'Here in the Castle we are like those gaudy parrots in the Royal Gardens – curious creatures kept for the entertainment of others and shackled to the trees with a golden chain. Much needs to be done in the world – and I am not doing it here. Will you come with me, Lukas? Will you still be my apprentice? And you, Otka? Will you come too?'

# CHAPTER FORTY

To Etienne Lambert
c/o The Three Violins
Mala Strana
Prague

21st November, 1598

Dear Etienne,
We have now been at the hospital for three
weeks. My Uncle Anselmus has been given an
imposing residence overlooking the river. I
continue with my medical studies and often
accompany him on his rounds.

Uncle was disappointed that Otka chose to
stay with her stepfather in Golden Lane. She has
been greatly distressed by these recent events. But
this has worked out well. Aunt Elfriede refused
to come away with us, much to my great relief!
Now Otka has promised to look in on her as
often as she can. She also promises to visit us
frequently. It is not too arduous a journey from
Prague to Plzen. We are greatly in need of a
housekeeper and cook, and Anselmus has
written to Celestina and Perpetua in Zidice to
offer them accommodation and work, should
they be willing to accept it.

*I miss Prague, but I feel safer here. When I went for a last look around the city before we left, I saw Hlava's head up there on the Stone Bridge tower, next to Dorantes's. Are they still there now? Over the last few months I often wondered if our own heads would end up there too, but we've been lucky so far.*

*When we first met you said you would help me get to Prague but I would have to do something for you in return. You never kept me to this, but I would like to do so now. The last time we spoke you said you had had enough of Prague, so perhaps you would like to make a fresh start in Plzen. There is a flourishing market here, with merchants from all over the Empire, and someone with your talent for foreign tongues will find his services in great demand.*

*My uncle has said you can stay with us until you are able to afford to rent somewhere. I hope you will decide to come here.*

*Your friend,*
*Lukas*

# FACT AND FICTION

This book was inspired by Giuseppe Arcimboldo's fruit and vegetable portrait of Rudolph II, *Vertumnus* – easy to find on the internet. A culture that produced something so magnificently strange and original sparked further investigation.

Prague and its Castle are well worth a visit. Woodcuts and engravings from the era show that much of the city remains from Rudolph's time. The contents of his Cabinet of Curiosities are well documented. Many of these artefacts were scattered to the four corners of Europe when Prague fell to Swedish troops during the Thirty Years' War. A fraction remain in Prague. The rest can be found in museums and art galleries around the world.

Rudolph was plagued throughout his life by severe depression – all the more reason to admire his open-mindedness, tolerance and passion for art and science. In a Europe haunted by the Inquisition, his Prague was an oasis of freethinking, where Catholics, Protestants and Jews lived side by side. Here, 'natural philosophers' could investigate and share their knowledge of the newly emerging sciences without fear of being burned at the stake as heretics. In his patronage of alchemy, and fascination with the world, Rudolph was an early champion of the Scientific Revolution of the seventeenth century.

I have tried to portray Rudolph as I imagine he would have been, and Anselmus Declercq is very loosely based on Rudolph's Belgian physician, and curator of his Cabinet, Anselmus de Boodt. Father Johannes Pistorius, who makes a brief appearance at the end of the story, was Rudolph's real-life confessor. All other characters in the book are fictitious.

Although the plot by Spanish envoys to remove him is also invented, Rudolph had plenty of enemies in the Holy Roman Empire and there were many court intrigues and even assassination attempts against him.

I based Hrusosky Hlava's alchemy confidence trick on an incident reported in Henry Carrington Bolton's book described below.

Dorantes's Aztec knife can be seen in the British Museum. You can also see it on their website.

If you would like to read more about Rudolph and his era, you might like to dip into *The Mercurial Emperor: The Magic Circle of Rudolph II in Renaissance Prague*, Peter Marshall (Pimlico 2007), which I think is the most accessible introduction to this subject.

There's also:

*Rudolph II and Prague: The court and the city*, edited by Eliska Fucikova (Thames and Hudson 1997). This features acres of academic articles – many in translation – but it is also crammed with fascinating illustrations.

*The Follies of Science at the Court of Rudolph II: 1576–1612*, by Henry Carrington Bolton is worth a look. It was originally published in 1904. You can download it from the internet.

You could also try John Hale's very readable *The Civilization of Europe in the Renaissance* (Harper Perennial 1993 and new edition 2008), which is a more general introduction to the era.

# ACKNOWLEDGEMENTS

Many thanks to Ele Fountain at Bloomsbury for her patient moulding of the story, Talya Baker and Margaret Histed for their sterling edits, and Dilys Dowswell for wading through the first drafts. Their advice is much appreciated. Kate Clarke and The Parish produced the evocative cover.

Thanks also to Jenny and Josie Dowswell and Charlie Viney for looking after me; Sally Hoban and Christine Whitney for lending me two beautiful books; Adam Guy, Jeremy Lavender and John Dowswell for their sound advice, and Ben and Jana Anderson, and Nina Jelnikova of Prague Tours, for making me so welcome in Prague.

# ABOUT THE AUTHOR

Paul Dowswell is a former researcher and editor. Published in the UK and internationally, he has written over sixty books and has twice been shortlisted for the Blue Peter Book Award. Paul lives in Wolverhampton with his family.

Praise for Ausländer

'A thrilling tale, exceptionally well written and affecting'
*The Times*

'More vivid than a Patrick O'Brian novel'
*The Independent*

Praise for the Sam Witchall adventures

'Prepare to have your timbers well and truly shivered'
*The Scotsman*

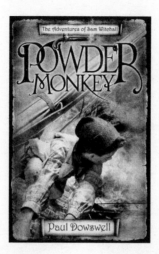